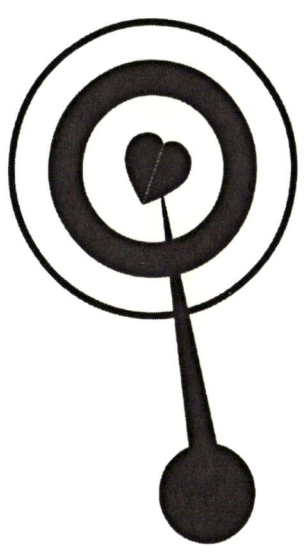

THE INTIMIDATOR STILL LIVES
IN OUR HEARTS
STORIES BY GARY AMDAHL

artistically declined press
oregon

The Amdahl Library
Published by Artistically Declined Press

The characters and events of these stories are works of fiction. Any resemblance to real events or persons, living or dead, is entirely coincidental.

Copyright 2013, Gary Amdahl
All rights reserved, including rights of reproduction in any form

Cover & Interior Design by Ryan W. Bradley

ISBN 978-1-4675-5854-9
Artistically Declined Press
artisticallydeclined@gmail.com
www.artisticallydeclined.net

Sonata for Small Dreaming Spaces

I.
The Breezeway   11
lento, triste, ma allargando

II.
The Lesser Evil   31
scherzo serioso, pazzesco

III.
More Geese Than Swans   41
notturno, ubriaco

Two Symphonies of Fear, Wrath, and the Death Wish

The Cold, Cold Water   51
D-sharp minor

The Intimidator Still Lives In Our Hearts   81
D-flat major

Favole per musica senza musica

We Whistled While We Worked   141

San Luis el Brujo   191

Saddling the Sorry Ass of Self   243

Coda

Night, Mystery, Secresie, and Sleep   281

for Leslie

"Like imperfect sleep which, instead of giving more strength to the head, doth but leave it the more exhausted, the result of mere operations of the imagination is but to weaken the soul. Instead of nourishment and energy she reaps only lassitude and disgust: whereas a genuine heavenly vision yields to her a harvest of ineffable spiritual riches, and and an admirable renewal of bodily strength."
—Saint Theresa, *Autobiography*

"In the Louvre there is a picture, by Guido Reni, of St. Michael with his foot on Satan's neck. The richness of the picture is in large part due to the fiend's figure being there. The richness of its allegorical meaning is also due to his being there—that is, the world is all the richer for having a devil in it, so long as we keep our foot upon his neck."
—William James, *Varieties of Religious Experience*

"This is one of the secrets of success in human relationships. He has much who can give himself away frequently and lavishly."
—Christina Stead, *Letty Fox: Her Luck*

THE BREEZEWAY

"The Holy Scripture points clearly to the vanity of sorrow, and so does reflection... but why does the heart grieve and refuse to listen to reason? Why does one want to weep bitterly?"
—Anton Chekhov, "Easter Eve"

When, for Christ's sake, when did I come to know what I know now? How could I have failed to mark the date, the moment, how could I not remember where I was? I must have known something from the very beginning, but did not, could not, understand it. And consequently, because I did not, could not, understand it, forgot about it? Is that possible? Children are selective, highly and carefully, consciously careful, selective about what they profess to know, what they appear to know, about what they will allow themselves to know, or even consider—and if understanding eludes them, baffles them, do they not divest themselves of the concern? Immediately, in an almost business-like and practical way? No feelings of resentment or frustration or inferiority, something like the beta male in any but human society, who rolls on his back, admits his loss without the faintest taste of shame, occupies himself with a piece of fruit that was not being contested? Maybe that is the way of the healthy child, the whole and unwounded child. Maybe the damage comes when they are forced to consider something they cannot understand. Maybe that's when they become lost in the woods and preyed upon—when someone or something refuses to let them turn around and run away. I must have been a healthy, whole, unwounded, undamaged child. My mother and my father must have been very gentle with me, with my brother...my aunts and uncles and grandparents, my older cousins, so superbly and mysteriously princely in their older-ness...they must have known and understood so well that they were able to let me run away, rather than clutch and grab at me in their own confusion and, who knows, terror—it's not too strong a word,

I don't think, it doesn't take much to terrify a child, and my older cousins must have steeled themselves with what they knew and understood, must have been very brave and strong not to cry out to me—or even to just let something slip, a warning, a look, an obscure reference. I can only guess, but I must have known something from the very beginning, and must have come to that knowledge as I sat next to the humming, faintly rattling freezer in the breezeway. I cannot account otherwise for the primacy, in my imagination, in my memory, of the breezeway. What a wonderful place it was.

My grandfather, my father's father, built the house in 1954. He and my grandmother moved in on All Saints Day, a Catholic holy day that meant nothing to them, as they were Lutherans —and not just Lutherans, but "Hauge Lutherans," a relatively stern and austere variation on the Protestant theme that had swept the western fjords of Norway in their grandparents' day. I mention it only because that was also the day the French-Algerian war began: my future sister-in-law was two years old at the time, and lived in Algiers. It was also the year, a month or so earlier, that Martin Luther King, Jr., ascended his first pulpit, at Dexter Baptist in Montgomery, Alabama, and Joe DiMaggio married Marilyn Monroe. I mention those historical events not in order to make the demographics of my childhood more clear, my story's setting more effectively detailed, but to suggest a far greater world of things I did not, could not, know: the nearest darkies (term of choice—never either negro or nigger) and professional baseball teams were both at such a remove, in Chicago and Minneapolis, as to not exist, or rather, to exist only in lurid and exciting fables. Technically speaking, darkies had been encountered in Waterloo and Des Moines, where my grandfather had worked, at a government job, for a year in the middle of World War II, and my uncles had been in the Navy, island-hopping in the dreamy deadly South Pacific with every sort of Negro imaginable...but the college in town was as white as Ole Miss. Not by design or policy, of course, simply because of circumstances. Nobody in our extended family drank, either, but I saw reeling drunks before I saw blacks.

The property abutted the campus. Its handful of buildings were situated on rolling hills with steeper hills, limestone outcroppings, and bluffs spreading east to the Mississippi, black loam farmland flattening out to the west. The Upper Iowa flowed shallowly through the middle of town. Caves, some of them big enough to attract and sustain a small tourist trade, issued currents of cold air that allowed more northerly species like balsam fir and lady-slippers to flourish on some slopes—my grandparents' property, for instance. A broad avenue of bigger, older homes, and oak trees led past the front of the house up to the college, and a steep narrow street went up one side. The other side was college parkland, and the backyard was a wall of cracked limestone plates and ledges twice as high as a man. Sometimes flowers from the neighbor's garden could be seen nodding over that height, but her house was far enough back so that only its roof could be seen. The backyard was consequently quite secluded, a narrow strip of thick green grass. The limestone seemed like the wall of a fortress to me. And my grandfather's tiny tool shed was like an enchanted cabin in the wilderness: dark and musty and full of ancient hand-tools, awls and adzes and files, handles dark with dirt and sweat and smooth with use, edges bright and sharp, trays and jars of nuts and washers and bolts and screws, sacks of fertilizer, boxes of old issues of National Geographic, sawdust, cans of paint and turpentine, soft old brushes, a stiff red bristle here and there, heavy boxes of nails, clamps, vises, spider-webs...a bench to work on, a fluorescent lamp hung swaying over it, and a small desk with post-office style pigeon holes for his documents. It was his ambition, when he retired from the county relief office he had retired from farming to take over, to read a set of World Book encyclopedias from A to Z, and to write his memoirs. The documents in the tool shop were arranged in file folders marked by year, one folder for every year of his life, 1900 to the year I am writing of, 1960. There was also a map of Military Township, on the border of Winneshiek and Fayette counties, with the names of the farmers who owned land typed carefully over their sections: the Uhlenhakes and the Tinderholts and the Linderbaums (Conley and Viola I knew), the Hemesaths and the Zweibohmers (the old bachelor brothers Alphonse and Aloysius), the Schissels and the Schweinfusses, the Kipps and Bohrs and Dibbles. Little areas of variously-styled cross-hatching with an ink pen (a *nink pin* we used to say they pronounced it "down south"—which was anywhere from south of the Fayette line to Little Rock, and, a real howler, *lat bubs*) indicated, according to a inked-in legend the home place and the place my parents built after and the Nesvik #6 School and Stavanger Church. It was an ordinary, if well-appointed, tool shed, in other, less nostalgic, less elegiac, words; but like certain discrete, out-of-the-way, poetic spaces, it could exert subtle magnetism or focus the power to bind gentle spells upon an occupant, to induce and amplify day-dreaming. We only lived there for a short while, a little more than two years, but much of that house worked on me in that way—in fact continues to work on me fifty years later. The jagged broken shelves of limestone rising up to the flowers in the clouds, the tool-shed, the breakfast nook with electric percolater, the steamy surge of coffee into the clear glass cap atop the cover, and the clock with the fish that floated around with the hands, the door in the ceiling in the hallway that became a ladder up to the attic when you pulled the rope attached to it, the kitchenette apartment in the basement where we lived, the rooms for students in the garage, the breezeway: just a roof covering the space between the house and garage, narrow, no more than a couple yards wide, no more than four or five long, wooden arches, sawn plywood like a stage-set, at either end, through which eddies and gusts of hot humid summer winds were channeled and in the shade, on the mossy concrete, made to seem brisker, drier, cooler. In the winter the snow came from the west and would drift across the mouths of the breezeway but never penetrate it; sometimes we would get Minnesota-level accumulations and I could tunnel into it. I feel somehow as if I have never been anywhere else but in the breezeway, sitting next to the freezer, humming, rattling to a stop, rattling up again to a shaky hum...that everything that has happened to me has happened in the breezeway. I could be in Australia, for example, in vast and glittering Sydney harbor, listening to an opera, as I once in fact did, in 1986, an opera about an early explorer of the outback by David Meale and David Malouf, based on Patrick White's novel *Voss*...and somehow be in the breezeway at the same time. I will try to say this as simply and prosaically as I can: I seem to view life as if I'm at one end of the breezeway, the back end, looking out towards the street, through that carefully sawn but false archway. The sky is gray but the sun breaks through unpredictably, the house across the street is shuttered, leaves and in the bursts of pale sunlight the faint shadows of leaves are moving up and down the sidewalk, and it is so humid there seems to be mist in the air, or the grass is simply wet and thick, time to mow again so soon but too wet, the blades of grass would simply fold around the blades of the mower and my father would slow his walk, push harder and harder, back up and take a mighty run at it, and finally be forced to stop. I was married on an island in Lake Superior, in 1989, under a chuppa, with a klezmer band playing, but it was as if my wife were coming slowly up the steep sidewalk toward a little housee in a little town in northeastern Iowa, crunching acorns, then appearing as if in a dream in that arch with her dress blowing wildly around her. The door to the garage rooms is open, and The Crew-Cuts are singing "Crazy 'Bout You Baby." My mother and father are looking up at me from the basement kitchenette, just the tops of their faces visible, hands waving close to their faces peering sharply upward, through the window well. The freezer is humming. My grandfather is hammering something in his shed. That sounds too much like Faulkner, the bang   bang   bang of the hammer, but there it is.

The first two, not quite three, years of my life, I was in and out of the hospital. I had croup and nearly ceased to breathe, I pulled a pot of very hot water off the stove on top of myself, and I drove my "car" out the front door and down the steps, five of them, at some point flinging myself from the vehicle and rolling down the steep front yard to the retaining wall, rolling over it, and dropping maybe three feet to the sidewalk. I could have rolled off the sidewalk, down three more steps to the street, but had lost momentum, having more or less fetched up against the iron-pipe handrail. But Iowa in any case is not as flat as popular conception has it. My grandfather is reported to have said, "Well, now you know about that." My grandmother had a brand new electronic organ which allowed the user to create special sound effects, and to accompany him or herself with a variety of "beats" or rhythm patterns: a couple of my older cousins were said to have been playing a very fast bossa nova beat, much faster than any human organist or dancer could have kept up with, when I shot out of the door. I cried a lot, and was fussy, generally, but by the time I was three I had calmed down and was making attempts to be a good son. One day, for instance, my mother was washing and drying and ironing some very large pieces of fabric—I don't know what they were, curtains, bedsheets, tablecloths, maybe an assortment of these things—hard, time-consuming work, and it was naturally exhausting her. So I decided to cheer her up by bundling my toys and presenting them to her as a birthday present, even though I knew it was not her birthday. This act of spontaneous generosity, however, did not cheer her much.

In fact it angered her, though a long practice of resisting anger, now almost a habit, kept her from any demonstration of real feeling—beyond, at most, a sharp word and brusque handling. Maybe she swatted my rear, but I doubt it, as physical violence was another routine we as a family were habituated against. The problem was that I had used one of the carefully ironed curtains as wrapping paper. I believe after she scattered my toys and threw the curtain back onto the ironing board, she sat down and cried. She must have. I can certainly see myself doing so. I am sure she put me on her lap and hugged me. Of course I am relying on a perforce unreliable memory, but the memories are there, crystal clear, panoramic, and as effectively detailed as any novice storyteller could hope for. What I do not know, what I do not know with certainty or even the hope of the possibility someday of certainty, is this: was I three years old? *Or was I four?* It makes a great deal of difference.

I retired to the breezeway. I sat next to the freezer and probably sulked a little, only to be lulled, as I almost always was, by the music coming from the rooms of the students in the garage. Maybe it was Elvis Presley or other pioneers of darkie music. As a young mother and father, my parents didn't listen to rock-and-roll, and I believe my oldest cousin, closer to my father in age than to me, was coming to prefer jazz. He played the trombone, and in photographs looks very cool. It could be that the kids in the garage liked folk music, The Weavers, Pete Seeger, but not Bob Dylan yet, though he must have been playing in Dinkytown at that point, near the University of Minnesota campus. I don't know what kind of music it was, but I liked it. Not too many years later I was able to get a transistor radio which I was allowed to take to bed with me. It was red and white, had a collapsible antenna, and a volume control dial that clicked most satisfyingly when nudged on with my thumb, the static-fuzzy speaker up tight to my ear.

The students intrigued me, and when I learned that my mother and father had been students just like them, at the very college I could see if I went down to the sidewalk, I pored over their annuals, the only evidence easily to hand of their studenthood. I was learning to read and write and draw rather precociously, to render convincing shapes, and so, noting the fond addresses penned around the photographs, scrawled some valedictory hieroglyph over my mother's pretty face.

No memory of anger. Maybe she laughed. I would not have. But maybe she did.

I have suggested that I was a difficult child, but one, I hope, that seems ordinarily so. And that I grew up in a place that was, if incredibly, even dangerously homogenous, safe and peaceful and beautiful. And that my extended family was comprised entirely of decent, intelligent, loving people. I have also suggested, I think, that there was some mystery, some unhappiness that was being lived through about which I had not the slightest idea—at the same time I was experiencing full sensory privileges and quickly learning about both the world and the people around me. I saw and understood so much that I am not just baffled but angry about the things I did not see and understand, or saw but did not understand, or saw and understood and ran away from, forgetting either naturally or unnaturally but so completely as to be surprised by it all now. I am not, and must make this very clear, not dealing in anything so specious and dangerous as "recovered memory." No depraved or evil or defective person abused me or threatened to abuse me—I knew no such people, such people might just as well have been living on Mars. I was surrounded, for miles and miles around, it seemed, by people who valued decency and reason and kindness even more than money! (My nostalgia is simple, simple-minded: for days that had less money in them.) No. I plainly refused to accept something that had happened as clearly as everything else happened, refused to contemplate the consequences as I had every other consequence I'd had in my purview, declined to, as I have said my grandfather liked to put it, know about that now. And my question to myself is what else did you not know about? Certainly it's ridiculous to hold one's infantile consciousness to account, to hold it in contempt as I evidently am doing, and it's equally certain that children have little or no interest in the lives of their parents until, usually, it's too late, the wonder beginning to grow only as mother and father age and slow and weaken, their memories become chalky and nebulous, their interest in the value of stories dissipates. They become wan and enigmatic, or daffy, difficult chatterboxes, and the wish of the child to know is overwhelmed by sadness and annoyance, or outright fear. No no, we want to live and ignorance is bliss.

Sometimes the births of our own children will cause some uneasiness to well up as we recall the blitheness with which we demanded selfless and absolute fealty from our parents, along with food and shelter and clothing—and our dismay and petulance when they were other than selfless. We ask them how things were to assuage our consciences, we are rueful over our selfishness, amused at our capering, and we come away wiser and gentler, we know about that now, we understand, we are only human and we are doing the best we can. But I have no children, and cannot therefore claim this smug satisfaction with the miracle of emotional development. Nor can I look to the ordinary comparisons that come of achieving benchmark ages: what was my mother like at nineteen? A bobby-soxer? To some extent, yes, but what else? A mother? Yes, but what else? And my father at twenty: leaner? Certainly, wiry and handsome—nearly broken in pieces by his time as a soldier? Perhaps, I didn't know and apparently didn't care when I was twenty and breaking myself into pieces. How about Mom and Dad at forty? They were millionaires and about to divorce, but I knew nothing about it at the time—nothing, not the least inkling—and by the time I was forty, I was too concerned with alcohol and art to see beyond the whirling room I was in.

I am fifty now. Fifty-one, actually—mustn't forget that crucial extra year of insight. It is a ludicrous age to be so confused, so needy of exemplary anecdotes, so bereft. All I have is this memory of the breezeway, the green fuzz, the moss and mildew, spreading out across the stones and up the bricks.

My brother's birth inaugurated an era of peace and goodwill of many months. There had been some concern about the "Rh-negative factor" in his and my mother's blood, and he had to wear a brace, two little shoes bolted to a chrome-plated bar, for a little while, that kept his feet from turning inward so severely, but he was by all accounts a quiet and content baby, and I must have seen how well that worked: a photograph from that year shows me sitting in a cleft of rock on a lakeshore with a pipe in my mouth and a look of thoughtful indolence on my three-year-old face.

Another photograph, taken on Christmas Eve, after we'd opened our presents, shows my brother with a look of excited pleasure that was, for him, relative to his usual amiable sangfroid, suggestive of lust and madness, arms outstretched, about to roll up and take what must have been very early steps. He has been moved to this show by my new aluminum model of a service station, complete with mechanic's bay, lube-station, gas pumps, pump jockeys, you name it, it had it. He is staring at it and I am staring, in disbelief, at him, as if it was all too clear to me what he was about to do: lumber toward it, fall on it, and utterly crush and destroy it. You can see it in my eyes, just as I saw it in his.

A photo from a few months later, early spring, no snow on the ground but the earflaps of my cap tied under my chin, clutching a puppy fiercely, protectively, jealously to my bosom. We are on the top step under the streetside arch of the breezeway. I may have been given the puppy as a kind of substitute for the gas station, but no one remembers how he came to be in my care, nor what happened to him. I believe his name was Scamp, but no one else remembers that name. It's almost as if the puppy never existed, and yet there is the photograph, for which I am very grateful. At what point did I come to remember the puppy as "Scamp"? Because I cannot say, conclusively, without doubt, that I remember the puppy, just as I cannot the gas station or the pipe or the birth of my brother.... I remember looking at the photograph sometime later and believing the puppy's name to be Scamp. Why would I do that for a life so briefly and tenuously part of my own? Was the puppy mine? Was it a stray? Why would my mother or father adhere to my pronouncement that not only was it mine, its name was Scamp, if in fact, in truth, it was a nameless stray that I'd held on my lap long enough for a photograph to be taken? Did this belief seem to them somehow essential to my well-being? And did it then simply become habit? I do not believe that is the case. I refuse to believe it. Scamp is something I have not forgotten. The memory is all but gone. I have only the memory of the memory, a photograph whose context, whose "truth"—the documents, the things you could point to if Oprah accused you of lying—is as lost to time as... as what, as Kertesz's picture of a wandering half-grinning beggar-violinist, his son or apprentice and another very small child standing in the middle of a dirt road in somewhere in Hungary, but I believe it, I believe steadfastly in the memory of the memory, and I therefore remember Scamp. I believe that he was mine and that something unhappy, unpleasant, unfortunate happened to him. You can see the foreboding in my eyes. If you don't have access to the goddamn photograph, you can see it in my eyes right now. That such things happen all the time to everybody fails to alter the character of my grief —that is to say, of inexplicable loss. You can in fact see it in anybody's eyes: that's what life is. You see the recognition, and it is either one of gentle sympathy or of violent outrage.

My grandmother, my mother's mother, Clara, not Mae, in whose basement we lived, died shortly after the appearance and disappearance of Scamp. We drove several hundred miles northwest, to a crossroads town in the Red River Valley of North Dakota, close to the Manitoba border, called Pittsburgh. My mother's family had farmed barley and potatoes and sheep there, back in the days when socialists ran the state legislature and fought the railroads, and later, sunflowers and sugar beets. The funeral was held in the basement of the Pittsburgh Lutheran Church, a little white building with a steeple. I was lifted up so that I could see over the edge of the casket. I remember being grasped under the arms and the edge of the casket slowly lowering before my eyes, revealing my grandmother. Her eyes were closed. I remember all this very clearly: rising up over the casket, and the difference between her eyes when they were open and when they were closed. Certainly my perception and understanding of my grandmother's eyes has been strengthened, even, possibly, to the point of modification, by my perception and understanding of my mother's eyes, and it is much too much to say that there has ever been violent outrage there...but the change, the simultaneous and perhaps paradoxical darkening and brightening of their eyes, the precipitous fall from kindness and sympathy to something else, that is something I understand very well.

The drive home must have been a long and sad one, but whenever I drive those roads now I am flooded with feelings of peace. Grief brings people physically together at the same time, I think, that it isolates them emotionally. The car was crowded: my father driving, unlatching the vent window and tipping his face toward the rushing air, my mother, pregnant for the third time, between my toddler brother and myself in the backseat, my grandfather in front, adjusting the other vent and allowing me to study his leathery wrinkled neck—and I must have found some hypnotic pleasure in the flat green eternity of the valley, the Pembina hills in the northwest subtle but fantastic evidence of another world entirely. My father's struggle with himself, initiated by those terrible nights in the Army, had abated to the point where he'd decided not to enroll in the seminary: his religious conviction had deepened, and, he believed, saved him, but the idea of being a pastor had given way to a plan to follow one of my uncles into banking. My mother was not quite twenty-four and given over wholly to motherhood, which she felt saved her from an excess of grief. My grandfather had always been very quiet, and continued to be so, though I had seen him unable to walk past the casket without the support of my mother and my aunt.

It is now July 3rd, my second brother's birthday. He would have been forty-seven today, but he lived only to the 5th. I can find no trace of him in my memory. I can find no trace of him in my memories of my family, my mother, my father, my grandparents, my uncles and aunts and cousins, no trace of sorrow or grief or pain of any kind. No memories of the hospital, no memories of hearing the news, no memories of those long hours stretching into days and weeks and finally years. No memory of having been told how the great happiness that surrounded the expectation of his birth could possibly have given way to such incredible reserve, and silence. No memory of silence. It's as if it never happened. There was once again a potentially lethal antagonism between the blood of the mother and the blood of the child—but the antagonism was expected, and a relatively simple matter of a blood transfusion would resolve it. The transfusion was botched. Air entered my brother's bloodstream. I was taken by my father's father, and two or three of my oldest cousins, to the river, the Upper Iowa, to spend the afternoon fishing. I still have the tackle box, with its rusty old spoons and daredevils and cracked plastic bobbers, and my cousins must have been guffawing and snorting and snickering because I never saw them not laughing, they are the funniest men on Earth, and my father tells me that my grandfather put on his waders and went upstream to cast flies for trout, which is where my father says he saw him weeping, up around the bend, standing in the middle of that shallow rippling river, rod in the water, line all spooled out downstream and following the current, holding his other hand over his face. It has taken me forty-seven years to come to his grave, and my brother says that he does not think he ever will, there are millions and millions of lives that could have been but never were, and he is satisfied with the brother he has always had, enough so that he feels no grief, no need to mourn—and I understand that. I understand as well why there are injunctions against grief, why holy books and common sense both counsel against it...but what I do not understand is why I so often feel I am sitting in the breezeway, looking out through the little arch at the dark gray sky, feeling the humid air just begin to move, hearing a soft and comforting roll of distant thunder, absolutely certain that something is about to appear.

THE LESSER EVIL

"The simple-hearted and the sincere never do more than half-deceive themselves."
—Joseph Joubert, *Pensees*

Many years ago, I published a collection of short stories, called *Ostrogoth*. It sold very poorly—forty-eight copies to libraries whose librarians were not playing close attention and thought it was a work of late Roman Empire history, and thirteen copies to family, friends, and a couple of my students, and five to people I didn't know at all. If you can bear to go online and read customer reviews, you will be amused, I think, as a handful of the librarians struggle to understand what they perceived as either an outright swindle, or postmodern nonsense. They give my book zero stars, unanimously, while my students brazenly kiss my ass. "He is our next Lolita," one of them declared, confusing, as he often did, book and author of book, just as he confused characters on television shows, and the actors playing the characters. I, of course, was very attached to my stories: they were like my children, and if, for example, we were hosting a cocktail or dinner party, I would bring them out before their bedtime and have them do card-tricks, sing songs, perform somersaults, sit up and beg, and so on. I was very fond of my characters, too, so fond that I really don't have a leg to stand on when I ridicule my former student. During the earliest years of my writing, I was all but psychotically convinced I would meet one of them walking down the street, a particular character in whom I had invested a great deal of my own secret yearnings and beliefs—along with some not-so-secret personality traits and nervous tics, like actually staggering when someone tells me something that is "hard to believe," or hopping up and down when I am happy, or blinking excessively when my social footing is uncertain, when I am crossing the no man's land between my life and the lives of others. But as more and more of my characters came to resemble me, either in pathetic Walter Mitty disguises or even more pathetic confessional hair-shirts, I saw the effect had grown too diffuse: all that psychological bravado seemed to depend on a laugh-track that you couldn't really hear. Eventually the thought of "another me" became sickening. The artist can sit in his cell looking at a skull for years, abandon his family, lose his friends, and remain as powerless and confused as the day he began his spiritual exercises: the origin of other people, the source of the continuous production of new life, the means of the extinction and creation of souls...must have something to do— mustn't it?—with the imagination of...for lack of a better phrase...highly trained sorcerers. And by extension, artists. We must, I mean to say, we artists must be the visible end of that spectrum. We must have something to do with the creation of something out of nothing, and therefore ought not be driven from town for thinking, for suspecting, that we can make "another self." But in the end there's nothing you can do about it. You can't prove it's even possible much less produce the goods—or the bads, as the case may be, the evils—and you have to give it up and learn to enjoy the simple things in life. Literature is a weedy meadow made terribly soft and lumpy with the graves of doppelgangers, with "secret sharers" and twins and doubles and dream narrators who can be no one else but ourselves, and men coming back to life to claim lost identities, or feigning death to shake and slough off unsatisfactory selves, Jekylls, Hydes, princes, paupers, nature stomping the shit out of nurture...and I was immersed in this literature. Hawthorne and Poe and

Stevenson and Conrad, Shakespeare's *Comedy of Errors* (the BBC production from the early 80s with Michael Kitchen and Roger Daltrey, whenever I needed a break and a laugh) and at the same time, just after Kirkus Reviews gave *Ostrogoth* a starred review, I got letters, five of them, from the five people I didn't know who'd bought the book. One asked, "Are you the Gary Amdahl who lived in Rochester in the late 60s and dated my sister Karen for a while?" I had lived in Rochester in the late 60s, but I had no memory of a Karen, and in any case had been too young for dating in those days. The second asked if I had lived in Saint Paul in the late 80s and early 90s and played guitar in a blues band called Ceremony in Lone Tree: yes to the former and no, I wish, to the latter. The third wondered if I had lived in Rhode Island (no mention of dates) and was heir to the Amdahl Computer fortune. Again: yes, then no. The fourth: had I been to a party in northwestern Connecticut where I'd met Arthur Miller and refused to shake Henry Kissinger's hand? Met Arthur Miller, yes indeed, great moment, told him I'd played Biff and Hap on alternating nights, but no idea Kissinger had been there. The fifth was from an address in Madrid. I had just finished reading a pile of Spanish, Latin American, and Portuguese writers, concluding with José Saramago's *Homem Duplicado*, but this was from a writer, a rather famous and important one, with whose work I had yet to acquaint myself: Javier Marías. It was a large but not bulky envelope, hand-addressed, and the letter was formal but very friendly in tone, written on a typewriter: was I this Gary Amdahl? He referred me to the enclosed, beautifully produced, chapbook, an early story of his called El Noruego.

The Norwegian in the story is named Gary Amdahl, and works in the Barcelona office of a US company, in whose Madrid office works another Gary Amdahl. They are alike in every way, down to the most minute details and urges, and the very short story describes the struggle of the narrator Gary to become different from the other Gary. The letter said Señor Marías had come across the strange name in the phonebook of Palma, Mallorca, where my father, whose middle name is Garrison, had indeed once lived for a few months while trying to straighten out what was in effect an extortion deal in the setting-up of a "legal entity" in Spain for the beverage-dispensing company he worked for. But he had lived in a hotel, and didn't in any case ever go by "Gary." You can search the antiquarian internet for days, weeks, you can google the hell out my name, Javier Marías, noruego, and find absolutely nothing. I apparently have the only copy, and Señor Marías no longer replies to my letters, which, I admit, may have become a little oppressive.

Eventually, of course, no surprise here, the world being what it is, I met the other Gary Amdahl. He looked exactly like me—according to our families, anyway; we were unwilling to accept the shortness of our legs, and how bowed they were—you could drive a truck between his—the immensity of our foreheads, the tininess of our eyes, the featureless tomatoes we became when we blushed, which was often and easily. I said I would grow a beard, which made him shudder with distaste, and he offered to try contact lenses, which you couldn't pay me enough to wear. The differences in our personalities, however, were appalling. It's not too strong a word. I am not a strong believer in the infallibility of first impressions, not a believer at all, but I do know what it's like to meet someone you almost instantaneously do not like. We all do. It's instinctive. These people alarm us. The other Gary Amdahl alarmed me. My instinct was to nod and smile and move on. He set my teeth on edge. He evidently had a short fuse, would raise his voice or give menacing looks in public, and had a terrible gift for sarcasm, which he would use with full *commedia dell-arte* gestures at the drop of a hat. If people were being witty, he became desperate to top everything off with devastating satire of the entire *mise en scène*. He laughed too much, explosively, nervously, pre-emptively, and at his own jokes. He was extremely, pathologically sensitive to criticism, very defensive, and even though he had lots of money, always let other people pay. He tailgated at a hundred miles an hour, simultaneously laying on the horn and flipping the bird, hated crowds, was very impatient in lines, and had the table manners of a starving dog. It was repulsive, almost sad, to watch him eat. Finally, he had a way with women that I thought was transparently disingenuous but which seemed to work very well for him. He was married, his wife was beautiful, and appeared to suffer him gladly, but I saw her once, much later, actually swing a big heavy sack of potato peelings at him and hit him smack in the side of the neck. Almost knocked him off his feet, and you could see he was seeing stars. On the plus side, he had a really fine singing voice, was a real guitar-slinger, and had a great job (Amdahl Corp.) with the kind of responsibility and authority that not just any asshole can get, or hold onto, for very long. He loved his dogs and cats, and was very gentle and sweet with them.

As for his observations and analyses of my character...! He said, "I'll make this brief. You are a misanthropic artiste manqué. You are lazy and cowardly. You make a big show of being a lone wolf, with only your principles and vision for company, but I have never met anyone more thoroughly dependent on the goodness of other people. You have sacrificed everything that makes life worth living: hearth, home, the love of a good woman, the hopes of your family, the esteem of your fellows...self esteem. You want to canonize Chekhov but he would never have gone in for your kind of deceit."

"Say what you like," I said serenely. "But I am a maker. I am a creator. I am probably, though I can't prove it, responsible for your existence. Everything you think you know about me, you know because I want you to know. Required you to know, so as properly to employ you, in my creations."

One of us laughed. I think it was him, given his predisposition to it.

"You didn't create me you fucking dimwit."

"How do you know that I did not create you?"

"I don't know that."

"Very good. I do know. I did create you. That's what I do."

"Fine. You created me. If that's your story—stick to it, buddy."

"But stay with me for just a sec. Given, for the sake of argument, that I'm right, and I did in fact create you—What does that make you?"

It was a ridiculous question, and I knew it. I was angry and wanted to humiliate him. We went back and forth for a while trying to come to an understanding of what sort of answer I was looking for. He paused and appeared to be giving serious, even troubled thought to it. "If you made me, what does that make me?" he asked sincerely.

"Yes," I said.

He seemed to take pity and exact his revenge at the same time. "The lesser evil," he said, "just for starters."

And I say yes, yes, yes, easy for him to say, but where is he now? Better still: where am I? No, no, Samuel Beckett said it best when, upon noting voices in or near his head, demanded to know who was speaking? and who was listening? And refused to go on until he got it sorted out. Certainly there can be another man in the world named Gary Amdahl, who looks a lot like me. Just as certainly I can imagine, I can create, a Gary Amdahl who is all the things I can never be—because I am too lazy or cowardly, sure, I admit it, it's easy, it's almost a part of human nature to imagine ourselves as decent, attractive, accomplished when we are mean-spirited, ugly, paralyzed by anxiety. Or maybe I am thinking of Rimbaud: "*Je est un autre*." I is another. I am not me. Me is someone else. Me is someone else. Me is someone else. That makes sense, doesn't it? I think it does. Me is someone else. Thank god.

MORE GEESE THAN SWANS

I

The American Legion's club 432 holds a book sale every summer in the Veteran's Memorial Hall in Cambria. The hall is like many others: plain, sturdy, well-kept, lots of folding chairs and long tables, big windows and a little stage, moved from the camp at San Luis Obispo to Cambria just after the war; and Cambria is not much more than a single long street winding around a cool and foggy range of hills on California's central coast, just a few miles south of San Simeon, where Hearst built his castle. We rent an old cottage, simple and sturdy and well-kept like the hall, a block from the ocean for a week, sometimes two, during the summer, when temperatures where we live, east of Los Angeles, rise unremarkably to 110, and 120 is merely remarked. I am most comfortable in cold and rain: the glaring sun and furnace-like heat depress me just as the brief cold days and long cold winter nights depress others. It actually makes me suicidal. My brain overheats and doesn't work the way I need it to work. It often doesn't rise to even the most minimal standards. I hover on the edge of sunstroke even in the middle of the night with the air conditioning running at warp ten and an industrial-strength fan, the kind used to ventilate musty warehouses, inches from my face. So Cambria is a good place, in my estimation. Cool and quiet, rocky, often peopleless beaches, and the ocean to remind me that I am just a complicated and momentary manifestation of non-human elements, mostly water, a wave, like six billion others perhaps for a time but in the end simply water. The people who own the cottage don't mind dogs one little bit—there is even a triptych of photographs of one of the family's beloved old fellows on the mantle, and another of my many quirks is that I would rather roast in Hell (yes, burning hot for eternity—how would I know I was dead?) with my dogs than be in Heaven without them. I come to Cambria and I am reduced to thoughts like this: Good good good place. Paradise. Thank you. Please let me stay. There is also in Cambria a good independent bookstore, new and used, Potter Books, and a tiny cramped dusty musty used shop in which nine-tenths of the stock is in cardboard boxes, open, spines facing up, with duct tape straps for easy lifting. These are the kind of bookstores I like. I won't set foot, to tell the truth, in a (unintelligible muttering with suggestions of obscenity), and I much prefer forgotten authors to (unintelligible muttering with suggestions of biliousness), so the American Legion sale was a pleasure within a pleasure within a pleasure. I was of course not likely to happen across anything truly valuable—if I'm no antiquarian there are nevertheless some books for which I would gladly, immediately, remorselessly plunge myself into even deeper credit card debt—but I did expect to find several novels of which I would be the sole reader on the planet. (I encourage lawsuits from people who think that's perverse, or childish, or whatever combination of attitude, principle, and dysfunction it takes to trigger automatic exclusion from Oprah's Book Club.) And so I did: I picked up Norman Lewis's The Volcanoes Above Us, published almost simultaneously with the death of Malcolm Lowry, who wrote Under the Volcano; The Norton Book of Scores; an omnibus edition of three novels by Louis Bromfield; A Distant Drum

(1957) by Charles Bracelen Flood (who was a student in Archibald Macleish's writing seminar at Harvard not long after John Hawkes passed through a similar seminar there, taught by Albert Guerrard); the Rembrandt volume in the Pocket Library of Great Art; Flight from Ashiya (1959) by Elliot Arnold; The Living Lotus (1956) by Ethel Mannin; a book of Italian verse I didn't recognize and which was in poor enough shape to be lacking the least trace of author, title, and publishing information; and two romances by Catherine Gaskin: Blake's Reach and Sara Dane. They stack the books up and measure the collective width of the spines. You pay by the inch. I had about three dollars' worth of books and was about to pay when I saw the flashy glossy spine of a brand new book. Like I said before, I'm no cagey ruthless antiquarian, but this book stopped me dead. I gulped, maybe even gasped aloud, I don't know, and shot glances left and right. I could not believe what I was looking at: I Am Death (2008), by Gary Amdahl. For no good reason—no reason that holds up when recounted to others, even loved ones—I was in something very like a state of shock. I paged through the book and found the writing only vaguely familiar. Good, certainly! Innovative, startling— but not altogether familiar, in the sense that the familiar makes you feel comfortable. Then I looked at the author photograph: again only faint recognition, mostly of the Indonesian print shirt I wore for every day for five years, and of the magazine shelves at the bookstore where I worked. Without conscious decision, and walking a very long walk I could not recall making only seconds later, I was getting my books measured and pulling a five dollar bill from my pocket. I thought what fun, I should ask this volunteer lady if it looks like me, and then I thought—panicked is not too strong a word—that I should just leave, just get the hell out of there before something happened.

II

The feeling of psychospatial dislocation persisted, and something did indeed happen, but not until I'd left Cambria and been home in the desert long enough to want to drive through hours and hours of blisteringly surreal traffic to feel an ocean breeze again, to join the MENTALLY ILL ON THE THIRD STREET PROMENADE IN SANTA MONICA. I don't mean to imply there are only mentally ill people on the Promenade—there are thousands of shoppers, moviegoers, eaters, drinkers, and so on—nor do I mean to suggest that the proportion of visibly mentally ill people to invisibly mentally ill people is any higher in Southern California than anywhere else...though I think that's actually true. Suffice it to say that people shouting obscene non sequiturs is not particularly remarkable anywhere on the planet (unless the speaker has a weapon strapped to his thigh and is ostensibly debating health care reform). But the Third Street Promenade is just a one-minute helicopter ride from Hollywood, a proximity that makes everything seem like an audition. For instance, I was auditioning for a spot as myself, author of the acclaimed American Legion Club 432 bestseller, I Am Death. I was also rehearsing "just another face lost in the crowd," a role that had garnered me more than one kudo, a "Minnie," to tell the truth, an award given to Minneapolis playwrights who fail to get a play not only on Broadway (that's easy) but at the O'Neill Conference or the Humana Festival at the Actor's Theater of Louisville as well (both of those places require participants to win something like a hot-dog eating contest, the hot-dogs replaced by cold turds), but who nevertheless get lots of work as actors in stimulus vignettes produced by corporations specializing in "learning" (the kind of faux earnestness that calls for the actor to use his common-sense accent), the kind of blather you might see if you work for a company that doesn't specialize in learning but which gives you as a benefit, a half-day at a seminar on how to whistle while you work). I was, in other words, all alone on the Promenade: no friends, no loved ones, no dogs, no bookstore. There was once a really good one there, The Midnight Special, just as there used to be another good one, Dutton's, at which I worked, just up San Vicente into Brentwood where we had regular laugh riots with Dustin Hoffman ("What do you call a black guy who flies a plane? A pilot, you racist!"), Norman Lloyd (very old, dwarfed by his Panama hat, but with an incredibly loud stentorian voice, cornering Linda Hunt: "I HEAR YOU'RE IN A MOTION PICTURE, LINDA! I HOPE THEY'RE PAYING YOU A GODDAMNED LOT OF MONEY, LINDA! THEY ARE? THAT'S WONDERFUL, LINDA! THE BASTARDS SHOULD BE PAYING YOU A LOT OF GODDAMNED MONEY! YOUR WORK IS EXCELLENT, LINDA, GODDAMNED EXCELLENT I TELL YOU!") and Ben Affleck (please see my new collection, The Intimidator Still Lives In Our Hearts, for details—no, sorry, wait, it's not out yet, probably won't ever be despite the contract: the sales reps are telling my publisher they have GOT to be joking, please tell us you're joking, you're joking, right...? They can't even sell them at American Legion sales unless the author himself comes in and has a nervous breakdown). So there I am, memories of my friends the movie stars, pretending to be me, watching cellists pretending to be Jamie Foxx in The Soloist, while their partners pretend to be Robert Downey, Junior; mimes pretending (ironically, I think) to be Marcel Marceau; men and women painted entirely in silver pretending to be statues while people pretending to be dogs piss on them. There are homeless people and runaways and people, doing exercises for acting class, pretending to homeless runaways. And of course there are the Christians with Microphones, and their shadows, the shouters of obscene non sequitirs. I could hear one such fellow long before I could see him. His voice was not nearly as rich as Norman Lloyd's, but just as loud, and I was... well, this is the weird part: I was drawn to him. When I was about twenty-five yards away, the crowd began to thin out, the extra-wide sidewalk quite quickly becoming a no-man's land. While I was being drawn in, everybody else was keeping clear. Because I was in effect the only one there, our eyes met and locked. Before they locked up, I had noticed that he was a normal looking young man, heavy-set, dressed in stained rags, baseball cap on backwards, sitting on a bench, bellowing so fervently that his body was jumping. I won't repeat what he was saying because I am so very very tired of those words, you hear them everywhere, on the playground, in church—and I am simply and stupidly a guy who has given up everything for the sake of uncommon utterance. The point is that we locked eyes. I continued my long slow walk towards him, and he continued to fulminate. When it registered that I was approaching him, the volume dropped. He began to pause after every few words, then to stutter and mutter. Finally I was standing over him, my back straight, eyes wide open and tilted down to his, which were also wide open. He fell silent. I could feel people turning their attention to us. I said nothing because I had nothing to say. I had walked up to him for absolutely no reason, and now stood over him, expecting, I guess, that he would say something, something other than what he had been saying. We were locked in our silent observation of each other for some time. His eyes grew wider and wider and finally he exploded: "WHAT DO YOU WANT, YOU FUCKING ASSHOLE?" and I snapped out of the trance. I said I was sorry. Then I showed him the book I was carrying. "Would you like to buy my book?" With this effrontery he ceased to scream. He got up and stormed away into the crowd. And I thought there he goes, the one guy in a million that I could talk to.

THE COLD, COLD WATER

"Thou'dst shun a bear;
But if thy flight lay toward the roaring sea,
Thou'dst meet the bear i' th' mouth."

1

Oh, the cold, cold water. It was such a relief. Billions of gallons. As cold as a glass of ice-water, sweating on a picnic table. They no longer pour cold water on the heads of maniacs. They give them balls and parties instead. Even so: it was relief on a scale beyond pleasure, of another order—closer, perhaps, to lobotomy. Not that he was not perfectly clear on how attractive water was to people, any water, and shores and beaches, any sort of shore or beach, any kind of proximity—a boat, a puddle on a sidewalk. But the idea, the picture of people stacked and frying, or even all by themselves in advertisements, on the more tropical, the more commonly popular beaches, called to mind thoughts of disaster, even horror, before it did pleasure or ease. Even if they were laughing and tossing frisbees. Especially if they were laughing and tossing frisbees. He needed cold water poured on his head, and if that made him a maniac, okay: he was a maniac. He detested people. There: he had said so. He needed cold, cold water, and some elbow room. The first purchase he made after he married, more or less accidentally, the department store heiress, was twenty acres on the island, a little sandstone shelf of boulders and sweet white clover with bog spruce and popple cantilevering out over it as the lake continued its erosion of the little cliff that rose up over it. The cabin was in a stand of birch trees. A mossy, rotten, tangled cedar swamp comprised most of the rest of it.

It was early in the spring and still quite cold. The only flowers blooming were tiny white Canada violets. Bobby and Patricia, on a trip to the island to celebrate their first wedding anniversary, crossed the dirt road that ran between cabin and shore and circled the island, holding their cups of coffee carefully level as they swung their legs over the Armco barrier and descended the embankment the county had only just recently built up to keep the road from falling into the lake. They stopped for a moment at the top of the steps that led down to the shore and made a tentative identification.

"Next year we'll know for sure," said Patricia, a tall, handsome woman who was dressed for warmer weather and so held her husband's arm and snuggled closely to his side. Bobby too was lightly dressed but felt the icy wind and ripped-up gray clouds had been made to order. He put his hands in his pockets and let the wind buffet him for a while, his wife safely in his lee. Then he put his arm around her and hugged her tightly. They clumped slowly down the steps. With his foot raised to leave the last one, she suddenly stopped him.

"Look at that." She pointed and he looked.

Precise impressions of large deer-hooves in the cold hard sand were surrounded by a delicate pattern of much smaller hoof-prints.

"And look there," he said, stepping gingerly down onto the sand, "the national bird. Those mean-looking crosses there. And tiny birds too. Maybe the white-throated sparrow we heard when we shut the car off." He whistled the three clear descending notes of that bird's singular call—poor Tom Peabody Peabody Peabody—but it was lost in the rising wind.

"It looks like a dog ran through here too. Do you see?" He pointed and walked a little way into this perfectly preserved evidence of life on their little island, and Patricia followed. Then it was his turn to stop suddenly. Patricia had folded her arms tightly under her breasts and hunched her head low and so bumped into him, but he remained silent and unmoved.

"Bear, too." He stepped closer to inspect the paw-print, then turned to look back at her. Her eyes grew wide behind the huge lenses of her stylish glasses.

"A bear!" she laughed. She smiled for a moment then stopped.

"A little one, I think."

"I didn't know there were bears on the island!"

"Evidently there are!" he shouted, laughing, and came back to her.

"Should I be afraid?"

"No," he said and stopped laughing. "You should be delighted."

"Well, I am!" she shouted over the wind. "Afraid."

"You shouldn't be."

Waves rolling into the shore were getting bigger and noisier as they slammed into the boulders that had been dumped into a crib designed to promote the build-up of sandy beach over the course of the next decade. They stood on the bottom step and stared as some of the prints were washed away.

"What a marvelous natural narrative," said Patricia.

It didn't seem quite the thing to say, somehow, but he let it stand.

They had met in Singapore, he researching various forms of Asian theater, she a cookbook, so for the celebratory dinner they put together a menu that had everything but monkey-brain soup in it. Patricia of course was a splendid cook, and he was no slouch either: the meal was magnificent, and they enhanced it significantly beyond their expectations with one, two, then three bottles of wine that might have sufficed for a down payment on another few acres of interior forest. They joked about buying the island, piece by piece, over the next twenty years.

"By the time we get a decent beach built up," he said, "we'll be able to boot everybody the fuck back to the mainland."

"Would you do that, if you could? Boot everybody off?"

"Really?" he asked. "No."

"Why not?" Patricia seemed intrigued.

"I don't know."

"You like the feudal model?"

"Oh come on!" he laughed. "I'm not that bad!"

But he saw that, despite his charming manners and resourceful sociability he could count on in the clutch, that perhaps he was that bad. He sensed it, or thought he sensed it, hidden away, but lurking, biding its time…but was fortunately appalled by it, and consequently a little bit afraid of clear and ordinary demonstrations of a self that could, without warning, throw people out of their homes. He staggered and wheeled around the cabin's big main room, arranging pieces of priceless furniture he'd trailered up himself from Minneapolis.

"Next thing I gotta do," he said, "is buy a nice sailing vessel. It's not enough to be near all that cold, cold, lovely water. I want to be out in it."

"Uncle Dickie likes to sail," said Patricia.

This was a quiet and sympathetically tender reference to a meeting at the Minneapolis Athletic Club that hadn't gone, apparently, very well. Uncle Dickie had the reins of the family business, and he had summoned two of his newest nephews-in-law to lunch. Bobby ordered extravagantly and had every drink course imaginable, while Uncle Dickie and the other nephew had requested tuna sandwiches and Pepsi.

"Uncle Dickie," said Bobby, "and me, alone in a little boat, in the middle of Lake Superior." He began to sing the Gordon Lightfoot hit about the sinking of the ore tanker *Edmund Fitzgerald*, a *Titanic*-like tragedy that had happened in 1975, the year Patricia and Bobby had graduated from high-school. " 'The gales of November came earl-EEEEEE,' " he bawled in a drunken but well-trained tenor.

A little later, after a few swirling slugs of brandy, he suggested they go down to the lake and take in its stormy passionate darkness, but Patricia said she was afraid of the bear. He went brusquely outside and shouted comic greetings to the bear, which eventually became challenges to come out and fight. He closed this performance with an improvised ballad, something out of Shakespeare about a bear and the raging sea. He was actually quite a decent singer, and was moved by the sound of his voice. It was as if he were singing in a dream. He stopped and stood silently still on his deck, protected from the wind and the rain. Then he came in laughing, tears slipping down his cheeks.

"He's not out there."

"Oh but Bobby it's too cold!"

He put on a sweater and a rain poncho and walked with headlong esprit down his drive, stumbling in the ruts but maintaining a steady pace. He bumped into a couple of little scrubby trees that couldn't be made out in a darkness he now realized was swirling and roaring, but didn't take it personally, and was impeded only briefly. Emerging at last into the less dark open space of the county road, he took his bearings, crossed it, walked full speed into the Armco barrier, and fell over it. Tumbling down the embankment he came to rest in a grassy declivity a little bit out of the wind, and still dry. It was a little nest, and he listened to the thundering waves, sighing with "contentment deep," as the lake itself and making a kind of obeisance to its immensity and power. Then he fell asleep.

In retrospect, it seemed he had never awakened from that mythic slumber, not truly awakened, but simply dreamed himself aboard a sailboat. He was gently rocking in his berth while a Haydn piano trio beautifully revealed itself and something delicious sizzled in the galley. There were five men in the boat, including himself; they had done a few days of cruising about the archipelago to warm themselves up for a voyage that would take them through the locks at Sault Sainte Marie, south through Huron and into the lower lakes, then up the Saint Lawrence to the Atlantic, ending in Boston. They were about to make the crossing from the Apostles to the

Keeweenaw Peninsula. What was left of the three billion-year-old Penokee Range, now called the Porcupine Mountains, was a band of purple on the horizon.

Bobby was the only man onboard who was not a lawyer, but that didn't matter because they were sailors first and foremost. Short, dark, effusive Rob also owned a restaurant in Boston's North End, and Jonathon, who looked like a Congregational minister, was a good friend of Martin Pearlman and a primary patron of the Boston Baroque. Jerry was the captain and had been more or less around the world in sailboats. His silver hair was quite long for someone with a history of accomplishment like he had (but never boasted about or bullied with), and while he was fit, he was clearly a man who liked to eat and drink. Bobby was the busboy, and after he had cleaned up breakfast, Jerry gathered them all in the main cabin and told them that it looked like something quite possibly wicked was that way coming. It was a friendly jibe at Bobby who was never at a loss for a quotation out of Shakespeare, but which nevertheless got everybody's attention. The radio crackled as if in confirmation. They were going up and down rather excitingly now.

They all went on deck. What had begun as a hot sunny day was now a cloudy cold one. A few columns of pale sunlight slanted down from what looked like ruptures in armor plating. The ridge of the Porkies to the east was still visible but less distinct, a shade of gray only slightly darker than the sky. Part of it was actually black, a color difference that was disturbingly strange, a darkness visible.

The barometer had dropped, and after a few hours Bobby took to staring at it. He said nothing about it and tried to be discreet, but he had come with rather astonishing speed to depend on the idea that careful observance of the instrument would reveal a slight rise in the reading, and that that would be a very good sign. If he saw such a sign he would cast discretion to the howling wind and share his good news unabashedly. But the wind had begun to shift as well. Bobby and the last of the five men, a former Marine whom everybody called Digger, were momentarily alone in the cabin, and Digger remarked casually that if the wind shifted just a few more degrees it would be coming from the northeast and their lives would be in danger. Bobby nodded and returned helplessly to scrutiny of the barometer. He realized that he was a terrified supplicant who could, if he felt abandoned, smash his god to pieces.

The wave chains that were coming at them were strong and relentless. The boat had been surfing at a speed faster than its design indicated was possible, and Digger, who had raced little boats singlehandedly, had been holding them all in a kind of endless tube—but now there was some concern that the mast would pound a hole through the hull. Or that they would simply capsize. They would lay on their side, way over, but the massive lead mine of a rudder would hold at always the same place and they would come back up. Shriek forward and be slammed back and forth, as if they were being slapped in the face, over and over and over again, by a giant. Then it became more like being in a plastic cement-mixer. All five men were now sea-sick, Rob and Jonathon miserably, incapacitatingly so. They were wet and cold and could not change clothes in the confines of the cement-mixer, making hypothermia a possibility drawing nearer and nearer. Bobby was relatively well, and the thought that he could smash the barometer and break the spell had given him a kind of comfort. He made his way on deck, clipped a line to his jacket, and joined Jerry in the cockpit, which was protected enough to allow speech. The black ellipse along the distant purple-gray swerve east of the Upper Peninsula was now larger and more amorphous. It seemed to have overwhelmed itself and was throwing black arms out at them, billowing and throbbing, but the sky was dark enough now for the contrast to be less striking, and therefore less frightening.

"It's a northeaster," said Jerry.

"Yes!" agreed Bobby. "Northeaster!" he shouted, as if to prove he was not afraid of saying its name.

"We will make for Ontonagon."

"Ontonagon!" shouted Bobby. "Good!" He had spent many nights at the top of his steps with a compass and a pair of binoculars, staring steadfastly due east. He could almost always see the Saxon Harbor, Black River Falls, and Marble Point lights to the southeast, but if he was lucky he would see the red flash of the Ontonagon light, something like sixty miles of nothing but heaving cold water away. On one or two very clear nights he could see it with his naked eyes. It was a sight that never failed to make his heart rise in his throat, and the Ontonagon light had become a kind of mantra for him. He spoke it rarely and never repeated it like a true mantra, but it had the same power to concentrate his soul.

And now, here, the beloved light seemed to be drawing his soul toward it.

"Rogue wave," said Jerry.

"What?" asked Bobby.

Moving across the wave chains that were slamming and stopping the boat, a rogue wave appeared. It rose up and up and up and was magnificent and glossy, molten and yet cold, certainly not real because it lacked the context of cause and effect that human beings require of reality, a fluid glacier, and it moved with the great slow grandeur of a glacier, years and years it took to reach them and yet they could not move, making it almost laughingly obvious that it was a dream, the boat was motionless, fixed in a single eerie silent moment of maelstrom. And then they were in it and everything was blinding white. And then they were out of it and everything was black. Slowly light seeped into the blackness and the screaming and slamming of the little boat continued.

They came out of a fog bank and were very near the light. Its red flash seemed to take up the entire sky. Bobby was below-deck throwing up with the somewhat improved Jonathon and Rob when Jerry and Digger came down again. The troughs of the waves—it was now clear and had to be admitted, and accepted, and faced, like men—were as deep as the waves were tall. If they attempted the harbor, in other words, they would almost certainly run aground. They would have to, in other, more or less final words, go back out into the storm. Jerry led them in prayer.

"Dear Lord, please help us. And if you can't help us, at least don't help the bear."

Bobby again thought of Lear's raging sea and bear. Jerry's joke-prayer obviously equated "the bear" with "the storm," but Bobby thought of the little bear that had tracked across his beach. He felt a great deal of sympathy for it, in that moment, almost as if it were in the cold, cold water with them.

2

Some years later, not many, two or three, Bobby and his second wife, Eugenia, drove up to the island with another couple. He was winding up his tale just as they turned into the ferry parking lot. "We entered the Waterway pretty much like an arrow shot at a very small bullseye, and we couldn't slow down. We were going twice as fast as the boat was designed to go, and there was a drawbridge ahead. We radioed ahead and the bridge was up, but this is like racing down some little town's main drag at a hundred miles an hour. Anyway, we did eventually slow down and were able to steer ourselves into little bit of a lake. We dried off and warmed up and called our wives."

"My god," said his friend Alex, a tall, rangy, rugged-looking actor. "That's right out of Conrad!"

"Well," said Bobby, "no, it's not, but I'm glad you liked the story."

"I mean to ask earlier," said Eugenia. "What is 'clocking'?"

"When the wind is shifting clockwise around the compass. The wind is said to be 'backing' when it's going counterclockwise."

"And you were on a 'beam reach' before the storm caught you? Is that what it was?"

"Yes."

"What's a beam reach?"

"I'll explain later."

They bought a ticket for the ferry and were directed aboard. Once the ferry got underway, Alex's wife Josie (also an actor, an extremely resourceful character actor with oak-blonde hair and green eyes who was always working) asked what his ex-wife said when he called her.

"Oh," said Bobby, "you know, she was glad I was alive, there was no question about that, but I wasn't supposed to come home when I got back to Minneapolis, because she no longer wanted to be married to me. She'd met someone else who liked people, who sincerely liked people, and she couldn't believe what a difference that made in her life."

"Well!" exclaimed Josie. "That makes absolutely no sense to me."

"Me neither!" shouted the adorable Eugnenia.

"It's a crock of shit," said Alex, "is what it is. You're one of the nicest guys on the planet."

Bobby grinned and Eugenia tickled him. The four were silent for a moment, and then Bobby said, "Well, there's a difference between being likeable and liking."

"Well hell," said Alex roughly, warmly, "you appear to not only be as well-liked as Biff—" whom he had just played in a very small but surprisingly popular production of *Death of a Salesman*, "but to like well, as well." It was a complicated utterance but they liked to talk that way. Bobby had improved to the point where he could ignore the fraudulence of it.

When they got the cabin, they unloaded only the food and drink, burgers and brats and bourbon and beer, set up the charcoal grill, and began to eat and drink. When they finished eating, the continued drinking and got out their guitars. All four of them played and they eventually became a kind of demented, drunken flamenco quartet, lips and teeth working fiercely over difficult fingerings, dripping sweat. When that was over, they turned on the radio and listened to a show called "Honky-tonk Saturday Night" being broadcast from a nearby Indian reservation. The show's host was very old, they thought, and had an all but completely indecipherable mélange of mumbling lisping accents for a speaking voice. They fell in love with him immediately, and when he would do things like get up to go to the bathroom and forget both to put a record on before he left and forget to close the door after he flushed, they swooned with delight. It was nothing but very old country and western songs for several hours, and then they began to play Yahtzee. Alex was wearing his cowboy hat and frequently jumped up to say, "Go fer yer Yahtzee, stranger," which precipitated them all into hilarity every time he did so. The radio show host, whose name was Maylon, dropped most of the "y"s and "ie"s at the end of names, and compensated by drawing out the last names, sometimes lisping the "s," sometimes turning it into a harder "d." so it would be "Here'd a dong by John Ca-a-a-a-sh," or "here'd Kit We-e-e-llth," and he would put a 45 on at 78, scrape the needle across the record as he removed it, curse softly but audibly, apologize, and put it on at 33 and a third, scrape the needle again and say, "Oh for Pete dake." When he got it right, he'd say, "Dis is goin' out to the Wallinsky Thithters at Lunker La-a-a-ke."

Bobby and his friends were so moved, so inspired by the superiority, the unabashed and unadorned authenticity, modesty, and joy of the broadcast that they began to speak freely of the theater collective they hoped to form, its principles and ideal performances. Josie, who could sing and dance, wanted to sing and dance. Every play that came over their transom, she insisted, could be improved by cutting twenty minutes out of its middle, and adding songs and jokes. Bobby had been somewhat caught up in postcolonial studies while a grad student and said he would not suffer the least taint of Gilbert and Sullivan and all that corrupt empire crap. Alex was about to begin rehearsals for Shepard's *Fool for Love*, and had brought a lariat with him. He started roping things around the big room and said he wanted to make theater that was acrobatic and dangerous, circus-like but with Artaudian cruelty that would make audience members sit up and understand there were live human beings on the stage before them. Eugenia, who came from a theatrical family and whose name was actually O'Neill, nicknamed Hughie after one of the master's less well-known works, stopped the discussion dead by saying she believed theater was a tool of the people. Bobby got up and made another round of drinks. When he came back he handed the drinks around and said as he did so that the tool of the people was a television set and that the people loathed theater: production values were so low as to seem silly, amateurish, childish. Only Disney could get the production values of live theater right.

The next day was one of sweet blue skies alternating with driving rain storms. Around noon, as they were eating lunch and the rain was falling nearly horizontally in sheets sometimes luminous and translucent, sometimes smokey and dark, so heavily that they couldn't see the road from the front door, a bear appeared. He was in the front yard, a swamp of little trees, old stumps, and thick brush, but the rain was so heavy he was merely a black and shifting shape. He was not small, though. He charged at one of the great old stumps and pawed at it. He then stood his entire awesome length up on end and seemed to dance around the stump. He made several revolutions around it, waving his arms, or forelegs, above his head. Then he went back down on all fours and hopped around it. Because they were theater folk, they were inclined to see ancient and primitive ritual in this performance, and it was Hughie who said what they were all thinking:

"He's trying to tell us something!"

"When I die," said Bobby, "that's where I want my ashes buried."

After the excitement of the dancing bear, the food, the steady rain, sleepiness overcame them. Hughie fell immediately asleep on the couch in the big room and began to snore so loudly the freckles seemed to lift from her face. Alex and Josie went into their little bedroom and were soon deep asleep as well. Bobby mounted to the loft and closed his eyes, only to have them pop open again a minute later. He still had a little divorce money leftover (along with of course the cabin itself and the land and the Mies van der Rohe chairs), and had purchased scuba equipment. He had learned to dive as a teenager, and been certified in his open-water test by a Frenchman who had been a member of Cousteau's *Calypso* crew. Abineau was never without a cigarette pasted to his lower lip and it was believed he could smoke underwater, thirty feet below in a muck-dark Minnesota lake, removing the regulator's mouthpiece, taking a soggy drag, replacing the mouthpiece, while with his free hand snatching face masks and mouthpieces from student divers about to make their free ascents, popping them in the stomach to encourage the steady exhalation required of the maneuver. Fifteen students were demonstrating their basic skills to Abineau and two assistants, and as they did so, a county sheriff roared up in a rowboat vastly overpowered by the massive outboard mounted so heavily on its transom that the bow was pointing at the sky even when they'd drifted to a stop. The sheriff demanded to know who was in charge and what the hell was going on, and when Abineau answered those questions, informed him that a Minnesota state law required all divers to be tethered to their dive-flag floats at all times.

Abineau was so incredulous he sputtered the cigarette from his lower lip.

"Zat is AHB-surrrd."

"Zat is the LAW," mocked the sheriff.

"But you seely bahs-TAHRD-uh! Captain Cousteau develop zis equipmaw to be SELF-uh CONTAIN underwater breeezing equipmaw! You see? So zat no line is attach to the diver-uh. He iz free-uh. Zat is zuh hull goddamn pwant."

Generations of technological improvements had come and gone in the twenty years since Bobby had first donned gear. His idea of a scuba diver had been formed first and foremost by Lloyd Bridges in the television show *Sea Hunt*, with bad guys constantly going after Bridges's big corrugated regulator hoses with their serrated shark knives; the sophisticated and worldly Cousteau crowd and their stocking caps had come later. And though there were many wrecks in southwestern Superior water to dive, some of them promising the ultimate sight-seeing sensation—cabins of perfectly preserved corpses —his intention now was only to familiarize himself with the latest gizmos with a brief swim, half an hour out into the lake and half an hour back.

The sun had appeared and shone hotly as Bobby lugged the big mesh bag of equipment from the trunk of his beloved Volvo, down the drive, across the road, down the embankment and down the steps, and as he wrestled himself into the wetsuit he broke into a tremendous sweat. The angle of the sun was one that always seemed to draw his attention to his neighbor's buoy, a beachball-sized tie-up to which he had never seen a vessel tied-up, a couple hundred yards off the neighbor's dock, where the deeper water began. Panting and sweating, Bobby stared at it: it compelled him in a way he had never succeeded in describing. It was a melancholy object, certainly, possessed of some kind of deep, end-of-summer loneliness, and yet pleasingly steadfast, almost cheerful in the way it bobbed up and down in its ceaseless duty. In a strange way that would always be his secret, he loved the little buoy and would grieve its loss if his boatless neighbor ever pulled it up and threw it in his shed.

Lost in this meditation, and superficially distracted by the "octopus gauge," a many-tentacled device that could tell him everything about air supply, the condition of the water, and his personal position and welfare that he could imagine wanting to know, Bobby failed to notice that the weather was changing yet again. The water had turned purple, whitecaps had been whipped up and were turning a greenish hue in the increasingly strange light. Along the horizon, where Chequamegon Bay opened into the big lake, a band of gray and a band of black were being transformed into electrified streams of charcoal and ash, shot through with blue lightning. But he did not see these wonders. He pointed himself to the southeast and duckwalked his immense lead-belted, rubber-bound weight around the boulders into the surging water. Up to his knees, he gently stretched himself out and took the snorkel in his mouth. Swimming a few strokes, the cold water seeping in through the suit and warming against his skin, he saw the bottom sloping away and replaced the snorkel's mouthpiece with the regulator's, purging it and beginning to breathe the air in his tank, valves sucking open and shut, vents roaring bubbles. Bending slightly at the waist, he made two pulls down through the water with his arms, then flippered his way along the mostly empty bottom, adjusting his buoyancy compensator, checking his compass, removing his mask and replacing it just for practice, feeling the bracing blast of very cold water on his face, looking this way and that into what was finally registering as surprisingly murky water. It was supposed to be crystal clear. He was troubled by the murkiness, but more as if he'd been sold a bill of goods than anything else. A few minutes later, he saw something flash, and he wondered doubtfully if it had been the flank of a big fish, reflecting sunlight, but this seemed unlikely as it was difficult to see even his gauges in the weakly lit swirl of murk around him. He was only twenty-five feet deep and should have been able to see for hundreds of yards, but could see precisely nothing and had used up half his tank. He decided to surface and see how far from shore he'd actually swum.

It seemed night had fallen. The sky was black as coal but eerily luminous. A wave smashed him in the face and stripped both mask and regulator from him. Coughing and choking, he spun around in a panic as wave after wave blinded him. The only land he could see—thought he could see—was a pencil line below a faintly lightening horizon, miles and miles away, it was impossible, maybe it wasn't even land, and then he looked up. Out of that roiling blackness a seam of white hot lava appeared to open. It boiled down at him like a waterfall, or like a vein of white blood in the arm of a god reaching down for him.

The crash of thunder awoke Hughie. She saw another blaze of light and heard almost immediately another boom of thunder: it was right on top of them and she could not prevent a yelp of fear escaping her. She called out Bobby's name, then ran around the cabin, inside and out, shouting for him. Alex and Josie meanwhile had heard the thunder and the scream and the shouting and were struggling into their clothes. Hughie appeared in the doorway of the nearly night-dark room, her white face livid in the terrible flashing light. "Bobby is out in the lake," she said.

"Jesus Christ," Alex whispered.

"Oh dear," said Josie. "Oh no. Do you—has he...? But can't he...?"

"He must be dead," said Hughie. She said it matter-of-factly, and they all took it calmly as they pulled big rain ponchos over their heads and went one by one out the door, across the deck and down the little steps, where they turned around a corner of the cabin and nearly ran into Bobby.

The cowls of the ponchos obscured the faces of his wife and friends quite thoroughly; they looked like a tribunal of evil monks, and they said nothing, moved no limb, no finger, no eyelash around an eyeball lit faintly in its cave of darkness by lightning. Bobby, panting so hard he was bent double, resting his hands on his knees, lifted his soaked head but could see nothing but three hooded figures beyond the curtain of rain, and so remained silent too.

3

Two years later Hughie got a job with Garrison Keillor and divorced Bobby; another year passed and Alex landed a substantial part in a Coen Brothers movie, and divorced Josie. Josie and Bobby got married and had two children, Martine and Marcus. Martine was dark and bookish like Bobby, Marcus blonde and vivacious like Josie. Josie was a tenured professor in an MFA program at a Lutheran college in St. Peter, Minnesota, and Bobby taught extension classes in a variety of subjects at the University of Minnesota. Their friends were all teachers now, too, and they invited two of them, Rex and Virginia, and their two small children, up to the island one very hot summer weekend.

They rented canoes in the Town Park and floated across a lagoon so untouched by the commonplace technologies and developments of their time that they imagined they would see French voyageurs around the next bend, their huge canoes piled with pelts, singing lusty songs in humorous accents. Then they went hiking in the State Park, just down a sandy road another couple miles, and clambered over the huge sandstone boulders of the shore, pointing out to the children mysterious caves, some of which ran very deep into the island's interior. Waves surged through these caves, Bobby told the children, and sometimes, on very quiet nights, you could lie on the ground and hear the beating of Indian drums in the earth below.

They climbed higher and higher until it seemed they were on the top of the island and could see it all. In Bobby's mind's eye he could see all the islands of the archipelago like little gardens floating in a bowl of cold water, gardens of black spruce and quaking aspen and white sweet clover, red clover, hawkweed and fireweed and purple vetch, oxeye daisies, blue flags hidden in the deeps of the swampy woods in sacred grottoes, buttercups and bunchberries and thimbleberries and bearberries, here and there a small stand of the old magnificent white pines and Christmasy firs, and darting through it all like arrows the yellow-bellied sapsucking woodpeckers, reincarnations, he had heard it said and believed, of people who had died on the island, and after which the Indians, the Chippewa, the Ojibwe, the anishinabe, "the people," had named the island: moningwaunakuning.

Evening fell as a smokey pink band along the horizon, deepening to purple in the east, toward Ontonogan, and to a halo of orange in the west, over Bayfield. The water was pale blue and luminous white with dark blue streaks moving through it and somehow suffused with red.

In the twilight, they saw a bear, two or three hundred yards away, crossing the road, and Bobby said, murmuring but loud enough in that serene stillness to be quite clear, "Dear Lord, please forget all about me, and help the bear." They went inside and ate dinner and listened to Ralph Vaughan Williams's "Oboe Concerto," which Bobby played several times, claiming it was the island's song, reflecting all its moods, the wind in the trees, the waves on the shore, the birds—especially the loon, late at night, when the lake was quiet—and even its darkness, its coldness, its depth and its indifference to life.

Then he and Josie tried to teach Rex and Virginia how to play poker. Rex had been a newspaper reporter but was in no way hard-boiled, and was quite amusingly wry about his dislike of games. They set up a game of five-card-draw and when the betting commenced, Rex pushed all his pennies into the center of the big felt table.

"You can't do that," laughed Bobby.

"Why not?" asked Rex with his usual dead-pan.

"No one here can match you, so even if you win, which is unlikely since we haven't finished drawing all our cards yet, you'll only be taking your own money back, and three of our pennies. And if you lose, you're done, you're out, you're finished."

"That was my objective."

So they gave up on poker and around midnight went outside: fireflies, starlight, a falling star (don't point at it, said Josie, it's bad luck) reflected on the glassy smooth water, an orange moon on the horizon, two red lighthouse lights, revolving beams of a searchlight, northern lights in a curtain from east to north to west, shooting in waves overhead from the north almost into the southern sky, the Milky Way visible all the way to the horizon so that it appeared to falling into the big bowl of reflcted glow from the city of Ashland to the south-southeast.

I can do card tricks, thought Bobby, and tell jokes in funny voices. I am generous with money when I have it and I am a good listener, but I am on my third wife in what, a decade? I like her, and I like these people standing near me, I do, I really do, I love them. But I am sick. I have always been and will always be sick....

The next day was very hot again. It had been a hot month and the water near the shore was warm enough to swim in. Waist-deep it was almost like bathwater, cooling off sharply with each step further into the lake. The children played in the sand and sat in the water, and Rex and Virginia and Josie swam a few strokes back and forth past the little beach. Bobby decided to swim out to his sad little friend the buoy.

"It's too far," said Josie. "And look how big the waves are out there."

"It's less than a hundred yards and the waves only look big because we're so low in the water. I'm a good swimmer."

"You're fifty years old. You're out of shape. And it's farther away than you think."

It was hard to say how far away the buoy was; some days it looked like you could dive off the neighbor's dock and surface right next to it, while other days it seemed all by itself, very far away.

Bobby felt invigorated and strong and began to swim. After what he estimated was about two lengths of a pool, fifty yards, he paused and looked up for the buoy: it was as far away as it had ever been. Perhaps even further. He struck out with new determination, even though the waves, as his wife had suggested, were bigger than he'd thought. He swam hard for several minutes, fighting his way through the waves, and then began to feel cold. Of course the water here, he thought, is much deeper. So of course it's colder. I am tired because I have been swimming hard through big waves of cold water for many minutes now. He breast-stroked a bit, keeping an eye on the buoy as it appeared and disappeared. I could turn around here, he thought, since the water is so much colder and since I am more tired than I'd like to admit I am. But that really runs against the grain. I set out to swim to the buoy because I've wanted to do that for many years now, it's an object that has had a special place in my imagination for years, it has called out to me in its loneliness and heartiness for years and I believe I will make a few more strokes, reach the buoy, and rest for a while holding on to it.

Which he did. On the shore, Rex, Virginia, and Josie watched him appear and disappear with the buoy. They saw him wave, and Rex asked if that was a greeting or a call for help. Josie thought he was just waving: it looked like an ordinary wave, just a flip of the hand, nothing frantic about it all. "He's just saying to me, see? I made it after all!"

Clinging to the buoy, after he'd waved to his friends ashore in attempt at reassurance he now had less faith in than seconds before, when he'd raised his arm, Bobby realized he was not getting very well rested. He was in fact getting no rest at all. He was more tired than when he'd begun to rest because he was freezing to death. He was already cold enough for the panic he felt to be a very cold and small flare indeed, but still it was with panic that he pushed away from the buoy and tried to swim.

His legs moved very slowly in the water, almost as if without volition. And his arms felt like lead. The waves were with him, though, he felt that and was grateful for it. He swam a few languid floating strokes and then rolled over on his back, wishing to keep his mouth further from the water, and trusting that the waves would continue their gentle transit of his body toward the shore even if he failed to move his arms and legs, which now seemed if not altogether out of the question at least ineffective and possibly, he thought, ridiculous. The little flare of panic was cold and dead and he felt very much at ease. If he could move his arms, he would. He could, and he did. It was a tremendous success, a kind of success he thought he'd never known before because it was so perfectly in keeping with what was natural and reasonable, a simple movement rooted in the present, like a breath. Memories of other similar movements of his arms and legs did not trouble him with thoughts that they had been imperfect, that they had failed, that he had failed, and his imagination of such movements to come, of the future, of a future of those same failing movements repeated uselessly over and over again, did not trouble him either, because he expected nothing of them. He desired nothing, nothing at all, and was completely happy to turn over again on his stomach and press his arms forward and draw them back to his side. This is how it happens, he thought. This. This is easy. This is wonderful. And then his foot brushed the bottom. After a moment his other foot too brushed the bottom, and soon he was walking weightlessly and his head and chest were entirely out of the water and the walking was slower now, and heavier, and heavier still, his torso was fully exposed to the warmth of the sun, his thighs were out and his knees until at last he was dragging his ankles water that was as thick as glue and he was sitting on a log. He told Josie he was fine, but tired, and cold, and that he was going to take a nap. He waved and smiled at Rex and Virginia, who were very near and holding their arms tentatively out to him, but who seemed very far away. He made his way up the steep steps to the cabin's loft, where it must have been close to 100, and he wrapped himself in one of his old winter woolen blankets and slept for three hours. When he awoke, he turned his head away from the wall and looked at the long rectangle of pale yellow light appearing to support both window and wall. It was full of dust motes and cob-webs and microscopic pieces of decomposing insects, little clouds of these things drifting as if toward the bottom of a warm clear lake, and even though the window was high enough to make the angling beam seem almost like a empty glass coffin, he rose and walked over to the light, examining it in a way that struck him as perfectly gentle. He stepped into the warm box of light and he understood that, sick as he was, he was alive, and ought not be so foolishly in love with the idea of the end of it.

for John Richardson
August 9th, 2006 Cambria, California

THE INTIMIDATOR STILL LIVES IN OUR HEARTS

OR, CONVERSATIONS IN CALIFORNIA

omaggio a Elio Vittorini

1

I drove into the gas station, taking care not to scrape my bumper in the flood runoff channel. The price of gas was higher than it had been the day before, which had been higher than the day before that, and so on, for months. It was now broadly considered very high. There was only one other vehicle at the pumps, a truck of the kind that are common where I live: body lifted from the wheels with heavy-duty after-market suspension equipment, big tires, wheels as shiny and intricate as diamonds, cabs spacious enough for large families, glossy spotless beds. I say, frankly and at the very outset, that these sparkling luxury toys set my teeth on edge. I thought instaneous and terrible things about the men and women and children who drove them. I understood, even then, that those feelings were rather hysterically prejudicial, poisoned, poisonous—but I had owned trucks: these were not trucks. Trucks were beat-up and dirty. Their tires were bald and their rusty fenders flapped, at any speed over an idle, like the wings of the first failed aircraft. One of my trucks was so rust-eaten and overused that I could—had to—turn the key with one hand and tap the starter motor with a hammer with the other; and another was a three-quarter ton Chevy, a big sturdy vehicle by the standards of the day, but it would hardly register on the local spectrum. If it was immaculately restored and driven by a longboarder with a silver handlebar moustache, it would be acceptable, even desirable; but otherwise be written off as the truck of a Mexican leaf-blower or Vietnamese housepainter.

I suppose I thought that only poor working people drove trucks—down-on-their-luck Jeffersonian yoemen—and that these other vehicles were props for a kind of Republican poseur, whose fundamental conceit and deceit was that he was not posing, that he was a straight-talkin' American bottom-liner who would stomp or sue your ass if you called him a French name again. Or, lower down on the feeding-chain, garden-variety Sweet Timothys, McVeigh-types who would run you over or sacrifice the dear ol' truck with a fertilizer bomb and the mingled blood of people given a head-start on the Rapture.

I recognized the truck and then the man standing next to it watching the numbers click on the pump. It was a neighbor of mine; I wasn't sure what he did for a living, but I did know he enjoyed stock-car racing: the back window of his truck was tastefully decorated with a small number of decals of brand names and logos of companies who sponsored racing teams involved in the billion-dollar NASCAR industry—and which fit the truck's color scheme. Featured most prominently were the numbers of the cars of his favorite drivers. He also had a bumper sticker, but just one: THE INTIMIDATOR STILL LIVES IN OUR HEARTS. This was a reference to a hard-driving villain/hero of millions who had died in a crash on the last lap of the Daytona 500, a few years earlier, in 2001, before everything changed.

"Is the number eight car going to get turned around this year?" I asked him.

He didn't seem to recognize me, so I stepped closer, into the circle of light around his truck. I saw that it was possible he was drunk.

He sized me up.

"You're into NASCAR?"

"Yes." I did not say that I could watch a race and listen to Schubert's Quintet in C, the one Thomas Mann wanted to hear when he was dying, but it was true, I could, and did.

Again he weighed me in a dubious balance.

"They were way fucked up to take Junior's crew chief away from him."

I nodded. Junior was the more-famous son of The Intimidator, his fame due certainly in part to the spectacular and violent death of his father but due at least as much to the easy conviction with which he played a charming and not altogether unintelligent young gun.

"Every Sunday they had the best car in the field. Junior had a shot at winning every race he was in."

"Why'd they bust it up if it was working so well?"

My neighbor paused and scrutinized me a third time. His tank was finally full and the pump clicked off. I think he suspected me of being a liberal, of condescension toward his sport, of veiled derision of his religion, Elvis & Earnhardt, Bible & Flag, of his life.

"It was family politics," he said.

I nodded. "Families can be tough."

"They got to where they hated each other."

"That's a tough way to spend a weekend."

"Junior said, I want to be able to come over to your house for a beer and just be cousins. We can't work together and be a family too."

"So you think Junior's responsible for the breakup of the team?"

My neighbor was tall and dark. He wore a heavy, drooping black moustache, and though he must have been forty or even fifty and well-off, a ballcap (advertising a service I didn't recognize) turned backwards, cutoffs, and a sleeveless t-shirt that showed off his muscular arms. With what I perceived as hostile incredulity, he yanked the nozzle from the spout of his truck's gas tank and turned away from me. He fumbled at the pump, trying to replace the nozzle in its niche, then turned back to me, still holding it, almost weapon-like, before him.

"Junior's fault!" He shouted but laughed. "Junior's fault! He was trying to make peace with those fucking idiots! They made him do it! They could have had a happy family and a championship racing operation if they'd listened to him but they fucked it up and now they're lucky if they finish thirty-fucking-second!"

"Well," I said, "maybe they'll turn things around this year."

And I turned back to my car. It was a winter night in Southern California, inland, more or less equidistant from coast and high desert. Because it was winter I could see the mountains: the smog that removes those eight, ten, twelve-thousand-foot peaks from view as surely and completely as if a spell of evil magic had been cast over them remains pooled for a few months over Los Angeles. I could see the mountains clearly even though it was midnight. Lights twinkled in the tiny clusters of the mountain towns and villages and gave way, at a faint but clear line of ridges and peaks, to a darkness only just barely perceptible as deeper, and starlight.

It was the kind of night that made me want to drive until dawn, east over the mountains and into the desert and over the mountains again, across the plains, across the Mississippi; but I drove west instead, for only a few minutes, to the airport in Ontario.

I circled the parking lots several times before my father appeared on the sidewalk outside the terminal, standing placidly alone with a small bag at his feet. I thought you could tell even from that distance what a good man he was.

He opened the back door and tucked his little bag in the backseat, then got in front. We hugged awkwardly but warmly over the console and shift lever.

"Well," he said, "I made it."

"You are here," I agreed. "How was the flight?"

"Oh pretty good. Most flights are okay with me. I sleep pretty well on planes."

He looked a little puffy, it was true, and sounded a little foggy.

"I learned how to sleep when I traveled for Cornelius in the Sixties." The Cornelius Company manufactured soft-drink dispensing equipment and my father had traveled to Europe and Japan frequently when my brother and I were quite small.

"I remember those trips very well," I said. "At least I remember you coming home with transistor radios and those big clunky tape recorders that seemed so small and portable then."

"That was high-tech for the time."

"Yes. And those mechanical pencils that showed the Buckingham Palace guards sliding back and forth in the whatever you call it, the barrel of the pencil, in that fluid, whatever it was. What was that fluid anyway? Was it just water?" I could hear the tape recorder's parts clunking in place as I pressed the big black lever pads. My brother and I saying something ridiculous.

"I don't know."

"And the miniature Eiffel Tower...."

I tried to think of more gifts he'd brought home for us, but was too distracted by the traffic, fast and heavy even at midnight. My father smiled the family smile, which was mostly a softening of downcast eyes and a slight tilt of the head —my grandmother's smile. My grandparents and their brothers and sisters and my parents and their brothers and sisters were all warm-hearted people, but not overly demonstrative. The smile, however, was soft and sweet.

"Did you enjoy those trips, Dad?"

"Oh," he said, "yes and no. It was hard not knowing the languages even though everyone spoke perfect English. And it seemed like a lot of responsibility for an Iowa farm boy to shoulder. Your grandfather thought business would be a good way for me to get off the farm if I wanted to, and I told him that I thought I did. He did too."

"He wanted you to get off the farm?"

"No," my father smiled. "He wanted to get off the farm himself. That was why we were in Waterloo for several years of the war."

"And he ran for county office, too, didn't he?"

"Oh yes."

"Was that before or after the war?"

"Before. He lost the election by one vote, which my mother would have cast had she not been giving birth to me. The doctor was also a supporter of my father. I don't know if he voted or not."

"Did he hate it on the farm?"

"Oh, I don't know, I think hate is probably too strong a term. He wouldn't have put it that way, at any rate. Love and hate were words he used sparingly."

"I wish I could do the same."

"I don't use them much either."

"No, you don't. I think that's admirable."

"Well, I don't know about that."

"But I wonder…did he use actual love and actual hate sparingly too? I mean not the words but the emotions…?"

"Well he certainly wasn't one for emotional displays."

"He would have seemed crazy if he was."

"That's true. Pretty quiet bunch those Norwegians."

"I've always thought I must seem crazy."

My father smiled. "No, no."

"To you and Mom and Eric. And to the extended family to the extent that they know me at all."

"You've got a temper, that's true. But so did your grandfather. He had a terrible temper, they say, but I can't confirm that because he had pretty much got it under control by the time I was born. I never saw much evidence of it. But my sisters did, every once in a while. He never got angry at them, or my mother, because he confined it to the barnyard. But evidently there were some displays of pretty high emotion once he was out of the house."

"Did he throw his tools around?" That was something I was famous for, infamous for, around our house when I was a teenager. One wall of the garage bore the marks of maybe a hundred hammer blows, incontrovertible and unrelenting testimony to my frustration at not being able to repair the derailleur of my ten-speed, or the strange moaning of the universal joint on the three-quarter ton. The *ghostly goddurnits*, my brother and I had called the sound.

"Yes," mused my father, "I think I remember seeing him throw things. I remember particularly, though, one incident. Well, I shouldn't say I remember because I wasn't born yet, but I remember hearing about this incident many times. My parents were going to take a couple days off to visit Mother's family in Ostrander. Now you know, dairy farmers don't take days off. It's a seven-days-a-week job, fifty-two weeks a year."

"I do know that. And I know you think I'm nuts, but it sounds almost like a paradise to me."

My father laughed loudly. "I have to tell you in all seriousness, you don't know what you're talking about."

"Well I'm sure that's true. But it seems like a paradise nevertheless."

He smiled and shook his head. "They got Leo to agree to take care of things while they were gone." Leo was my grandfather's younger brother. "He had been sober for a year or more, and was farming a few acres just a mile or so to the west, on the other side of the hill. His trouble with alcohol had been pretty serious, though."

"I guess I got that gene," I said. "Me and Leo and those two uncles of Mom's who killed themselves."

"Yes," my father said in gentle agreement. "Alcohol can cause a lot of grief."

"I'm sorry, Dad," I said quietly but suddenly.

"You're forgiven. We all are."

We let a moment pass and then my father resumed his story. "Leo was actually very grateful to my father, for all the help he'd given him, and he was eager to return some of that help. He thought my father needed a vacation. That was what he said. And a few extra rounds of chores were just what he, Leo, needed."

"How long had he been sober? A year you said?"

"Off and on for many years. Mostly sober with a few benders thrown in every half year or so. But I think he'd been sober for at least a year at that point and it seemed like he had really turned a corner."

I dreaded hearing what I was about to hear. I felt like Leo's sins were my own.

"But it turned out that Leo's alcoholism wasn't the problem that day. And though he fell off the wagon a few more times over the years, that year really was something of a turning-point. What happened was your grandfather's fault, not Leo's at all. He was nervous, I think, about leaving the farm, even for a long weekend, and even though he had faith in his brother. I gather he fussed around quite a lot the morning they were to leave, tending to things he didn't need to tend to, and little things were going wrong everywhere he went, which just made him more nervous and frustrated. When Leo showed up he was already pretty irritable, so my sisters said anyway. The car was loaded and everybody was ready to go, and just as they were about to drive off, a calf got loose. He jumped over the fence and took some of the fence with him, which I gather was an accident waiting to happen because the fence wasn't in great shape and my father blamed himself for not repairing it. But a loose yearling was a pretty ordinary problem, not really a problem at all. It just seemed that way to my father because he was already upset. And the unmended fence wasn't something he needed to take himself to task over either."

"Didn't they have a dog?"

"I'm not sure that they did."

"Woody would have had that calf trembling with fear and begging to get back in his pen." Woody was my dog; she'd died a couple years earlier and I still felt so much grief that the mention of her (admittedly incongruous) name brought tears to my eyes. I had once painted the very farmhouse my father was talking about, and Woody and I had stayed in a tent next to the rhubarb patch backyard while I was doing it. A yearling got out of his pen several times while we were there, and Woody had him backed into a corner within seconds every time. She was an Australian Shepherd, a blue merle, so I have to assume it was in her blood, but she'd never seen cattle until that trip.

"She was a good dog," said my father.

"It was purely delightful to watch her work like that," I said. "Maybe that's why I persist in thinking of farmlife as a paradise."

My father laughed. "A good dog would have been a great help that day, I'm sure. But I guess we didn't have one. Dog or no dog, though, my father should have just laughed and wished Leo good luck. Gotten into the car and driven away. But he decided he needed to at least temporarily fix the fence, and while he was doing that, the calf was getting playful with him, dashing here and there, upsetting things and running off, and even nudging my father as if to kid him a little over his frustration. But my father was by now quite angry and he would bat the calf away or lunge after him, then try to pick up where he left off, and Leo was trying to help but evidently not helping in the right way, and finally the calf came up behind my father and butted him in the rump. My father stumbled, then picked up a two-by-four, swung around, and hit the calf over the head with it."

I smiled and started to laugh.

"Killed it," said my father.

I swallowed the laugh and more tears formed involuntarily in the corners of my eyes.

"When Leo tells the story, he gives everybody a knowing look at this point, and says, Oh was John mad then!" The image of the short stumpy goggle-eyed drunk (Leo) and the tall lean virtuous yeoman farmer (my grandfather) in this reversal of roles should have been funny, and both my father and I did laugh, but I was unutterably sad. I thought of the dead calf, my dead dog, my dead grandfather and his dead brother—and I thought of my wife, from whom I had been separated for half a year, at whom I had hurled so many angry and cruel words. It may be childishly banal to say so, but I wanted her back, and I would have done anything, made any sacrifice—yearned for a chance to sacrifice myself in some way that would restore her to happiness. I wanted to be humble. I wanted to work quietly and hard and be content in that work. I wanted my dog back and I wanted my wife back and I wanted everything to be as it had been. I wanted my grandfather sitting there in the living-room with us, talking quietly but good-humoredly, smiling every now and then, laughing once or twice, and always finding a wise word or two to speak.

"I think," said my father, "that that was last time he ever lost his temper. Maybe it was a turning point in his life more than in Leo's. I don't know. He had a good relationship with Jesus Christ, and he knew his sins were forgiven. But I don't think he ever really forgave himself for killing that calf."

I knew I would never be able, or even willing, to do such a thing, but said nothing.

A little later, to shake off the somberness that had crept into our conversation, we went out to eat, at an Indian restaurant in the corner of a strip mall. The food was spicy enough, and so completely alien to the food we had both grown up eating, that we became quite jolly.

"We'll have to blow this pop-stand," said my father, "and head to Kalmar for some cold-eats." Kalmar was the nearest "big" town in Winneshiek County, on the southern border of which the farm was situated. Ossian, where my father had gone to high school, was considered hicksville in relation to the Babylon of Kalmar. "Pop" was sweet carbonated beverages, and "cold-eats" was what the old-timers in Ossian called ice-cream. My father imitated an old Scandinavian yahoo: "Yah shore den, you boyce, if you want cold-eats you got to go to Kalmar den!"

And I thought of a picture taken of my grandfather at one of his last birthday parties. He was sitting at a table in front of a cake with candles on it, and he was wearing a long, stringy, black wig. He looked a little like Tiny Tim, the folk-singing oddity from the late 60s. Nothing could have been more out of keeping with the somber wisdom that characterized him, but you could see he was clearly enjoying himself, the outright silliness of it; and yet there was a look of very great seriousness in his eyes, the look, I thought, of a man who had struggled with a demon a long long time ago, who remembered it with painful clarity, and who did not wish to forget it.

2

The next day I had to go to work. That meant one-and-a-half hours on the harrowing I-10 Freeway, if traffic was good, the 10, all the way into Los Angeles and beyond, the 10, almost to the ocean. I worked in a bookstore, one of the last bookstores in the city operated by its owner, a small place compared to the spacious and luxuriously furnished superstores, but a good place. We had books piled to the ceiling, in double and triples rows on the floor, pressed on shelves wherever they would fit and often where they did not—something out of Dickens, I used to tell people, dark for a bookstore and a little dank at times, especially considering it was a bookstore in sunny, breezy southern California. But that's what our customers liked about the place, they said. That and our "knowledgeable service"—like most booksellers, we were able to name authors and titles based on the (often wrongly recollected) color of the cover. The store was spread out, in little rooms, around the small palm-treed courtyard of a typical Angeleno building from the 50s, before malls. The municipality, Brentwood, had resisted malls and chain stores and big buildings, but our days were clearly numbered. Our customers were staggeringly wealthy, many of them movie stars (you may not know Brentwood, but you certainly know O.J. and have probably heard of The Getty) and their purchases of gigantic art books and bestselling hardcover thrillers and romances went a long way toward keeping us in business. The movie stars themselves were surprisingly friendly and modest and intelligent—usually —but the people with money, just money, were very often insufferable. This surprised me too, but it shouldn't have. I guess I thought people who bought books would be more decent, somehow, than people who didn't buy books. Or at least decent while buying the books.

I thought bookselling would be a quiet business too. It was not. It was retail, and the product, books, mattered only nominally.

The clamor began as soon as I walked in. We had six phone lines coming in, and no one specifically designated to answer them. This was one of the primary responsibilities of people on the sales floor, the other two being the ringing up of sales and the hunting for books requested by customers daunted by the seeming disarray of the shelves. There were four of us on the sales floor, and six lines ringing. Customers were lining up at the registers in each room, also four in number, and the intercom that connected the rooms and the offices was squawking continuously as well.

"Line four has a children's book question."

"Line three wants to know when we're going to pay them."

"Line one isn't making any sense, but I think she wants mysteries."

"Isn't anybody answering phones down there?" asked someone from the office upstairs. "I just took a call from someone who said she rang and rang and rang for fifteen minutes and nobody picked up! Answer the phone, answer the phone, answer the phone, please, it's the most important thing we do!"

I took line one because I had no choice.

"Do you have any books by Agatha Christie?"

I could just barely make this out; the connection was bad, the store was noisy, the woman either very old or very sick or both, and speaking with something, I was sure, in her mouth.

"Yes, ma'am, we have lots of books by Agatha Christie."

"I don't know which ones I've got, but I'd recognize the titles if you said them to me."

Though the phone cord was long enough to reach a computer, two considerations prevented me from stepping over to it: one, the great age of the equipment and the idiosyncratic nature of the information it could be counted on to supply; and two, the fact that I had never managed to learn now to cradle the phone between cheek and shoulder like everybody else in the universe seemed to be able to do. I thought maybe it was physiognomic, length of neck or slope of shoulder or something like that, but couldn't see anything terribly wrong with the parts of my body that might have effected the problem. So I simply put the woman on hold, got an armload of books from the shelf, found a little space on the crowded counter for them, got back on the phone, and proceeded to recite the titles. The poor old woman gamely fought off despair as she vaguely replied "no" to each one I listed. Then she perked up and began to ask me what certain titles were about. I tried reading some jacket copy, but it only seemed to deepen her despair as we went on. Meanwhile the intercom was blaring like something in a Marx Brothers movie, and people were lining up and getting impatient.

"I just want to know where the ladies' room is."

"It's upstairs, ma'am."

"Upstairs?"

"Second floor, yes, in that corner of the courtyard," I said, pointing.

"But where are the stairs?"

"They are outside. Two of them." I pointed like a flight attendant.

"I don't see any stairs!"

"You will if you go outside. You have to trust me."

"I," said another woman, "want this gift-wrapped!"

"Across the courtyard in the gift shop," I said, altering the angle of my point.

"But I was just over there."

"Miss Marple has her hands full in this delightfully wicked —"

"Where across the courtyard."

"In the gift shop," I repeated. "Next to the café."

"Yes, that's exactly where I was and I didn't see anyone wrapping gifts."

"I do not see any stairs anywhere!" shouted the first woman from the doorway. "No I'm not talking to you!" she shouted into her cell phone.

"Ma'am," I said to the Agatha Christie fan, "I am going to have to let you go to help some other customers here."

"Can you just send me a few books? Maybe ten or so...? If I've read them, I'll be able to compare them, you see, right here, on the spot, and be sure. And if I have read them, I can mail them back to you."

"All right," I said. "I'll need your address and phone and credit card."

"A what?"

"Credit card...?"

"Oh dear."

"Don't you have one?"

"Oh I've got one, all right," she said with surprising vehemence. "Just let me look here...."

While she was looking, I decided to gamble and run the first woman upstairs to the ladies' room and the second to the gift shop, but they both shook me off. In the courtyard, a homeless man who sometimes slept in the men's room hailed me. He was usually quiet, and liked to read in the corner of our darkest room. He had a colostomy bag and of course rare access to a shower, so the close quarters of the history section were sometimes a little much for other customers, but we liked Kenny a lot, some of us, anyway, so when he gestured, I stopped.

"I'm not feeling so good."

"What's the matter?"

"I don't know."

"Do you want me to call a paramedic or the Veteran's Hospital?"

"No, no, not that, not that, not that."

"Well, okay…."

"I just wanted," he said, "to warn you."

"Okay," I said.

He saluted me and marched off, feeling a little better for having warned me. I checked in on the gift-wrapping situation and found the woman staring angrily into space. I apologized and sat down to do it myself.

She said, "These are my options?"

"These are the complimentary papers, yes ma'am."

"They are absolutely revolting."

"They're free."

"Can't I have this paper?"

"That I will have to charge you for."

"Unbelievable," she muttered. "But okay." She slipped the paper from its rack and slapped it down on the gift-wrapping table.

"I will have to charge you for it," I said, getting up and going over to the cash register encouragingly.

She came over and paid me.

"You know what?" she asked.

"No," I said, "what."

"If I have to pay for this crap, you had better wrap it perfectly."

I suppose I could have taken it as mock-rudeness between a good customer and a jolly tradesman, and in that spirit decided to chuckle, but when I was done, she snatched the gift from the table and swirled off without thanks or farewell. I trotted back across the courtyard and picked up line one, which was still blinking in readiness for me. The line was still alive but the old woman wasn't responding to my greetings. I tried to cradle the phone so I could ring up purchases, but it kept slipping out and falling to the floor. Since we didn't have a UPC scanner, we had to enter the ISBN numbers by hand, and I had a hard time going from back of book to computer screen and back again, a difficulty compounded infinitely by the continual dropping of the phone, retrieving of it, and saying hello into it. Then the thing you slide the magnetic strip of a credit card through fell off the side of the monitor where it had been taped. The phones had been quiet, but all of a sudden lines two three four five and six started ringing. The intercom came to life of course as well.

"I've got my credit card," the old Agatha Christie fan murmured in my neck. "Hello?"

"Hello," I said. "If you can give me just a sec here, I'll take that number down and ship these novels right off to you."

"Novels?" she asked.

"The Agatha Christie novels...?"

"Oh I didn't know they were novels. What color are they?"

"The books whose titles I was reading to you all had light blue covers, with dark blue trim and black lettering. They—"

"Look," said someone else, a woman who'd been standing there but to whom I hadn't yet spoken, a big woman, older, lots of jewelry and plastic surgery, carrying several bags from other stores. "Look, whoever you're talking to certainly has a right to good service, and this gentleman does too," and she indicated the man whose books I had rung up and was now trying to get into a bag, holding the phone in my armpit, "but my friend is in a hospital and she is dying! Do you understand me? She is dying, she is hemorrhaging right now and I have got to get there."

"Yes," I agreed, "you really ought to."

"Now I special-ordered some books and I have been waiting weeks for them and I have to see them before I go to the hospital because they might not be appropriate for my friend."

I hit the intercom with mock urgency and asked for immediate help in the west. (Each room of the store was name after a cardinal compass point.) I knew the help would not be forthcoming, but rang up another purchase and returned to the descriptions of the Agatha Christie book-covers. The woman waited with imperfect patience for a few seconds, then lost it.

"WHAT ARE YOU DOING?"

"Trying to help several customers at once, ma'am." I was smiling and suddenly felt great.

"I TOLD YOU MY FRIEND IS DYING!"

"I'm sorry, ma'am, very sorry, but there's only so much I can do for you."

She stormed out. That wasn't my whole day, of course, just the worst of it, a couple hours maybe, but that kind of turmoil does take its toll; as emotionally and ethically sound as I'd felt at the end with the dying woman's friend, I was exhausted by 9:00 that evening, when we closed the store, exhausted in a way that felt dangerous. I was in no condition to make a long commute in heavy high-speed traffic, but I wanted to get home.

Conversations in cars with single occupants tend to be psychotic; and that's maybe why talk radio is so popular: the conversations go on around you, for you, but at absolutely no expense to you. This might be unhealthy too, in the end, but I can understand the difficulty in resisting it. So I turned the radio on just in time to catch a discussion of traffic in southern California.

"It's outrageous," said a caller. "When is the government going to do something about it?"

"What would you like them to do?" demanded the talkshow host.

"Add some lanes! Build a new highway! Anything!"

"That would cost quite a lot of money!"

"Not if they didn't charge $137 for a screwdriver it wouldn't!"

"Who is 'they'?"

"Washington insiders."

"Well all right but just a minute ago you were complaining about big government. You said you wanted government off your back. You said you wanted to get it so small you could drown it in a bathtub. You can't have it both ways. A government you drowned in the bathtub wouldn't be able to dig a ditch much less add a lane to a highway."

Another caller suggested that the problem was that most of the people in southern California were actually country people with country habits.

"What do you mean by 'country habits'?"

"Every family has five cars and they all drive at once. You can get away with that in the country."

"Very few people in this country live in the country."

"Well they used to."

"Not for generations. I think you're talking about suburban people."

"I'm talking about country folks."

"No you're not."

"I'm talking about country folks who are used to having elbow room."

"You're talking about Daniel Boone," said the host. "I'm talking about greedy selfish people who take their traffic jams with them, deeper and deeper into what used to be the country a century ago."

I sighed very loudly, almost a cry of despair, and switched to a Haydn piano trio: there were nearly fifty of them, and I would listen to them all, over and over again, for days and days, for months, driving eating sleeping. It was all so tedious, so dispiriting and annoying. Even "my side" made me weary, even tearful. I made myself weary and tearful.

Headlights were now in my mirror, very close and very bright. I had seen them coming, from out of the thousands, the millions of lights behind me, for miles and miles. It was almost as if I had seen them coming from the moment I left the bookstore parking lot, that I could see into the future and knew he would soon arrive, the preternatural stalker in a big ol' truck with Toby Keith droning nightmarishly through my Haydn.

The beams of course were elevated along with the rest of the truck, and so they illuminated the entire interior of my hybrid. (Did I have a bumper-sticker? Yes, along with the decals that gave me special entitlement to be in the commuter lanes—entitlement! to be drowned in the bath-tub!—there was a sticker asking people to howl if they loved City Lights Bookstore.) It was like being caught in a prison-yard spotlight, and I turned instantly into what my wife, pummeling my shoulder and arm and screaming at me to stop, once called "The Man of Marble." I could deflect even very strong blows when I became the Man of Marble, feel absolutely nothing, and even punish my attackers with at least the psychological equivalent of broken knuckles.

But because I had now entered a new phase of life in which meekness and compassion were the cardinal state and reflex, I did not lose my temper. I was no longer in what my AA sponsor called the honeymoon of early sobriety, certainly no longer floating in the pink cloud of bliss, so I couldn't greet my tailgater with friendly capitulation or even indifference, but I had vowed I would never raise my voice again, inside the car or out.

In a whisper I asked him to get off my ass. Then I slowed down. I kept slowing down and asking in a whisper what my friend was going to do now. Finally he flashed his high-beams at me.

It was as if a silent bomb had exploded inside my Prius.

I stomped on my brakes and whispered something like yes asshole, what now, what now you fucking piece of shit.

He engaged his horn, and kept it blaring until he found room to get around me. He pulled up next to me and made the usual gesture, which I returned. He then shot forward, into the next knot of cars, jerkily darting from one of the six lanes to another, looking for a chance to demonstrate his Hemi's dominant power (I should point out he was towing four personal watercraft). Whispering still, but demanding still who he thought he was and what he thought he was accomplishing with his pathetic jockeying, I bided my time, picked my moment, found a very fast way through the traffic, got way out in front of Toby, waited for him to close the gap, then pulled in front of him and slowed down. I asked him very quietly who he thought the Intimidator was now. Was he supporting the troops now? Would his belief in the unity and omnipotence of the Raider Nation see him through this dark time when a latte drinker could have his way with him, could dog, harass, and baffle his every move? If you whisper long enough, a kind of calm does in fact take over, and I found myself chuckling with genuine light-heartedness as I pressed the question, at a hundred miles an hour through two windows: who's the fucking Intimidator now you shitsucking pinhead?

I got home despite the fact that I was dangerously insane, and went for a walk with my dogs and my father. It was mid-December, so every other house was decorated for Christmas. My father admired these elaborate displays, but observed that they had become something other than decoration.

"We used to put up a string of colored lights along the front of the house," he said.

"I remember."

"That was as wild as we got. And your mother would put up that little wreath, the red one."

"I remember. It wasn't really a wreath, though. I don't know what you'd call it. Just a circle with that red fuzzy material wrapped around it. That soft nubbiny stuff. Kind of like the stuff they make pipe cleaners with. With an electric candle in the middle."

"Very old. That was one of the first electrical devices her folks bought when Rural Electrification went through. I think it must be as old as she is. That was the only decoration they had on the farm-house."

"We've come a long way," I said.

"I like these displays," my father replied. "Some people in our church think it detracts or distracts us from the true meaning of Christmas, but I think that's a little bit of an overstatement."

"Awful lot of money involved in these operations."

"Yes, maybe that's true, in some cases."

"There was a guy a couple years ago—not here, somewhere in Orange County or northern San Diego County or southern Riverside County, those are the hot-spots—"

"Hot-spots for Christmas ornaments?"

My father was not a sarcastic man, but was, I think, anticipating some more cultural vitriol from me.

"For Christmas ornaments, yes, and high-school shootings, and hatred of corporations when they are enslaved by them and hatred of government when they are not, and tension between workers left high and dry by the demise of the aerospace industry and money-people who left them high and dry when they moved on to some other money but stayed in their baronial castles. There's a lot of hatred and it gets disguised with Christmas lights."

"Oh now come on," said my father with what passed in him for impatience. "That's not why I put up my strings of lights, and I'm sure that's the case with most of these people too."

"Well," I said, "okay. But this guy I'm talking about spent $150,000 on his display, and he got over a thousand cars a day, on weekends, idling past his house to gawk at it. Lived in a cul de sac, so you can imagine the traffic problem. His neighbors complained but he ignored them, calling them Scrooges. They went to City Hall, and after a protracted and expensive legal battle, the city forced him to shut his display down."

"There are always exceptions like that. I'm sure nobody intended things to work out like that."

"No, you're probably right," I admitted. "Those kinds of things rattle me, though. I can't help it. They rattle me more than they should, no question, but there I am, rattled."

We walked without talking for a while, and the cypresses and palms grew black against the clear darkening sky. The cypresses were spooky, gothic spires that looked funereal for some reason, and the palms were goofy, with little tassels waving atop very thin trunks maybe a hundred feet high. A nighthawk clicked and screeched overhead, circling for a minute or so, then disappearing. We turned a corner and could see the lights of the towns in the mountains. We turned another corner and came upon a particularly elaborate display.

"This is nice," said my father.

There were four big ol' trucks parked on the expansive driveway, each of them sporting tasteful little #3 and #8 NASCAR decals; and one of them had the THE INTIMIDATOR STILL LIVES IN OUR HEARTS bumpersticker on its bumper.

"The lady of the house here once sprayed us with her garden hose," I said. I pointed at one of my dogs: "He was peeing on the trunk of that palm tree there, and she came flying out of her backyard gate in her nightgown with the garden hose splashing all over the place, no peeing on the trees, no peeing on the trees, no peeing on the trees! Then she put her thumb over the end of it and actually sprayed us."

My father smiled in gentle deprecation. "She must have been very unhappy."

"I think she struggles, yes," I said, "with her mental health."

"Did you get angry with her? I know you can be very protective of your boys...."

"No," I sighed. "I was surprised more than anything. I guess I felt sorry for her."

We had arrived at my house. There was no decoration on it whatsoever. I thought it was a lovely, splendid house. I suppose one of the reasons I felt that way was because I was losing it: though we seemed to be on increasingly amicable footing, my wife and I were divorcing, and I had signed away my claim on the house.

"The people," I said, "who owned this place before us had quite a holiday display themselves. It was a showstopper, they say. They had seven trees in the house, and what is now the library was Mrs. Claus's Candy Shoppe. They had life-size reindeer and a sleigh on the roof, and Santa of course, and a few elves. They re-wired the house to handle the demand."

My father laughed.

"When they sold the house to us, they concealed a leak in the roof. He was a fireman. Vietnam vet. She was a big fat harridan. Salt of the earth. Mr. and Mrs. Claus. Very jolly. Just doing their jobs, keeping their heads down and their mouths shut. Believed in the Bible and the Flag. Screw your neighbor unless he's far enough away to bomb."

"Oh well," my father said lightly. "Forgive them if you can. Try to, at least."

I laughed to show I was arguing in good faith. "What is the point of that, exactly? I know there's a lot of evidence suggesting people all over the planet and for thousands of years have believed it's a good thing to do—"

"It is a good thing to do. A great thing to do. The greatest."

"Yes but I think it's a concept that can only benefit from fresh and regular scrutiny. Why do you think I should forgive these hypocritical swindlers?"

I know I sound like an asshole when I talk like that, and I was pretty sure I sounded that way to my father, too, but he gave me the benefit of the doubt, hearing perhaps a little self-parody in my speech, in my manner, in my hateful confusion. And besides, there, directly across the street, was the mixed Christmas and reggae display of my other neighbors, my wise and friendly and caring neighbors. I was forced to consider the idea that only people I liked could display Christmas lights, and that people I did not like would suffer stiffly punitive fines if they did.

"It makes you feel better," my father said.

"Hmmm?" I asked, lost in what passed for thought.

"Forgiveness."

I found I could not refute it.

3

I had to go to work again the next day.

One of my fellow booksellers was a young man of Iranian descent. His parents were Iranian Jews who had fled with the fall of the Shah, to London, where my friend was born and where he lived for nine years. When his parents divorced, he moved with his mother and brother to Los Angeles, where a large expatriate community held many relatives.

He was tall, broad-shouldered, darkly handsome, and dressed like a hip-hop singer: baggy athletic clothing and lots of jewelry, a pencil-thin goatee, with all the accompanying gestures and affectations of speech that go with the fashion.

I walked in the back door and he sprang out at me from behind the door, grabbing me roughly and kneading my neck and shoulders with a vigor that was almost painful.

"You gotta loosen up, dawg."

"I know it."

"You're the only one I can do this to. Everybody else says it hurts."

"Not at all," I sighed and croaked. "It's great. It's just what the doctor ordered after a drive like I have to make. Look at my forearms: I look like Popeye the Sailor-man. Eighty fucking miles and a never-ending sense of being assaulted by would-be Intimidators. My hands feel like they're made out of stone."

"You're tight, man."

Since "tight" had several colloquial meanings, among them "satisfactory, often enthusiastically so," I kidded Amos about the shortcomings of fashionable language.

"Damn!" he shouted, "I have to watch every word I say around you, man! Okay Dad, yes Dad, yes Teacher, sieg heil Dad." Then he broke into a song from The Music Man: "Gary Indiana, Gary Indiana, Gary Indiana."

"You ought to study acting," I said. "Singing and dancing and stagecraft."

"Aw man that's bullshit. What I wanna do that for."

"You're good at it. You've got a great voice, you're handsome, you've got real presence—"

"I want to change the world, man. I want to help people who are oppressed."

"Well that's great, that's highly laudable. But there are indications that people who want to change the world just fuck it up worse. Oppress suppress repress in some new and equally horrible way."

"Okay, Dad. I won't give a shit. Fuck people. Are you happy with me now, Dad?"

I laughed and he began quoting lines at me from his favorite movie: *The Odd Couple*. He then segued into a rap lyric that described a way of handling difficult women (beating the shit out of them) and closed by singing more lines from *The Music Man* and pounding my neck and shoulders some more.

Then I took a phone call.

"Dutton's Brentwood."

"Hello Dutton's Brentwood!"

"Hello."

"This is Minnie Green! To whom am I speaking!"

"I'm Gary."

"Hello, Gary!"

"Hi, Minnie."

"How are you?"

"I'm doing pretty well, thank you."

"Oh that's terrific, I'm glad to hear that, Gary." Minnie had a strong New York accent, Bronx I thought, like my father-in-law, so "Gary" sounded more like "Gavvy."

"We've been buying our books from you for years, many, many years. We won't buy them anyplace else, and that's why I'm cawling you. We're in San Jose now, we moved several years ago, but we visit Los Angeles regularly to see our son, and we buy our books then, but we can't get down there now, George isn't feeling great—George is my husband—not bad but not great, and we want to give our friend Stanley who's in the hospital a nice big beautiful gift book. He's recovering from surgery and it was a very serious operation. He almost didn't make it, but he pulled through and we want to get him a book of really beautiful photographs that celebrate life. I don't think he's up to reading yet, though he's a terrific reader, Stan. But you know how it is when you're groggy and laid up like that."

"It's hard to concentrate, that's for sure."

"So what I'm hoping I can do, Gavvy, is have you recommend a good book, a great book if you can, of beautiful photographs."

"Well I can certainly try. We have a lot of great books, of course, so I wonder if we can maybe narrow it down a little…?"

"A friend of mine was in your store not too long ago and she suggested a book that I think is just the one, but I don't know. The last time I talked to you—I don't mean you personally, Gavvy, I mean the store—you had it. Do you still have it?"

Minnie named a book and its author and I put her on hold. Amos was meanwhile recommending several books on Islam to a woman not old but much older than Amos, who was clearly smitten with him.

The most salient feature of my friend's charismatic presence was not his good looks or theatrical energy, but his devotion to Allah. His conversion came about in this way.

Hard use of sedatives had slowed him down and spaced him out for a couple of years, and one day put him in a coma. He lay on the floor of his apartment, head twisted awkwardly against the couch, for three days. He was nearly dead when they got him to a hospital, and remained so for several months. Just as he was about to be given up on and the plug pulled, he woke up. Struggling violently back into consciousness and memory, he was easily enraged and would lash out at friends he did not recognize or was only just beginning to recall, so suddenly and frighteningly that he had to be restrained by friends he was not lashing out at. He would shout verses and slogans from the Qu'ran, in a Farsi he had not spoken for years, and several Black Muslim acquaintances were held in a kind of special esteem that precluded attacks. These men came and prayed with him every day; when he was released from the hospital, he went to as many meetings as he had the strength for, and was quickly admitted to the faith. At the bookstore, his religious beliefs were mainly in evidence in opinions about the war in Iraq, but he never missed a chance to declare his devotion and an ardent wish to take Islam back from the terrorists—a desire that was of course at odds with the hot blood natural to a young man, a highly refined and well informed sense of injustice, and the façade of gangsta machismo that the fashion of the street demanded from nearly everybody on it. So he would break into song one minute, then describe for me a situation in which violence might be justified and demand my approval. To which I would always reply something like, "Sure, you would want to blow those assholes up, and you could justify it pretty easily, but that doesn't make it right. You can't fight violence with violence. You can't defeat hate with hate."

"Dawg are you telling me that if they came and busted down your front door and shot your dogs you wouldn't fight back?"

I admitted it would be hard to restrain myself in such a situation.

"And what about those assholes in big trucks you keep whining about!"

I found the book Minnie wanted and got back on the phone.

"These are beautiful photos, no question about that."

"Can you describe them for me, Gavvy?"

"Well the colors are muted. Maybe you want something really colorful for your friend…?"

"He likes black-and-white photography, and so do we."

"So do I."

"These aren't black-and-white but they're muted, is that right?"

"Yes."

"And they're beautiful."

"Yes."

"What are they of?"

"Well," I said, flipping awkwardly through the big heavy pages, "still lifes, it seems. Fruit. A tiny figure of a man at the edge of a forest. Some sober urban landscapes."

"And you like them, Gavvy?"

"Yes, I do. My opinion, for what it's worth—"

"Oh it's worth a lot! I trust you, Gavvy! I can hear it in your voice. You're trustworthy. And we've trusted your store for many many years."

"Well, thank you, I appreciate that."

"So you're saying it's a good choice?"

"I think it is, yes."

"Well, okay...I wish I could be sure. I don't know what else to ask you, though."

"Here's something," I said. "The book is published in association with the Victoria and Albert Museum in London. Have you ever been there? Do you know that museum by any chance? It's a terrific place, and I would say that their involvement with the book is pretty persuasive."

"Victoria and Albert? No, we've never been to London. You think it's nice, though?"

"It's great."

"We don't travel much anymore."

"Ah."

"But okay, you sold me. Now. Can I dictate a get-well greeting to you, Gavvy? And have you send it along with the book?"

"Just let me get a pen and a piece of paper."

I did so, then tried to write the note while cradling the phone, making a nearly indecipherable scrawl and looking like a clown.

"Okay, Minnie, I'm ready."

"Dear Stan. Dear Stanley. We are sorry you're not feeling so hot. No: we are so sorry to hear you are not feeling well. Sorry you are feeling low. Which do you like best, Gavvy?"

"Hmmm," I said. "Is he a very close friend?"

"Let's go with feeling low."

"All right."

"We wish so much that we could be with you right now. But maybe this book will be good company. If you don't like it, you can return it to the bookstore and they will give you credit and you can pick out something you really like. Have a ball on us, Stan!"

Minnie started to sniffle a little, and then to openly cry.

"Love, George and Minnie. I'm sorry, Gavvy, he's just such a dear, dear man."

"Please don't apologize. I understand completely."

"Once he's up and around, he will enjoy coming to your bookstore so much."

"Well, that's great. That's really wonderful. Tell him to ask for me."

"Thank you, Gavvy, I will. Goodbye."

I hung up feeling quite good. I was happy to have had such a conversation. I felt like a human being. But trouble was brewing. A gentleman had engaged Amos in another kind of conversation altogether, one you could tell was wrong from a great distance. The customer had a dark but radiant look on his face and Amos was answering his questions with a very quiet, subdued voice. He looked uncomfortable and ungainly as he tried to stay as far back from the counter as he could. But before I could assess the situation, two other customers inserted themselves in my face.

"Do you have a guidebook to zombies?" an early middle-aged man asked me brightly.

"Zombies?" I asked.

"A guidebook for identifying zombies."

"A guidebook for identifying zuh—"

"Zombies, yes, that's right, that's what I said, a field guide to zombies and I need it right away because it's hard to tell the difference a lot of the time, especially in a crisis, and if I can't tell the difference, I'm just going to have to start killing people indiscriminately."

An older woman put her big purse noisily on the counter. She shot the zombie-hunter a glance, then rolled her eyes for me. The zombie-hunter merely smiled and waited. The woman showed me, with a dramatic gesture, her freshly-painted nails.

"They're still wet. I need you to get my credit card out of my purse for me."

"Certainly, madam," I said, "as soon as I make sure this gentleman isn't going to shoot us all."

"Shooting doesn't work," said the zombie-hunter with a great show of scorn.

"Right," I said, deciding that he was in fact trying to be amusing, as I had suspected at first, not simply insane, as I had suspected on second thought. The woman rattled her immense bag. The man who had begun to speak so ominously to Amos had disappeared.

"Amos, do you know if we have any books on zombies?"

"*A Field Guide for the Identification of Zombies,*" the zombie-hunter corrected me.

"Try humor," said Amos. He pointed out the door in the direction of the children's section, next to which we had a shelf of humorous books.

"It's no laughing matter!" shouted the zombie-hunter. "I told you I'm going to have to stah—"

"Yes," I interrupted firmly, "yes, please don't say it again. It's bad for business." I tried to make it sound like a joke.

The zombie-hunter changed tacks. "What about greeting cards?"

I couldn't help but ask what about them.

"While you people are looking for my book," he said pointedly, "I could browse the greeting card section and perhaps purchase one or two. Do you have any?"

"Yes we do. They are in the gift shop, next to the café."

"The café?"

I pointed out the door. "Out the door, on that side of the courtyard."

"How will I know it?" He stood at the door and pretended he was on a ship at sea.

"There, where those tables with umbrellas are."

"And the greeting cards are near the umbrellas?"

"Yes, you'll spot them if you just—"

"Good, because I don't see them now, and I'm going where you're pointing strictly on my faith in your goodwill."

"Well," I said, "I'm not a zombie."

"BUT HOW DO I KNOW THAT WITHOUT A FIELD GUIDE?"

"Excuse me," said the woman with the freshly painted nails. "Hello?"

"Yes ma'am," I said while still pointing out the door, perhaps imperiously.

"I need you to get my credit card for me." She indicated her many-zippered purse.

"All right," I said, "where do I begin?" I touched a zipper.

"No, not there!"

"Sorry."

"No, not there, either. That one, that one right there, no, no, yes, unzip that. Pull out the—no, not that one, pull out the yes that one. Unsnap it. Carefully. There they are." She said this last in a kind of celebratory way that I couldn't interpret. "Now," she continued jubilantly or mock-jubilantly, "take that card there, no, not that one, not that one, not that one, not—Yes. That one."

And I rang up her purchase.

"I can't sign the slip for you."

"Just put the pen in my hand—carefully—and I will manage the signature."

Then we had to retrace our steps. When she was finally gone, and the zombie-hunter had failed to return, I asked Amos what the other customer had been saying with such quiet intensity to him earlier.

"Guy's an asshole."

"I could smell it a mile off."

"Kick his fucking ass, man."

"You can't be kicking people's fucking asses and praying five times a day. You'll get too tired and confused to do anything. Eventually you'll just split down the middle, like a cartoon character. One side will fall one way, and the other the other."

"My anger is righteous, dawg."

"I'm going to pray six times a day then."

"Fuck you, man."

"One of us will have to kill the other, eventually."

"Oh HA HA, Dad. Very funny, dad. You're not my role model anymore, Dad. SEVENTY-SIX TROMBONES LED THE BIG PARADE, WITH A HUNDRED AND TEN CORNETS RIGHT BEHIND!"

Suddenly the troubling customer was again at the counter. He glanced at Amos and then at me.

"Who buys your books?" he asked in a friendly conversational tone.

"Lots of people," I said firmly, like a salesman.

"No, I don't mean who are your customers, I mean who selects the books you have for sale?"

I might have handed this question off to a manager, or the owner, but it was five in the afternoon and nobody was around.

"Well," I said, "the answer is the same: lots of us. We share that responsibility. Just about everybody in the store has a hand in the buying."

"I ask because I see a definite pattern here, and I'm simply wondering who is responsible for it."

"Lots of people," I repeated.

"Really. Because as I look around, I see a single mind at work. I see an adherence to ideology in a group of minds if not a single one. I'm trained and rather experienced in seeing such things, and I'm quite sure I'm not wrong."

"You're wrong, man," said Amos quietly, almost inaudibly, perhaps only for my benefit.

"And what," I asked, feeling truculence welling up in me that I wished I could channel away but did not, "sort of ideological pattern do you see here?"

"Anti-Semitism."

"Anti-Semitism!" I laughed.

"A particular kind: left-wing liberal pro-Muslim anti-Semitism."

I laughed again, dismissively I hoped.

"You can laugh, but it's very clear to me that that is the case."

He gestured at the books on the counter and on the shelves fronting the counter and on the table behind him and in the spinner-rack next to the table. Amos, it was true, had displayed many books that suggested strong interest in Islam, the war in Iraq, and U.S. imperialism on the part of someone, and that's what I said in our defense.

"Lots of people are interested in Islam these days. I think that's understandable, don't you?"

"It's not an interest in Islam. It's a prejudicial preference for books that advocate an Arab-only Middle East as well as general overthrow of U.S. influenced social and political institutions."

"That's simply not true," I insisted. "For every book you can point to about Islam, I can—"

"They are not about Islam. They are about a specific intolerant political ideology and the religious fanaticism that is its foundation."

"You could not be more wrong, sir."

"Anti-Semitic and treasonous."

"This young man happens to be an Iranian Jew."

"Yes, I saw his self-hate instantly."

Even though I knew I ought to back away from that kind of defensiveness, I said, "My wife is Jewish, and there are many Jews working here. Most of us who aren't Jewish are married to Jews as a matter of fact."

"Yes, yes, of course, some of your best friends are Jews."

"Yes that is true."

"None of that matters. I deal with what is in front of me. With clearly observable reality."

"If you can actually walk around our store and—"

"I can, and do."

"—and think that there's an anti-Semitic mind at work, you are suffering a very cruel delusion and I feel sorry for you."

"You don't really have a leg to stand on," said the customer, smiling with sympathetic kindness. "The evidence against you is right here in front of you."

"Are you calling me an ant-Semite? Because if you are...."

"I'm saying there's clear and incontrovertible evidence of it and you are defending it."

"That's preposterous," I spluttered angrily. "This is a ridiculous conversation and I'm not interested in carrying it on any further."

"If you just stop and think about it, you'll see that I'm right."

"I won't see any such thing."

"Your defense of yourself is just another aspect of anti-Semitism."

"Oh I see, I see! You accuse me of, say, being crazy, and anything I say to refute it is evidence of craziness! That's pretty slick! You alone have access to the truth and anyone else's truth is false! Wickedly wonderful! And you see it as your job to conduct inquisitions, is that it? Noble calling! Great tradition!"

"If you stop for just a minute and think calmly about what I'm saying, you'll see I'm right."

"If you stop for just a minute and think calmly about what I'm saying, you'll see I'm right!"

"Well, I'm going to go now, because I see you're getting angry, but I hope you'll think about what I'm saying. I'm quite confident you'll see I'm right."

"Oh, you're quite confident, are you? That's great. That and a subway token will get you the FUCK out of my store! Now go!" I pointed, once again, out the door.

4

The next day a strange meteorological condition subdued my petty grievances for a moment. It had rained most of the day, and the sky had been uniformly gray, but just before sunset, clear sky opened up in the southwest. My father and I had set out to get a cup of coffee and think about what we might like for dinner; as we turned north on a road that offered a view of the mountains, I saw something I had never seen before, and which, I believe, I am likely never to see again. What I saw did not seem possible to me, not in the moment that I saw it. That sense of simple physical impossibility lasted for several seconds, I think, a very long time under such conditions. But even when I saw how it was possible, saw what was real and how it had seemed unreal, when I understood the illusion, it still struck me as unearthly, magical, even terrible, and shivers ran up and down my spine.

An immense asteroid, as big as the town itself, as big as a foothill, seemed to have crashed, soundlessly and weightlessly, into the center of town.

Usually the foothills and the range of peaks behind them appear more or less the same distance away from any vantage point in town; they appear to be a single thing, even when you can make out lines and give yourself perspective and know what you are seeing and where it is in relation to other things and to yourself. But that day the mountains seemed incredibly far away, almost indiscernible against the mysterious milky gray of the sky; they seemed a part of the sky rather than the earth and ranged away to the north as infinitely as if they were clouds, or a fairy kingdom.

The sunlight, though, from the southwest, coming in at that terrible angle of late afternoon, that kind of sunlight that simultaneously bores into your eyes and casts ominously long shadows across your path, had lit up a single foothill, and when we turned the corner and saw it, it looked like a million tons of glittering ore, dark, rich, rusty brown, lit so brilliantly it seemed to be glowing from within. And I thought that something had happened. In that fraction of a second I thought that something terrible had happened, and I slowed my car down and put my foot on the brake pedal and I was prepared in that nanosecond of conflict between ontological time and something seen through a glass darkly to beg for forgiveness and bind myself to any labor or sacrifice that would appease the forces that had caused the disaster.

My father, of course, who had no history of ordinary viewing to compare it with, saw nothing unusual. When I pointed it out, he agreed that it was peculiar-looking, something of "a sight," but not what he would call strange. Even though I was long seconds past the shock of it and knew very well what I was looking at, I could not entirely convince myself that what I had, at first, thought had happened, had not in fact happened. I felt somehow as if a second world had appeared where the first one already was, and that in that small space, a different reality had come to pass. I felt a little haunted by it, and strangely comforted. Imperceptibly, the foothill asteroid's rich glitter faded and it stood out less sharply against the milky mountains; and slowly it moved into that darkening mass on which other smaller lights began to twinkle.

The conversation we overheard at the café could not have been more perfectly banal. The manager of the café was standing in the doorway, leaning against the frame with his hands in the pockets of his green apron, his English driving cap on backwards, talking to a young married couple with a baby in a stroller. We were sitting outside.

"It's clearing up at last!" said the young father.

"I like the rain," said the manager. "I like the clouds and the change. Summers here are so fucking horrible."

"This reminds me of Illinois, a little."

"How long have you been here now?"

"A year."

"How do you like it?"

"Oh, you know, it's great, but the housing market is really crazy. First-time buyers like us can forget about it. People from Orange County are selling their places for two million and buying estates here for $750 cash. That's great for them but it drives everything else up so you can't get a three bedroom ranch that needs a new roof for less than, shit, almost half a mill. We've seen some dumps going for $350, absolute shacks. No pool, not even AC. It's amazing. So we think we'll move again."

"Where would you go?"

"Nashville is the new hot city."

"If you like country music!"

"No, they've got a professional sports franchise now. It's different."

"I guess we'd like to move, too," said the café manager.

"Nashville, man, I'm telling you."

"I don't know...."

"You're into the arts, though, right?"

"Yeah."

"Try Eugene or Portland."

"We were thinking about that, yeah."

"Those are great cities if you're like the art scene."

"We like the art scene, that's true."

"We're in hospital administration so we can go fucking anywhere. We thought this was going to be it, we thought it would be perfect here but it's not perfect, you know, so...."

"No, it's not perfect, that's true too."

"Nashville's more temperate for one thing."

"Humid, though."

The young couple strolled themselves and their baby off to their car and the manager sighed and went back into the café. I thought, we are living out what seem to be years, what seems to be our lives in that tiny fragment of a second separating the impact of an asteroid that will destroy civilization, and our perception of that impact.

"When did you start taking cream in your coffee?" my father asked me.

"Special occasions only," I said.

"Didn't you think that was odd, the conversation about picking cities to live in? I mean, it used to be you'd maybe try for a nicer neighborhood or one that was closer to your job or more suited to your pastimes...but now we've got the whole continent to be choosy about."

My father chuckled. "I once had a chance to live in a very different part of the country, and I didn't take it. I often wonder if I should have...what my life would have been like if I had."

"When was this?"

My father paused. "In the Army."

I nodded my head; I knew 'the Army' hadn't been a good experience for my father, but didn't really know why. We were silent for a while and then I looked over at him and he said, "Maybe it's time I told you the story of my life."

"The story of your life."

"Yes."

"I think it is time, yes!"

"Well...the Army was quite a change for me. I wasn't used to rough talk and dirty jokes. I wasn't used to being yelled at and cursed and you know, called an asshole and so on. In spite of the famous but very rare episodes of my father's temper, which I never really saw anyway, I grew up in pretty sheltered circumstances. The atmosphere in our home was quite gentle. We were kind to each other. It was pretty quiet on the farm, generally speaking."

"And the Army was just the opposite."

"It was loud and rough and dirty."

"I suppose a farm could be considered rough and dirty, too, but in a different way, of course."

"Very different, yes."

"By people not used to cow manure."

"And I guess I felt, coming from a maybe rather stern religious background, that what I was seeing and hearing was terribly sinful. The way they talked about women was hard to believe. It was in any event way beyond the scope of duscussions I had with my friends in high school."

"Right, when you blew that pop-stand and headed for Kalmar for cold-eats."

"Yes. 'She's a looker!' we might say. 'She sure is, and how!' The talk in the barracks was of a different order altogether."

"I can imagine. Well, no, I don't have to imagine it. My generation had a different perspective on such things...."

"Sometimes it actually seemed like Hell to me."

"That bad, eh?"

"Yes, a genuine Hell on Earth. It scared me. It got on my nerves and just kept working on me. In some ways it's been working on me ever since. I used to think, or rather, I was afraid that it had ruined my life. That I had lost my nerve, so to speak, had broken down in a non-dramatic kind of way. I'm only just now beginning to understand it."

"But you've lived a pretty successful life, haven't you? It's hard to say you haven't by most standards of success. You had a great career in business. I mean, weren't you like in charge of half the world for Glaxo?"

"Well, not quite."

"But still...!"

"Yes, I did very well for many years. I was very fortunate. But I'm as good as broke right now, here near the end of my life maybe, with not much in the way of prospects, either."

I nodded.

"I don't even have a retirement account. It's all gone, all that Medtronic stock that split and split and split and seemed like it would go on forever. Luckily I built up my Social Security account when I was making money, or I'd be literally penniless right now!"

My father laughed. I had known for some time that he was in tough financial shape, and was truly amazed at how well he was taking it. It seemed he had sunk some good money after bad at least a couple of times and lost sums that made my head swim. My brother and I had grown up just as he was beginning to make really good money, so it was hard for me to imagine him any other way. But there he was; it was possible he had even less money than me, which was almost as unthinkable as an asteroid landing in downtown Redlands.

"I went through boot camp in Virginia. Afterwards I was picked as some kind of barracks leader, with one other guy. I don't know why we were chosen. Our names both started with "A" so maybe that's all there was to it. But we were given a little room to sleep in, at one end of the barracks, just he and I. And this guy used to talk to me all night long, or at me. Harangue me for hours. I didn't say much back to him. I was pretty shy, obviously, to begin with, and I didn't want to encourage him once I understood how he was going to go on. And I was scared of him after not too long. He may have been using me as part of some plan to get discharged as a Section Eight case, or maybe he didn't want a discharge but was in fact crazy. But whatever the case, he would describe in gruesome detail all the horrible things he wanted to do to people: other soldiers, the sergeant, officers, family and friends and what have you."

My father paused here. He didn't seem inclined to want to offer a sample of this other man's violent fantasies, and I didn't really want to hear any. I'm glad now, as I write, that he didn't go on about it, because I wouldn't want to repeat it. It seems to me the less said the better where such darkness and fear are concerned.

"But he played on my nerves something awful, and I got more and more anxious. I began to question my own mental balance. I began to obsess about whatever little urges toward violence I might have noticed in myself, and I began to be afraid that I might suddenly go haywire, lose my grip somehow, like this guy seemed to have done, and do something terrible. I didn't think I was capable of anything like that, but I became afraid of it, you see, afraid that craziness could happen to anyone, manifest itself no matter what I thought or wanted to the contrary. The Army, even in peacetime [this was just after the Korean War] was a crazy and violent place, and I was afraid that I was being introduced to something, or almost seduced if you will, by something alien to my character. Encouraged to act out things that frightened and disgusted me."

"Sounds more like repeated rape than seduction."

"Yes, maybe that's a more accurate way of looking at it. But whatever was going on, one day, or rather one night, one of the guys in the barracks started screaming that he was going to kill himself. He ran into the latrine and started banging his head against the wall and screaming and crying. Well of course that shook me up pretty badly, and I decided I had to talk to somebody about getting out of there. I got to my CO, talked to him pretty frankly a couple of times, and he was a fairly decent man, it seemed to me, and he convinced me to stay. Not too much later, I was transferred to Fort Sill in Oklahoma, and promoted to corporal. My plan was to get married to your mother on an upcoming leave, and we would live off-base in Lawton, until my time was up, at which point we would go to Minnesota and I would enroll in the University. But then one day the CO called me into his office. It seemed I had done particularly well on some kind of aptitude test for something or other, and he told me he wanted me to consider re-enlisting. If I did, he would send me back to Virginia, where I would teach some kind of class in whatever it was they thought I had an aptitude for. He said it would put me on a fast-track for advancement and that I could make a good career out of it, maybe even a really good one. I look back now and I wonder if I might not have made it into the political side of the military, ended up in the Pentagon. I wonder what my life would have been like if I'd moved to Virginia, to the DC area. A farmboy in the nation's captial."

"Mr. Smith Goes to Washington," I said.

"But I didn't want to do that at the time. I wanted to go on my leave, marry your mother, finish my time, and go to school in Minneapolis. I wanted to start my family and my career as a businessman. And that's what I ended up doing. I turned down the Army's actually somewhat attractive offer, and went ahead with my plans. Now that I'm bankrupt, of course, I often wonder if I made the right choice."

"Of course you did! You did what you thought was the right thing to do at the time. You can't second-guess that kind of thing."

"Maybe not. But it's the failure of my marriage to your mother that really pains me the most, and that's something I do in fact have to second-guess. I wonder if I wasn't ready for marriage. I wonder if I should have sorted out my mental health, so to speak, before I started a family."

"You were a good husband and a good father," I said firmly. "I don't want you thinking otherwise for another second."

"Well. Thank you. I appreciate that very much. But I have to think, I have to wonder or analyze myself, I have to come to terms with the possibility that I made life for your mother worse, not better."

"You didn't," I insisted. "If you want an example of a man making life harder for his wife, you should look at me, not you. I never hit her, Dad, never threatened to, never even suggested, I thought, that violence was possible, except in the form of angry yelling...but she's afraid of me. There's no way Mom could say such a thing of you in a million years."

My father said nothing.

"She told our marriage counselor that the neighbors were worried about her," I said after a while.

"You're not that kind of man."

"No," I agreed, "I'm not, but I scared her anyway, and that's just as bad."

We were silent again, for a long time.

"I was afraid of hurting your mother that way. I was afraid I might lose my grip, like I said, without warning, and hit her."

"You're not that kind of man, either."

"No, but I was afraid of it. Afraid I would lose control. I don't know that there's much difference between me and a man who does hit his wife. Some, maybe, but not much."

Again we fell silent.

"I carried that kind of senseless crippling anxiety with into my business life, too. I did very well anyway, but I have to wonder if it was doomed from the very beginning. I remember once, very early on, you couldn't have been more than two or three, I was working as an accountant with Ernst & Ernst. A very dignified and thoroughly scrupulous firm and we all behaved like that. But one day I had had a particularly hard time of it and I felt I was going to pieces. We'd gone out to lunch, and there was a little pressure, but I became so nervous I was almost unable to reach out for my silverware, or my glass of water. And I came home and I told your mother I thought I was cracking up. She was all set to go out to some ladies' function or event at our church, all dressed up and eager to get out of the house for a few hours, but I was so distraught I asked her to stay home with me. That's how afraid I was. Of course she did, but that's the last thing any woman wants to see or acknolwedge in her husband. And I have to think it was a terrible turning point in the marriage, though everything worked out well that night. I called our pastor over, and he came and we talked for several hours, and it really seemed to help. I had a kind of epiphany, and understood my faith as I never had before. I felt so good afterward that I kept your mother up almost all night telling her how good things were going to be from then on. But it must just have seemed like the other end of the spectrum to her. Just as bad in its way as the other."

5

I drove him to the airport the next day. My reconstruction of the conversation the night before seems overly grim to me, but I am helpless to make it seem less so. Suffice it to say that it was anything but grim: I came to understand something about him that I had been aching for all my life, and in so doing understand something about myself as well, which in turn helped me understand my wife and our ragged and torn marriage. I had taken her to the same airport a few days before my father arrived; it had been the first thing she had asked me to do in the many months since we had separated, and when we said goodbye, she kissed me. A feeling of hope that had been beating weakly but steadily in the iron fist of my heart began to throb.

So I made the exhausting drive into West Los Angeles with something less than the usual tense fury, and what could have been another ridiculous day of retail commerce turned into a comedy, complete with movie star. We had a book booked for a reading, but did not expect much of a crowd. The editor of the anthology, *The Modern Jewish Girl's Guide to Guilt* was told as much, and we had only ten copies of the book on hand. Some unexpected and extraordinarily effective publicity, however, changed, as we say now, everything. A crowd of about seventy-five or maybe as many as a hundred arrived early and quickly filled the courtyard. The editor brought three contributors and they gave a great show: people were laughing and shouting and clapping and then suddenly they were lining up at my cash register, which I was operating alone. I sold a couple copies and realized the line extended the entire length of the mystery shelf, was out the back door, and snaking around the courtyard. I began to make small noises that suggested we were running out of books. The women who had just paid for their copies, and the women who were just about to get them, looked at me in disbelief, and then the word began to spread. Soon there was a great deal of shouting, from inside and outside the store—not amusement or even incredulity, wry chagrin, and muted frustration, but anger. "YOU DON'T HAVE ANY BOOKS?" "HOW CAN YOU NOT HAVE ANY BOOKS?" "YOU HAVE A READING AND YOU DON'T HAVE BOOKS?" YOU CALL YOURSELVES A BOOKSTORE?" "I CAME ALL THE WAY FROM EL SEGUNDO!" "I TELL YOU WHAT YOU'RE GONNA DO," said the lone man in the crowd, shaking his fist at me, "YOU ARE GONNA FIND ME A BOOK AND YOU ARE GONNA SELL IT TO ME!"

I felt like it was turning into *The Day of the Locust*. Then, just like a Marvel Comics superhero, Ben Affleck appeared, a rosily pregnant Jennifer Garner at his side. He'd come in just before the shit hit the fan, and asked for books on Costa Rican architecture. Now here he was with about a grand's worth of such books. In the turmoil he stepped up to the register and I rang him up. Because his senses are hyper-acute, he quickly understood my life was in danger, and intervened.

He picked up the last book and said to the woman who was about to buy it, "I'm sorry, I'm taking the last copy. It's my fault." The woman looked up at him and went all dreamy.

"Oh!" she giggled, "no problem!" The people nearest us were in shock, and getting rather dreamy-eyed too, but everybody else in the little room was still shouting and cursing.

"That's great," I said. "They were going to tar and feather me, but you take it and they couldn't be happier."

"Watch this," he said, and stepped back from the counter. "I'm sorry folks, can I have your attention, please, begging your pardon, sorry, I'm really sorry, but I've bought up all the stock, there are no more books left, my fault, hope you understand."

And the whole place exploded in gushing titters. Some people even applauded. Cellphones were whipped out, and the story of how Ben Affleck bought the last copy of the book they were going to buy ("our hands were on the book at the same time!") went out across the land. The crowd quickly dispersed in laughter and loud cellphone voices. I found a little stool we use to get the high stacks, and sat down, because my knees were a little weak.

"Thanks, Ben."

"No problem." And he winked.

I got home late that night, walked the dogs, and made myself a cup of coffee: there was a chance that my wife would call from Paris, and I didn't want to doze off on the couch and be groggy when the phone rang. I wanted to be bright and cheerful, and there was also a chance that the grogginess would be mistaken for drunkenness.

Around midnight, the phone did indeed ring, and it was indeed my wife calling from Paris.

She was exultant. "Paris is full of light!" she said, "and so am I!"

"Oh that's wonderful! I am so glad to hear that!"

"I love you," she said. "Are you drunk?"

The fist that had been crushing my heart relaxed its grip. I could feel its bolted parts loosening and breaking off, the grip failing entirely, the iron melting, and my heart began to beat hard and fast and move up into my throat, so that it was almost impossible to speak. But I did.

*For my father
and for Josh Nouril*

*April 2006
Redlands, California*

WE WHiSTLED WHiLE WE WORKED

I

We lived out our lives in a worker's paradise. That was how I liked to put it, it made Rosemary laugh, and that was all there was to it. We were just little girls, and we liked to laugh. We called ourselves "The Champions of Work" and we whistled a great deal. The owners were in fact kind and generous people, decent, intelligent people, and were famous for those qualities in all the mill towns of southern New England. They built an opera house in which works by all the greatest composers were performed: Verdi, Rossini, Bellini, Donizetti, Ponchielli, Puccini, Giordano, Cilea, Catalani, Leoncavallo, Mascagni—oh I could go on and on! I remember German and French names as well—tip of my tongue, can't quite get to them, though I am sure I will remember once I'm done here. We never saw a performance, of course, but the owners made sure that singers with incredibly loud voices and insanely gorgeous clothing provided free concerts in the parts of the mill that weren't so noisy you couldn't hear even the loudest tenor wailing directly into your ear. Once there was a free concert by the lake in Coventry, on a Sunday. There were many, many people of Italian ancestry working in the mill (myself included) who could appreciate the lyrics just as they were sung (myself included), but we were proud of the diversity of our workforce: it's not much of an exaggeration to say that we came from the four corners of the earth. The owners, I know for a fact, subsidized the emigration of peoples from fourteen nations, including Syria, Borneo, and Patagonia. We enjoyed exotic foods, vibrant festivals celebrating ancient and obscure rites, and the glorious singing I have already mentioned, the singing of songs that made the whistling we engaged in while working something entirely out of the ordinary. We sang, too, once I'd taught the words to her, seeing who could sing the loudest. She fancied herself Italian because I was, and could have passed for Italian in all but the most rigorous of audits. Rosemary said she knew nothing of the circumstances of her birth. I could not imagine such a life. I could not believe it was true—but of course she was right: none of us can know. I was not at all sure but I think I envied her: all that trackless solitude where there was nothing for me but immensities of architecture. She did believe that the man and the woman with whom she lived in the earliest years in Willimantic were in fact her mother and father. The father had been employed for several years as a matchmaker, which meant that he worked unshielded over great tubs of white phosphorus, the fumes of which in that cramped and dirty, unventilated shop rose up and hung in the air like the ghosts of all the tyrants of history and prehistory, or like fallen angels from which even evil had been wasted, leaving only a radiant, naturally occurring poison. With his head in these clouds twelve hours a day and his hands in the tubs dipping and plucking thousands of little sticks, he began to come apart. At first made only nervous and irritable, he suffered headaches and losses of memory that he knew were so near and yet gone, she said, that they reduced him to weeping. Then he became simple and docile and yet somehow witty, full all of a sudden and for no reason with gems of wisdom. He spoke in a kind of sing-song that often rhymed. As his brain became desiccated, so did his bones become brittle. His jaw rotted and his teeth fell out, and one day, waiting for the Sunday excursion train to Coventry where we planning to sit by the lake and listen to the lapping water and hopefully the opera stars too, holding Rosemary's little hand in his frail yet still warm and big own, he stepped off the curb, found the street further below than he'd imagined, and broke his ankle when he touched down. In a kind of chain reaction, the bones of his left leg broke, and when he swung himself wildly to the right, the bones of that foot and leg snapped also. He collapsed in a bloody, powdery heap, pelvis, backbone, and neck cracking in swift succession. Finally his poor skull shivered like an egg-shell, leaving smiling face and cooling brain to rest softly on the cobbles of the street. Thus at any rate did my Rosemary narrate the tragedy, the tale of the matchmaker sick with phossy-jaw who broke his leg stepping off the curb: many times and in many places, for many different reasons. She did not understand what had happened. Neither did I. She did not understand where her father had gone, nor why. Neither did I. She blamed herself and yet could not understand where she had sinned or erred. And in what way, exactly, was she being held responsible? She had been a very small child and the truth, she suspected, was that she remembered nothing, that some other kind of activity was taking place in her mind, that, perhaps, an agency representing some other kind of reality, dreams, for example, that wasn't so difficult a concept, that an agent of dreams was operating while she was awake. It was dismissed in all but the most credulous quarters—even by sympathetic listeners—as apocryphal, as propaganda (propaganda of a different sort of deed, a story of a life), understood and made to function as a folk legend to comfort and amuse the weaker and more poor, who cannot understand the actual workings of alchemy, the medical arts, and the large scale drift of money—but believed devoutly by a few (myself included), who claimed to have seen it happen. (I will swear to it if need be.) And when, some time later, perhaps as short a time as a few days, perhaps as long a time as a year (Rosemary could not say and neither can I) her stricken, suffering, perhaps overly sensitive mother in turn died (whether of causes natural or unnatural, by her own hand or the hand of God, her story too is ambiguous) all that Rosemary could find in their meager belongings to tell her who they were, now that the testimony of their presence no longer sufficed, was a last will. It was written in a shockingly violent, nearly indecipherable scrawl and blot, and we treated it, in yet another of our games, as a treasure map. Places of birth were stated (Lower East Side and Canarsie) but believed to be false. More suitable nativities were imagined. Ages could be puzzled out with arithmetic. Her father, Rosemary calculated, was twenty, her mother nineteen. Lines at the bottom of the document, where their names would likely have been entered in less violent circumstances, were left blank. Rosemary thought she sewed it into her skirt. Wandering about the town, she found herself at the well. (That was how she put it: mother died and I wandered off to a public space where I might be afforded some amusement.) After drinking, looking around, drinking again, daydreaming out loud and drinking finally to soothe a throat now quite raw from talking to herself as she wandered, and from crying, I found her and we began to muse with the complicated fancy and helpless rigor that is the hallmark of the philosophy of children. We considered her condition—its causes, effects both immediate and clear and as yet unknown, and her prospects—then came out of what can only be described as a delightfully enchanted fugue, marked equally by a sorrow that was not indulged in and practical resolve that had little relation to reality, and saw three persons approaching. Used to the hustle and bustle of our small city, to herds of people being driven here and there with an urgency just shy of stampede, the sight of a small and isolated group, in the middle, as it were, of a nowhere we had conjured around ourselves, made us uneasy. They appeared to be dressed alike, too, in heavy black robes or cloaks or skirts and shawls, and this kind of uniformity of course makes ordinary people uneasy. Then we saw that they were old women and that their faces bore the look of kindness that only tremendous age and silent suffering can account for. They bid us a good afternoon, addressing Rosemary as "Little Girl" and me as "Friend of Little Girl," which I did not mind the least little bit. My name, and the strikingly pronounced emphasis on the "Little" of Rosemary's, gave us the strange impression that they were Indian names but the old women resembled in no other way Indian squaws as we had seen them, in illustrations. We had no idea, either, what time of day it was, but saw suddenly, as if invited by the immediate presence of the three women, how sharp and long the shadows were around us. We were surprised by the pale and empty sky, believing that it had been cloudy, turbulently and loweringly so. We then wondered if we hadn't simply imagined the clouds

—or, it occurred to Rosemary, strangely, for a reason she could not quite come to, but which she felt came from her father's ghost—had they not gathered in response to her histrionic sulking? The season, too, was middling and mysterious: were there buds on the trees, as she remembered it, or were they bare, as I remembered it; and if bare, had the leaves just fallen or were they about to appear? The air was warm but the wind was cold—or was it the other way around? Warmly reposing in a cleft of rock, or cooling pleasantly in its shade? We did not know, we did not know, we did not know. Clambering down from the rocks, she debated naming herself to these strangers, and decided not to, asking the women instead if they were Sisters of Mercy. It was a phrase she had heard and liked, one which she associated with the Maker of Heaven and Earth, and which seemed to describe them in the same way Little Girl did herself.

"Little Girl and the Sisters of Mercy!" chuckled one old woman.

"We have a fairy tale on our hands!" said the second, smiling but with an air of prudence regarding a serious if not grim responsibility.

"Sisters of Mercy," murmured the third. "I should say not."

"Are you servants of the Devil?

"No!" laughed the first woman.

"No, no," said the second, shaking her head judiciously.

"Yes," said the third in her odd but clear murmur.

Rosemary laughed as her father had often laughed, calling a bluff, and demanded to know which one of them was telling the truth. Or which two.

"The first to speak told the truth," giggled the first woman, "and so did the last. The second was a liar."

"Now, now," remonstrated the second. "Let's have no paradox here."

"Certainly we are sisters," said the third. "But we serve no one and do not know the meaning of mercy. Finally, Little Girl, if you must ask us which of us is telling the truth, then I simply do not understand what we are doing here talking to you, when there is a world full of people just as confused as you are but who frankly have their wits about them."

"I AM NOT AT ALL CONFUSED!" Rosemary shouted. The old women flinched, ducked, cowered, stepped back and drew closer together. When they had finished doing all this, Rosemary understood that they were only feigning alarm, and were in fact having some fun at her expense. When they saw that she saw, they left off pantomiming and came boldly around her.

"You are very bright, Little Girl," said the first. "It does my heart good to see such warmth of brain in one so young. I believe you will become wise as the years go by." A gust of wind blew the hood of her cloak from her head. Her blue eyes twinkled in her wrinkled, grizzled face.

"You are very brave, Little Girl," said the second. "It does my mind good to see such warmth of heart in one so young. I believe you will turn away from no fear in the war to come." Another gust blew the hood of her cloak back as well. Her eyes were green as emeralds.

"You are very dark and frightened, Little Girl," said the third. She was barely audible in the rising wind. "I have never seen such anger, confusion, and recklessness in one so young, and it quite undoes me to imagine how you will make your way in the years left to you. I believe you will find little peace in them."

The wind was very strong now, and loud, and gusts of it smote the three as if with fists. Their garments fluttered around their trembling limbs, flapped and snapped until finally the hood of the third lifted away from her head, billowing and falling away. Her eyes were black but the look in the old face was one of commiseration, not of hate or malice or fear. She looked at me in a sad and friendly way, too: I was to watch and tell. That was all. Then she reached up, putting one withered hand to the side of her skull, the other under her jaw, fitting them carefully, sighed, and pulled her head off. The first and second quickly followed suit. From their sagging old necks rose, like gnarled and crooked arrows from grotesque quivers made from the bodies of trolls, the branches of trees, stripped of bark and white as bone, bare of leaves, and tossing in the wind.

We were largely unmoved by this display of witchcraft. I recognized it as something out of a nightmare, but accepted it as yet one more grim aspect of a reality that, it was clear, had infinite powers of derangement and which we would never fully understand. Buds appeared on the branches and this seemed to be a sign of better times just around the corner. From the buds tiny leaves eased forth and grew. The old women nodded and swayed over her and the succulent green leaves grew larger and larger. Rosemary swooned with the majesty of it, and I lay down beside her. When we awoke we realized we were staring into the beady but strangely still and calm eyes of a squirrel. He was upside down, clinging to the trunk of the tree amongst the roots of which we lay, no more than a foot or two above her head. We began to converse about the pleasant weather and the indescribable pleasure of a nap in the afternoon on a day when there was wind in the trees. Then I fell silent. Rosemary asked the squirrel how it made ends meet, and the squirrel spoke of life in the tree, of ordinary successes and failures in the familiar places, stories of its vastness, trials and tragedies in its most remote reaches, of proper conduct and good government. The squirrel wanted Rosemary to understand that while they were free, the quality of that freedom depended utterly on circumstances. Rosemary tried to give the squirrel the impression that this was elementary reasoning, but the truth was that she could not grasp the meaning of it. Then the squirrel said, "The tree remains the tree no matter what I think about it," and Rosemary awoke. "Stop pretending your mother is dead. It hurts her terribly. Be dutiful and loving toward her." And Rosemary awoke a second time. I had either been awake the whole time and recording it, or asleep and dreaming too, dreaming that I was dreaming the same dream Rosemary was dreaming—and woke up when she did. Again: we did not know, we do not know.

II

Our mill was not merely a legendary worker's paradise; in fact it was famous for its looms—or rather, more precisely, for an innovation in the design of the looms' flying shuttles: they had lead tips and were ten times as durable as the all-wood shuttles, whose tips cracked and splintered and fell to pieces under the stress of the new high speeds with unacceptable frequency. But before we could get to a loom, we would have to spend several years ("the best years of our lives," I liked to say, making Rosemary laugh) on the drums, working the "jumbo exotic carders," as they were technically known. There were eleven drums of varying sizes connected by belts: the big central drum was called "the swift" and ran clockwise; two drums about half the size of the swift, "the doffer" and "the fancy" were high and low at the back of the swift, running counterclockwise. There was a little "stripper" between the fancy and the doffer, and above and below the feeding tray, which was in front of course, where the cotton fibers entered the carder, at tit-level, were two little drums called "nippers," with a little stripper on top of the top nipper. Going up over the swift were four medium-sized drums, two pairs of strippers and "workers." In the back, below the doffer, was the fly-comb, tit-level, where the cotton fibers left the carder, again at tit-level. (I stress this point of the description because we could never let our arms hang, they were always raised from the shoulder and spread.) This was a job considered especially suitable, for an unknown or undeclared reason, for little girls, teamed, as often as possible, with their mothers. Rosemary's "mother" was a devious and secretive harridan who hated Rosemary (hated me, too), again for an unknown or undeclared reason. Confronted with the truth, as she had been at the well by the witches, that harridan was Rosemary's actual, biological mother, Rosemary would hold up her hand and slowly shake her head: she was a distant relative who had hated Rosemary's parents because of their interest in unionism, and feared they had passed this interest on to a little girl who clearly had troublemaking on her mind anyway, and for whom she had an unpleasant but unavoidable responsibility. But whatever the cause of the hatred and the nature of the relationship, there was one constant in the acting out of it, and it required two actors and a long-forgotten understanding of who had started it. Rosemary, despite the fact that were living out the best years of lives in a worker's paradise, was deeply disturbed by the monotony and sensory assault of her job (it's hard for most people nowadays to imagine a child of six or eight or ten on the edge of nervous collapse, but not me). She would often fall to her knees in exhaustion and misery, or, if she had enough strength and will, would wander away from the drum. The mother would catch her by the arm and yank her to her feet, keeping one hand in her game at the other end of the carder, or, failing the catch the arm, Rosemary's hair, sometimes yanking so hard she would snatch Rosemary off her feet entirely, stretching her out like a no-holds-barred wrestler and slamming her to the floor with a thud. But while the floor was not the rumbling, screeching, eternally rotating drum, it was no picnic down there either. Its warped and clattering boards were coated thickly with oil and grease and mud, sawdust and cotton waste, tobacco juice and tubercular spittle, blood and pus and the dust of our very skins, but it was the only place where a little girl might powder her nose. Given the carefully regulated clockwork mechanisms of the mill's fundamental movements, we were encouraged to eliminate our waste prior to or after the bells. Company policy stated clearly that no employee would be, indeed could be, allowed to vacate a station for any reason whatsoever—not even to urinate. So Rosemary (and I, though not so regularly or with such blasé facility) learned to piss on the floor at her station. The mother would grab her arm as usual, but a sign from Rosemary that urination was underway would almost always result in a loosened grip and a general tolerance.

"You filthy little beast," the mother would chuckle.

"You are ignorant of the world below," piped Rosemary, drawing herself up like an opera star and delivering her lines with a recitative-like eloquence. She was annoyingly precocious and took a great deal of undisguised pleasure in unusual tropes and words dense with multifarious meaning (as did I—it was another one of the ways in which we in effect whistled while we worked). They had to shout to hear each other, and really couldn't make out much of it even when they did, but understood each other well enough, reading lips, remembering, imagining. In spite of the hatred that underlay it, the nervous tension that harried it, and the deafening thunder of the looms above, the constant but irregular banging of the rows of drums and creaking spools and thudding engines, the ordinary remorseless cries of horses and men and clanging bells and piercing shrieks of steam that overwhelmed their conversations, Rosemary and her drum-mother had somehow come to agree that whether or not there was "another world below them," they could at least argue about it. Somewhat in the manner of a prisoner and guard, they exchanged warm and candid, if not altogether friendly and sympathetic, observations, fanciful hypotheses, hilarious syllogisms, and straw men. Rosemary posited a world no bigger than the mill sunk a mile or so into the earth at the end of something like a mineshaft. It was an utopia in which hard but calm and therefore satisfying work alternated with intellectual seductions and sensual pleasures of the simplest and deepest kind: wind in the trees, water rushing over rocks, hugging, kissing. The people refused to take advantage of each other, and governed themselves with quiet talks and broad deliberations. They grew old very slowly, and death was almost unknown among them, but (and what a big but, I always liked to say at that point) they depended utterly on a magical precipitate, a gentle rain that fell upon them like mercy from their tiny heaven, coursing down their tiny mountains and running swiftly past their tiny mills, an elixir derived solely from the germ-laden phlegm and urine-sodden dust as it percolated down the shaft from the big mill above the ground. When they coughed in their anomalous illnesses, their germs sprayed up at her in turn, in faint puffs, like little angels of mercy. The drum-mother dismissed all this as fairy-tale nonsense, suggesting that whatever they got from the big mill came upon them like plague and flood. It was very likely a flammable liquid as well, igniting infernos where it didn't drown or cause pustules and lesions to form in the lung, the face, and the genitals.

"And as for the utopia—!"

"You are as ignorant of the world below as you are of this world!"

"Dream on, you little nincompoop!"

"I shall, allow me to assure you!"

"Why would they behave any differently down there than they do up here?"

"Because they wish to!"

"I do not wish you to speak of it again. You must pay attention to your work or risk a break in your concentration. You might fall behind, your work will pile up, something might snarl or jam or catch, and you will place not only the steady functioning of the line but yourself and your fellows in terrible jeopardy. If the line is destroyed, so are our jobs and consequently our lives and our souls. Yes, it is a sin. God will wonder what is wrong with you. You don't want God wondering what's wrong with you, Rosemary, do you understand me? Do you understand me? I will not have you starve to death!"

III

Because our drums were necessarily near the loading docks, we were privy to tantalizing portions of the conversations of the men who came and went there: the suggestive small talk and boasting and whispered rumors, the thick accents and humorous imitations, bits of news and gossip, jokes and the tag ends of strange lines of dialogue, oratory and performance of anecdotes to pass the time—and of course, observation, analysis, commentary, complaint and passionately-voiced frustration which became, with what seemed like the passage of the years of our childhood, slow-boiling anger and isolated bursts of terrifying outrage. It was, in the absence of real family and friends, with these men that we learned to speak—first to ourselves, but after not too long, publicly and socially, as well. Rosemary became a favorite of some of these men. (She was pretty, I was not.) They sought her out and kidded her while the drums turned and we pushed the dirty lumpy cotton along the feeding tray. She kidded them back, telling them of her merciful, nutrient-rich urine and the deep little people who prayed for it. The men found her inventions startlingly witty in one so young. It's not too much to say they found her fascinating, which attention in turn encouraged her to act more audaciously, to broaden the reach of her narratives, and to deepen their meaning. By the time we were fourteen, in the year 1910, she was the center of a devoted circle. The men (boys, really, not much older than she) would appear in the several proscenia of the open loading dock doors, lit and backdropped according to the weather, sometimes silhouettes against the bright sunlight, sometimes colorful heroes striding out of the ravages of a storm, conduct their business, tease her a little bit from a distance, making big obvious gestures and shouting, then drift nearer and nearer, refining remark and gesture as they came until at last they were speaking into each other's ears and there was fondling and wrestling and kissing and all our drum-mothers would scream abuse—early days, or, later, blow their whistle. It's not hard nowadays to imagine the extent to which the sexual play went, but we couldn't believe what was happening. Then, one day the next year, they stopped coming. We did not know why, but suspected that the drum-mothers had said something to someone, and someone perhaps had supplied them with the goddamned whistles, and now taken even harsher steps to restrict the flow of communication into and out of the mill. Rosemary fell into a deep depression (I did not) and kept climbing up and tumbling down the sides of it. Her old nervous unease and disorder—the tics only she noticed, the fluttering feeling and the feeling that something other than blood was coursing flammably through her veins, and her heart, racing for no reason until she felt ready to faint, then hovering on the edge of unconsciousness until it passed—began to take hold of her again. Her head ached ceaselessly, her whole body ached and trembled, and she fell into nearly incoherent rages over nothing. It was either that or weep, almost undetectably but uncontrollably, while staying physically steady, pushing and spreading the cotton as the drums screeched in their eternal revolutions. She became fixated on the idea that there were little girls inside her drum, dead little girls playing games and singing, girls who could be our dearest friends but for the fact that they were trapped in the drum and forever tumbling. Noises would suddenly sharpen and penetrate her head, then fade out again, there were dark curtains around the familiar shapes of her station. She could make out distinct and interesting conversations inside the drum and outside it simultaneously. She might hear bells ringing, horses knickering and snorting, greasy smoking engines thudding away, then suddenly clear human speech. If she looked up and saw her mother's mouth moving, she would sigh and stop listening; if a man's mouth and bushy moustache across the room were moving, she would listen as long as she could. On the worst days the noises would join and become unbearable, but then, as if under the control of a just and surprisingly merciful god, cease utterly. She might look up and see her mother's mouth working some terrible curse—she knew the patterns of lips and tongue and jaw by now—see that she was sobbing, but hear nothing. In that silence, when she knew perfectly well that something inside her had broken—or perhaps only relaxed?—she could hear the little girls, our friends, inside the slowly turning drum singing whispery mournful songs, simple little dirges in time with the drum's re-emergent banging and creaking. Dazed by this silence and the warmth of the sad songs, she would slip to her knees and, sometimes, urinate. One day she did fully and completely faint. She was having trouble hearing anything at all—the sounds of the mill were muffled and she could only see the drum-mother's lips moving as she hectored and judged almost good-naturedly, and she made a motion as if to squat and pee. The drum-mother reached out with her habitual gesture almost of comfort but of restraint too, but Rosemary went unsteadily down. She began to urinate, then blacked out and went over backwards. The drum-mother panicked. Fallen workers were to be left to their own devices and the assistance of floor managers, so she stepped over Rosemary, hurriedly pushed some cotton along the tray, then dashed to the back to the carder. Rosemary awoke a second or two later, having no idea what had happened or where she was. When it came to her—when she realized she was not in a strange white room but in the mill—she tried to get to her feet. Her mother reached out now without even looking at her and caught a hank of her long dark hair. She tipped over again but her mother wouldn't let go this time, bending awkwardly but keeping her fear-filled eyes and one hand on her work. Rosemary crawled toward her, grabbed her ankle and bit hard into her calf. Her mother yelped inaudibly under the noise of the machines, and let go of her hair. Rosemary stayed low, slapping and banging the filthy floor as she made her getaway. One man laughed at her, again inaudibly, a grotesque grimace of pain it looked like, and another shook his leg at her like he would a dog. The kick caught her a glancing blow, altering her direction and ultimately bringing her to her feet. The sound of the mill and its workers was now deafening but she could hear every note of it. She looked over her shoulder at her drum-mother, who stared back at her in panic and horror, and at me, wide-eyed, frightened—then bolted. I swallowed hard and followed her. She ran as fast as she could up the aisle into the heart of the mill, shouting "STRIKE! STRIKE! STRIKE!" (I suppose I hollered the same or similar.) Our fellow workers did pause in their movements, some for only a second or two, some for longer, and confusion began to mount. Leaping up the stairs to the second floor, we struggled—still dizzy as well as being ordinarily weak from the poor food we ate—with the weights and pulleys of the big iron door that led to the looms, pulled it open just enough to squeeze through, then lost our way in terrified inner darkness for a crucial moment. The door caught us as it swung heavily back into place. We screamed and fought the door and slipped through: the looms clattered and hummed. It was a noise on a higher register than the noise below, but more penetrating. Rosemary took a breath, started shouting "STRIKE! STRIKE! STRIKE!" again and dashed into the center of the room. It was exactly at that point that one of the mill's famous lead-tipped shuttles shot from its loom. It was "a convergence of the twain" worthy of Hardy. The shuttle traveled straight as an arrow, then, just as it began to lose momentum and descend, struck Rosemary in the temple. It was like the Hand of God. That she should faint, then revive and race to a distant point only to intercept a missile streaking toward the very spot where she would be— and not simply be but be in an act of outright rebellion— seemed incontrovertibly theological in its parabolic progression. Because the danger posed by these powerfully ejected and effectively rifled shuttles, the room was laid out so that no one who was standing where he or she was supposed to be standing would be hurt when one of them fired itself out of a loom; the obvious corollary revolved around the ancient belief that if you weren't where you were supposed to be, even for an instant!—you deserved what was coming to you. And it would always come to you. And because company policy was company policy no matter what floor you worked on, she was left in a heap on the floor. What had been coming for her for millenia had arrived. She was nervously glanced at over shoulders and under arms, and there was a great deal of surreptitious talk, but she remained where she was and as she was. Her long black skirt (in which was sown the flat little package of family documentation) was spread out around her and hid most of her body so that from a certain angle she looked like she'd fallen in a hole filled with black water, with only her head and arms above water, weakly hanging on to the edge.

IV

After He smote her, God spoke to her. He spoke to her for a very long time, and when she awoke, she knew The Almighty to be a fraud and a coward. A handsome young man had her in his arms and was standing up. He was whispering to her that it would be all right, she was fine and everything would be all right, she should not worry.

Rosemary was not to worry. The handsome young man repeated this injunction. No stranger to the protocols of the fairy tale, she immediately trusted the young man and found herself as incapable of worry as of suspicion. His princely, heroic beauty held no trace of treachery or even vulnerability to vice—and in fact his only fault seemed to lie in an apparent double standard: he was visibly worried, stricken, it was not too much to say, with anxiety. If he was outwardly reassuring, he was also clearly gripped by a fear of what might happen if he failed to get Rosemary off the filthy floor and into a warm bed in a clean room. He carried her across, it seemed, the whole of Willimantic, me bouncing along next to them, moaning and whispering and petting Rosemary's head, then through the door of a small house, up its main staircase, and into a room that was clean and warm but nearly empty. There was a bed in it, and he put her gently under its covers. I crawled in too, and he seemed not to think I was being presumptuous. He brought more blankets and more pillows. He brought some food, which we ate together, conversing with polite awkwardness about conditions at the mill, the weather, opera, and romantic poetry. There was evidence outside of a growing commotion, but we were able to ignore it. Rosemary was warm and happy and thoroughly amazed at the depth of the young man's knowledge of beautiful, truthful things (as was I, even though I saw very clearly that I was not the object of his tender little attentions, but merely an object). We were as well unspeakably grateful to him—so grateful and so admiring we found it impossible to find out who he was or even where we were. After a while, in which we must have dozed, the commotion outside became so loud and strange that we could ignore it no longer. We stood at the window, the young man holding the curtain back just enough so that we could see.

It was a strike.

"They're saying you started it," laughed the young man.

"Me?"

"Yes."

"Who is saying that?"

"The men who saw you take the shuttle to your head."

"Oh," said Rosemary falteringly. "Is that what happened…?"

"Yes. They think you're dead. Some of them do, anyway. It was too much for them to bear. You're a legend in your own time."

"I ought to join them."

"Certainly, if you feel better. But do you in fact feel better?"

Rosemary suddenly found herself sobbing. "No," she said.

"Then you must stay."

"Perhaps until the morning...?" Admitting her weakness made her feel even worse, and she sobbed wretchedly.

"Certainly. But while you are resting, think about those men who know you are not dead."

"There are men who believe I'm alive?"

"Of course there are, darling. But you're safe here. If you expose yourself, whether you feel better or not, you will be less safe. You may in fact find yourself in terrifying danger. You might get shot. You might go to prison for the rest of your life." The young man stared out the window. "I'd lie low for a while," he said, not turning around. "You too, of course," he said to me, turning abruptly and putting his hand on my shoulder.

Rosemary sat on the edge of the bed. Her feet were cold. It was hard to believe, but she thought she could eat some more, if more was available. The young man said he would find more if it was the last thing he did. His pose of ardency seemed even more authentic than it had been earlier, but what he actually did was give me some money and send me out. Earlier, prepossessingly resourceful, he had found a victrola and a complete recording, forty sides, by La Voce del Padrona of La Gioconda. We listened to this long masterpiece in its entirety, and then I went out for bread and cheese. Rosemary and the young man listened to it at again, in its entirety, playing over and over "The Dance of the Hours," because it took me, no surprise, quite a while to get the food. We listened to it yet again, mad for it, really, as who would not have been, given all that had happened, all that was happening? The next morning, the young man gone, we decided we were finished lying low. Rosemary was pregnant. Though of course we didn't know it at the time, she couldn't keep the news of the fuck to herself. The young man had disappeared. Had he fathered the presence she suddenly insisted she unmistakably felt within her? She did not know. She did not know. How was one to know? I did not know. She did not care. I cared but was helpless. Strangely, her skirt was missing, too, the one (the only) in which she believed she'd sewn the family document. Since her undergarments, stockings, boots, blouse and sweater were all still available to her, but strewn here and there about the room, the corridor, landing, and stairs, she concluded she was merely being hysterical and could not trust herself to look carefully and search thoroughly an environment in which so much had happened in so little time. I could be, she said, looking right at it. Wrapping herself in the bedsheet with snug ingenuity, she dressed herself and we went out into the crowded street. It was a cold day but not so cold that we shivered, and if the gray sky threatened snow, it was still dry.

 Rosemary liked to speak of herself, and perhaps to think of herself, as a fairy-tale innocent, but she was not naïve. She knew she hadn't caused the strike, but she felt in an obscure way responsible, even guilty. There is no explaining such guilt: it had something to do with a frivolous lightheartedness that informed or was at least present in or witness to her darkest deeds. There was no romance in a strike, and she knew it; it could only seem so in retrospect, in, as it were, a ballad. It took place in darkness and the light it shed was explosive. But it was not a darkness of evil, and that was the difference. It was a darkness of despair and fear, and a light of pain and anger, and so it was unreasoning and unrelenting. Good was not an inherent consequence. In fact no good could come of such a force, unless reason could be brought to bear upon it, unless people around whom the water was rising and swirling could be encouraged to somehow not mind the ominous roaring in the distance, could be encouraged to think and act calmly even in the face of (this is where Rosemary Thorndike eventually made her single historically documentable mark) brutal repression. And so we clung to the steps of the house while our people raged past us. If we had heard singing from the window earlier—it was possible but we viewed the possibility with suspicion, given what had been happening—no one was singing now. The flow of the crowd was so fast and turbid that it was impossible to stay in one place for longer than a few seconds. Some people we recognized who in turn recognized us, but nothing was made of these recognitions as nothing could be made of them in such uncertain circumstances: the mill had been struck and shut down and the street was a river in flood just as surely as if a dam had been dynamited. Men, women, and children would certainly drown, it was only a question of how many; and when their bodies finally fetched up in some psychological backwater, slowly rotating in the faint current, recognition would matter even less. We heard fragments of talk, asked a question here and there when we could, and, with what we already knew from the men on the docks and rumor, slowly fashioned a narrative, which went something like this: the Commonwealth of Massachusetts had begun to take measures that would raise the standard of living for millworkers, and protect them generally from the zealotry of mill-owners and other smaller-minded, meaner-spirited capitalists, but Connecticut was slow in following suit. There was a corresponding diminishment of patience for the scaling-down of the sixty-hour workweek. Fifty-four was the goal, and fifty-eight would be acceptable as a first step, but both goal and step were rejected as mill owners testified to insurmountable disadvantages in the marketplace: it could simply not be done, no matter what Massachusetts may, in its folly, have set out to do. Fifty-eight was nevertheless mandated. In acceptance of the mandate, the owners reduced wages. This was seen as a more or less reasonable compromise, but the three percent cut was felt by the workers receiving it as salt in a wound. Rosemary felt wounded, so wounded, as I have said, that she was in a nearly perpetual state of hallucination, and understood as well as was necessary, with a mind not at all at ease with numbers (with in fact a mind in which numbers elicited a kind of feverish loathing) that the weavers had been forced to work twelve looms at forty-nine cents a cut instead of seven looms at seventy-nine cents. This was probably why she ran upstairs when she regained consciousness on the floor before her drum. These men did in fact respond to her cry. They were ready to walk out, and when "the little girl" ran screaming into their presence, it was nearly impossible not to act. Most workers, however, in other parts of the mill, stayed at their stations. It wasn't until the next morning, when she was feeling the first uneasiness of pregnancy, that pay envelopes were opened and the wage cuts made incontrovertibly manifest, and violence broke out. After a period of nervousness and actual embarrassment (Rosemary's word for the general sentiment that universal principles of right conduct had somehow been subverted), shouts of anger could be heard here and there, and before anyone could think of doing it, some gear-works were smashed, and some drive-belts cut. One man, who seemed lost and who had obviously been crying (she could see the tracks in the grime on his face, and his eyes were puffy and red) told her that someone had been killed, a little girl had been shot down by soldiers.

"Soldiers?" she cried. "Where did soldiers come from so quickly?"

"They shot her. I saw it," said the man with sudden disturbing calm.

"No," said Rosemary. "No they didn't. There aren't any soldiers in this town."

"A little girl was shot and killed," insisted the man, now with a kind of indifference.

"NO SHE WASN'T!" shouted Rosemary. "THAT WAS ME! I AM THE LITTLE GIRL AND I'M NOT DEAD!"

Whereupon she spun away and staggered back up the steps to the door of the house. I followed. When we looked back, the man was gone. Confused and alarmed, suddenly and to the edge of panic, we went into the house and found its kitchen. There around a table were three Wobblies. We knew they were Wobblies because they were extremely dangerous-looking and handsome. Despite the dashing good lucks, however, Rosemary was instantly struck by their similarity to the women at the well. "One Big Union," said a big man, describing himself and his companions to her, telling her everything was going to be all right from now on. A woman told her that the young man who had saved her from her nearly fatal descent into unconsciousness was a friend of theirs. He was part of the one big union, but more specifically was from New Bedford. This she was told as if it meant something crucial to her understanding and well-being. "He's not exactly local, but it's not like he's from some mining camp in Colorado!" she laughed. "He grew up in a mill just like you two did. He writes songs for us. Did he play his guitar for you?" "No," said Rosemary, as if she was confident of her place not just in the conversation but in the greater scheme of things, in life itself. "I'm afraid he didn't." "You really missed a treat!" the woman assured her with a kindly smile. They told her they would take us to Lawrence, Massachusetts, where an even bigger strike was taking place, if we wanted to go. They made it clear they wanted Rosemary to come with them, myself as well (nodding smiling at me) and implied quite strongly that she would be considered highly valuable in a very short period of time, as the dreams of the One Big Union were beginning to be realized. So we went with them, Rosemary accepting a skirt from the woman and reconciling herself to the loss of her own, feeling a tremor of anxiety when she remembered what she was pretty sure she'd sewn into it. Someone had put the opera record back on upstairs, so that the last thing we ever heard in Willimantic, the door slamming shut on it, was "The Dance of the Hours."

V

The woman wore a tall red hat pinned to her hair, and Rosemary snuggled so close to her in the car that she could study with her diseased but powerfully concentrated imagination the whorls and folds of the little enamel rose at the head of the pin. She perceived it as a living thing. The woman seemed to know a lot about her, and Rosemary accepted this without worry or question. The woman said she understood that Rosemary had been very helpful in not just the triggering of the strike but the priming of it. The men she'd been briefed by had put it just that way, she said, narrowing her eyes and clearly implying that there was something wrong with what she'd just said. You will read Bakunin, she said, like I did, and Nechaev in the cool shadows of your delirium and in the bright fever of it, and you will believe as I did, for only an hour perhaps, or a day, but no longer, and say to yourself, honored sister, there are three classes of women. The first consists of empty-headed, senseless, and heartless women who must be exploited and made the slaves of men. The second consists of those who are eager and devoted and capable but not fully committed, who must be pushed until they do, or, more likely, perish. (I knew instantly, fatally, that I was part of the second group.) In the third class, the woman continued, are the women who are truly ours, our jewels, whose help is indispensable. I underscore this last phrase, and urge you, honored sisters, to compare your own knowledge of what you have done and what you will do to this corrupt and poisonous passage and believe it for as short a time as you possibly can.

"Who is Nechaev?" asked Rosemary.

The woman peered deeply into Rosemary's eyes as they jolted through Worcester and said, "He was a murderous twerp with a lot of moxie. You will find men like him all over the place." She sat back and pretended to fan herself, though it was quite cold in the car. "Don't get me wrong, honey," she said, "I am terribly interested in Mr. Bakunin's cult of violence, deeply so, it gives me goosebumps, but come, pull yourself together, we could not possibly have left you in that shit-hole, we'll all go to Lawrence together, where the woolen mills are bigger than ten Willimantics or wherever we were. The strike there has shut the whole town down. Can you speak any foreign languages? It will come in handy, believe me, in Lawrence. Oh you poor little things, you poor little women. There is another look, isn't there, in the bloodshot eyes of men when they see the only solution is to destroy and kill and maim and burn and pant like dogs in the light of the dying flames? When they lie down with us and how does it go? Jet the stuff of a superior race?"

When we got to Lawrence, we were immediately put to work: we were to mind the children, the ones who were hungry, the ones who were cold, the ones who were lost, the ones whose mothers and fathers were off rioting. Rosemary hatched a plan and insisted money be raised specifically and solely for her plan. It was a fantasy she had nursed for as long as she could remember, she told me, and then the others: to get the children out of danger. Money was found, and Rosemary's job became one of getting the children, more than one hundred of them, on a train bound for Philadelphia, where sponsor families would care for them until the strike was over. Management spies got wind of the plan, and it was quickly publicized as one in which the children, following a pied piper, would be precipitated off cliffs. When the day of departure came, however, there was no need of a cliff. At the station, mounted policemen bore down on the children and their mothers like Cossacks, herding them at first then knocking them flat with deft little movements of their great horses. Guns were fired into the air over shrieking little heads and several policemen lost their heads: they began laying about themselves with light batons, clubbing people to the ground indiscriminately. Panic overtook the brigade and the flight of the children out of Lawrence seemed doomed. The police and their henchmen managed to create a no-man's-land of the platform, charging up and down the length of the train upon their steeds, while cops on foot waded into the swarming hysterical crowd with whistles and fists.

Rosemary entered the no-man's-land.

It was the greatest thing I have ever and will ever see anybody do.

Three horsemen galloped towards her, fast as they could go. She was four feet tall and they were twelve feet tall—something like that. They were going thirty miles an hour, and Rosemary was standing still. (I am now looking at the old newspaper clipping that I keep in a frame on my writing desk: the headline reads LITTLE GIRL DEFIES COSSACKS. A grainy, faded yellow and torn photograph shows a train-shape on the right, crowd-shape on the left, a little girl half-standing, blurry with motion, a beached whale—the fallen horseman and his horse—in front of her, and two wide-eyed horsemen, still mounted, the whites of their eyes dominating their gray shapes, staring down at them.) "I felt," she once told me, "like a chicken buried up to my neck in the ground, waiting for them to come pluck my iddle head off. They came, I stayed, they came, I stayed. I stayed and stayed and still they came. The station was shaking with the thunder of their hooves, a ton of horses and riders bearing down on me, and still I stayed. At the last second, they reined back. One of them wasn't paying close enough attention, I guess, and he went over the top of his mount. Landed at my feet. Actually rolled into me and knocked me down. That's when the picture was taken. Just as I was scrambling to my feet."

For this show of fearlessness she was broadly denounced and publicly humiliated. Not only mill owners and conservative newspaper editors, but prominent socialists and leaders of mainstream unions—even some theorists within the dread I.W.W. itself—had characterized "the evacuation of the children" as a sensational stunt. It was a sordid piece of advertising. Parents were bullied and children all but abducted from their homes, a House investigative committee in Washington, D.C., was told. "We are to the labor movement what the high diver is to the circus," an old bearded Wobblie told her, in a stern but grandfatherly way. "Our big mouths can bind an audience with spells of hellfire and brimstone as surely as any old wild-eyed Puritan Scourge. We can foam at the mouth like mad dogs and wink at the same time, and the audience cries out for more, and more, and more, and finally gets bored with thrills and marvels and goes home and the workers remain unorganized. We are like drunkards: very amusing until we take a swing at somebody and pass out." Nobody formally blamed Rosemary, and certainly there were many who all but canonized her on the spot (myself included), but because she was the girl in the photograph, she endured, as proxy or figurehead, a great deal of frustrated haranguing and oblique vituperation. She was only vaguely aware of it, but was being used in some way as a pawn between Wobblies based in Chicago, who were thought of by Wobblies based in Detroit as lawless boys playing at revolution, who in turn characterized the Wobblies based in Detroit as parlor-room socialists with sticks up their asses. One of the more dashing and devilishly handsome Italian men from Chicago befriended Rosemary in Lawrence, began to school her, and, after he'd secured an abortion for her, to sleep with her. By the time we arrived in Paterson, New Jersey for a strike by silk-workers that would last nearly half a year and include twenty-five thousand weavers, loomfixers, twisters, and warpers, she was again pregnant and again in charge, at least nominally and picturesquely, of "the evacuation of the children." Many years, a lifetime, and no time at all, seemed to have been passed—or rather, a moment was imperceptibly repeating. Rosemary found it nearly impossible to fix herself in a secure and ordinary sense of time and place, in the life of the community —on which fixing, of course, sanity, almost solely, depends.

The irony of her situation was lost on no one, and the belief that her first child had been aborted not by a doctor but the fat Irish cop who fell off his horse and knocked her down, became common, and eventually legendary. Some versions even had her shoved off the platform and under the wheels of the train which had just begun to move, or within days and not months of delivery, that she had given birth to a dead baby in the cloakroom of the station. She was also informally apprenticed to the editor of the Passaic Weekly Issue, a socialist who was shortly to write an editorial critical of Paterson policemen which would land him in prison for fifteen years. In the course of becoming something like the press secretary for the Chicago I.W.W., she found some purchase, entered into some valuable routine, and remained more or less sound. She learned to defend herself calmly and articulately: she had hurt and coerced no one, she had not even argued with people, she had simply stood there looking out for the children, who would tell you if you cared to speak to them of lives the stink of which would never leave their nostrils. And in this way she began to develop as well a persona and philosophy: If you cannot obey (she wrote with the aid of the PW editor, who had also begun to fuck her) , you cannot command. I have found in my short life almost no one whom I wish to obey, and therefore must decline command. Obedience and commandment are the surest means of terror I know. She was something like a pacifist-anarchist, and people who could not conceive of anarchism as anything other than deeply, inherently violent—that is to say, nearly everybody, found her paradoxical stance, in a word, fascinating. Lusty young men who liked to sing songs in bars about mining camp massacres and stage free-speech fights on street-corners were particularly mesmerized by her, though it seemed to me she was growing less beautiful—more crazy-looking, sometimes even scarily so, with her huge bright eyes and the dark exhausted flesh surrounding them, lank, unkempt hair that not even the sturdiest hats could organize, the long, sharp nose, the extraordinary curves of her mouth, the big pigeon-toed feet and big-palmed, long-fingered hands. She had a charismatic but self-effacing presence: people liked, even longed, to be near her.) One night at Mabel Dodge's fashionable Greenwich Village salon, the Broadway producer David Belasco declared he would find a vehicle for her ascent to stardom.

"I can't act," said Rosemary. "Even speaking in a room like this makes me nervous." The room was blindingly white, from a burning white porcelain chandelier to a polar-bearskin rug before a white marble fireplace, wherein pale birch logs appeared to give off pure white flames. The furniture was delicate and Florentine. Rosemary was a dark quiet untidy center of gravity.

"Ah but we've all seen you act!" shouted Belasco, referring to her stand against the mounted policemen.

"That's not acting," said Rosemary.

"There's acting," said Belasco, "and there's acting. Shakespeare said that all the world is a stage."

"Who is Shakespeare?"

Tittering laughter failed to discourage Belasco. "If there's an audience and they applaud, you are acting."

"And if they throw rotten vegetables?"

"You are still acting, but less..." he searched for the right word, "popularly."

"Oh Mr. Belasco," said Rosemary coquettishly, "you say that to all your little Joans of Arc." And the titters became whoops and guffaws. He'd made a nearly identical sally at Elizabeth Gurley Flynn, whom the novelist Theodore Dreiser had called "the Eastside Joan of Arc," and who had brushed him famously aside saying she preferred to "speak her own piece." Though we hadn't known it until several weeks later, it was Gurley who had rescued us from Willimantic. Belasco settled back in his chair and smiled good-naturedly, undeterred. He was smitten not only with Rosemary's ungainly allure but with what he called "real realism," genuine objects on his stages and not props, walls that did not shake when doors were slammed, an apple pie one could eat and not painted cardboard. If he was going to do a show about a poor little mill girl, he wanted a poor little mill girl to play the part, wearing her own authentic clothing, usufructuary rights to which he was willing to pay handsomely for. (He had astonished beggars in this very way, his assistants stripping the shirts off their backs as he peeled notes from a wad.)

The idea of a play about the Paterson silkworkers did take hold that night. It would be a pageant, a series of more or less static tableau-like scenes depicting important episodes in the life of the strike, as vast and emotionally resonant as any ten productions in a cathedral by the great visionary of the theater Max Reinhardt, because it was real, with hundreds of workers on stage, playing themselves, moving from sorrow and desperation to triumph and glory via courage and principle. One of the wealthy intellectuals, John Reed, who had acceptable credentials as a daredevil journalist—he had ridden with the infamous bandido generale Pancho Villa, and had been in jail with scores of rank-and-filers in Paterson—made himself responsible for the mise en scene, both financial and artistic. A light-hearted lothario, he saw a lovely weird target painted on Rosemary's back, and endeavored to be the salient feature in a world that she was surely experiencing as more and more delightful by the second.

VI

Although it may indeed happen, I once read aloud to Rosemary, that when we believe the truth A, we escape as an incidental consequence from believing the falsehood B, it hardly ever happens that by merely disbelieving B we necessarily believe A. We may in escaping B fall into believing other falsehoods, C or D, just as bad as B; or we may escape B by not believing anything at all, not even A. I have to stop and think about it for quite some time, and all the thinking I've done about in the past never seems available to me or applicable when once again I turn to it, but that sums up our feelings quite as fully as is humanly possible. At least for me. At least in that wonderful moment when I am able to return to it, to think it again. We did not want to be caught up in belief and disbelief—and yet at the same time we wanted to act, we wanted to live! And you can't live freely and fully, you can't act boldly and easily, if you don't properly believe in something. Conversing in this way, we (Rosemary, myself, and a friend of John Reed's) turned on 23rd and walked up Madison to the Garden, its yellow bricks and terracotta fading in the twilight while at the top of the tower, thirty-two stories high, the St. Gaudens statue of Diana swiveled back and forth two or three degrees in the gusty spring wind and caught the last red light of the setting sun. We entered the ground floor arcades and I said that I liked arches, liked looking at them and walking through them. As the baffled wind blew through those arches, following us, gently carrying us, Rosemary asked me why I felt that way, but I had no answer. It was no great secret, I suggested, that people were drawn to archways, but whatever it was that was at work in that kind of architecture, I felt it very strongly. It makes me feel soft and safe, I said, an admission that would have astounded if not choked us—We were Wobblies!—in any other circumstances. John Reed's friend (whose name was also John) suggested we visit Seville and Florence someday, see the loggias and porticos and so on. I'm not even sure what those things are or where those places are in the world, Rosemary admitted with equal candor equal to my own, but I'd go there in a second. Anywhere in the world I would. She squeezed my hand. With you.

John wondered if there was a lift to the top of the tower. Thirty-two storeys seemed a great deal to ask, especially without authorization, but it turned out that we could get to the parapets and columns surrounding the little space, the lantern it was called, beneath the many-tonned but mobile Diana, almost without moving a muscle. Thus was the horrible noise of the city swallowed up. It was another world altogether. The city was not real. All we could hear was a faint but steady grinding of stone on stone, and the wind, buffeting one ear and then, turning to consider another aspect of the island city, the other. The arm of the ancient goddess moved above us, in the upper corners, as it were, of our eyes There were fewer and fewer people in the lantern lookout, night had swallowed up the city, there were only a few floating streams of light....

"Or we could just stay up here," murmured Rosemary. John had his arm around her. "We could move to San Francisco."

"Yes," he said. "We could just stay up here. We could move to San Francisco."

Diana groaned and creaked in the darkness and stone just above our heads. A week or two later, up in the lantern again, Rosemary had an idea, an image of something that might happen and somehow matter. We went down a flight of narrow stairs, painfully, then another and another until they came to a room that appeared to cater to unused utility: electricity! And based on what John thought he understood from the Beveridge engineers he had come to know and to talk to about this and that, he thought it could easily be drawn from this room. A little old man, so quiet and still we hadn't known he was in the room, Rosemary and I at least, John giving a faint impression of prior meetings if not old acquaintance, began to speak from a tiny triangular desk in a dark corner. When Diana had been unveiled twenty years earlier, they had draped her legs and belly with ten thousand incandescent electric bulbs, so that her lovely breasts and forbidding face could be seen by anyone who cared to look up, all night long. John said we were associated with the Paterson Strike Pageant, which would be performed in less than a week, surely the old man knew of this spectacle? Yes, yes, he thought he did. Well, we were wondering if Diana might be somehow relit, to help us advertise our show. The old man said that she would be lit now, lit eternally if he had anything to say about it, but that the scandal of gigantic titties lighting up Manhattan, mesmerizing people and drawing them nearer and nearer her magnificent safety like a light house—it had been too much for decent people to bear. Three hours later we were in the offices of the Passaic Weekly. Rosemary took care of a neglected duty—using a typewriter to make daily reports of news gathered shop-by-shop, job-by-job, everybody from the native-born, highly-skilled, and relatively well-paid ribbon workers and weavers, to the immigrant loomfixers and twisters and horizontal warpers—while John and I sought and found old light-bulb boards, electrical wire, flashers, and fuses. When he had everything he thought he needed, we hired a wagon, though it was nearly midnight now, and brought it all to the apartment in the Village he shared with John Reed, put as much as we could in three suitcases, and locked the in his bedroom. Then we had a late supper. (It was the first time in our lives when we could count on all the food we wanted whenever we wanted it, and we never tired of eating.) When we finished eating, we walked to the Garden, and ascended the tower once more. It made all the sense in the world as we listened rapturously to the sound of the goddess atop her little six-pillared lantern, grinding from one minute of perspective to the next. Here is what I see now. Here is what I see now. Here is what I see for a moment then never again. The lantern was evidently something of an attraction, and was filled with people even at that late hour, the lift going ceaselessly up and down, up and down, up and down, but John was quite sure there would be a slack period in the wee hours, when they could rig their lights. Secreting the contents of the suitcases wherever we could, here and there in the tower's highest rooms, another three suitcases each day, we waited for Opening Night.

An exhibition of the latest art was on display at the Armory. John (with whom, yes, as you have been suspecting, I had fallen hopelessly in love, he was so handsome and capable and so clearly desirous of the kind of life I had slowly been working up a description of with my friends) had seen many paintings and sculptures in his life, and been moved by a few, but Rosemary and I had not. But because the work in the Armory was new to everybody, John found no precedent for it in his imagination. He therefore thought he did not much care for most of what he saw, but as he and I and Rosemary walked— John and Rosemary hand in hand, me waiting patiently for the time when I knew someone would snatch Rosemary away and John would turn to me in astonished love, as if a storm had passed and I was the one who was still there—from one curtained gallery to the next, under the canopy of bright yellow streamers billowing up into the darkness of the somehow still military ceiling, amid the boughs and sprays of evergreens and baskets of flowers, I think he could not help but feel some of our amazement and excitement: the tumbling but suave sweep of geometric shapes in Duchamp's mockery of the "cult of big women," Nude Descending a Staircase, No. 2, the strange but vivid, too vivid colors and objects in Matisse—I heard someone call it "epileptic"—the hallucinated landscapes of van Gogh.... No, he could not deny what I was saying with such conviction: the affinity many of the paintings had with narcotic perception, or with narcotic thought, with what it was like to work in a mill. And so he was annoyed for our sake to hear people buzzing in every room about what former president Roosevelt—had he just been there? and if so, how had we missed him?—had said, suggesting Americans take the work no more seriously than they did P.T. Barnum's mermaids. Which was to say, somewhat seriously, as you could look far and wide and not find a more striking, beloved, archetypical example of an American than Barnum, but skeptically or at arm's length, with tongue in cheek, with an eye toward amusement and belly laughs rather than edification and sublimity. Certainly there was more repugnance than beauty in much of the work. One left a canvas too often irritated and confused, and there was even a sense of outright falseness in every one of the eighteen octagonal rooms, either the result of ineptitude and childishness, or the calculated deceit of a huckster. But Rosemary and I were thrilled with the recognition of something essential in our lives. She was holding my hand tightly now, and could say little more than oh oh ohhhh, as if she were having an orgasm—a sensation I could not help but feel drawn closer and closer to myself. We could only be responding, in our completely untutored, inexperienced way, to what we sensed was the life in the paintings. That too John could not deny: there was life and ecstasy in them, some of them. There was life somewhere. He could smell it. It stank but it was alive. I shivered. And then we came to Odilon Redon, whose first works were ridiculous and grotesque: the huge grinning spider, the hot-air balloon that looked like an eyeball, worms and deliquescent flowers, the puerile doodlings of a bored but gifted little boy. A sad, creepy Cyclops. Six lithographs inspired by Poe. Rosemary drifted away.

When she came back, her face was clouded. She stood over us and we could see her eyes were wet and that tears had run down her cheeks. Then she smiled and it seemed the tears were of joy. She pulled us to our feet and told us he must come and see The Druid Priestess.

She was in profile, and her head and neck and shoulder were clothed in a kind of silken fluid gold that became a reddish orange on her arm. Her jaw and cheek were darkened, and at first glance she would be taken for mannish, the dark staining an early growth of beard. But then it began to look more as if she were made of wood, the lower part of her face darkened with age or mold, or the nose and large dark eye and forehead bleached by the sun. The blue, green, and black background suggested a luminous forest at twilight, and there was a spattered yellowish moon in the upper left corner. Her golden hood appeared to be raining around her. Her eye grew deeper and darker, her sharp nose and thin lips more feminine. Hair flowed from under the golden rain, like a deeper, darker current. We were hypnotized. "I think that's my grandmother," said Rosemary. "She is a strange but lovely woman," said John. "Grandmother," I repeated reverently.

We waited for a large group of murmuring people to pass into the next room, then swung around the burlap-covered partition wall and came face to face with the first of the horses. It was a dark, earth-brown and gold demonic Pegasus, embroiled in its own fury, writhing and contorted as it struggled to fly, or having flown, to not fall. Next was a silver and white Pegasus, rearing up on a black, blue, and silver mountaintop, majestic, magical, and beautiful—but alone. The winged horse and rider in Roger and Angelica, or Perseus and Andromeda was purely golden, with very small wings. A kind of wormy serpent and mutant fish-monster—possibly the Medusa but possibly not—menaced them in the blue clouds. We decided these paintings were beautiful, but troubling, and admitted we had become distinctly uneasy. Finally we came to The Chariot of Apollo. There was the blue sky again, now frighteningly blue—not dawn, not noon, not dusk, not midnight—and the white horses in agony. Only a small smear of the sky was that shade of strange bedlam blue; the clouds were brown and green, as if the world were upside down, and the chariot, stolen from Apollo by the brash young reckless Phaeton...seemed to be falling. Phaeton's head appeared to be on fire, and the chariot was falling.

Though playgoers lined the sidewalk the length of the Garden, went around the block and nearly the length of its other side, most of them, assevering poverty or union brotherhood, would get in for pennies, or without charge, if they were

Paterson silkworkers not appearing in the show. The Pageant's backers, John told us as we stood in the park across the street, had been depending, in the face of sky-high—we all looked up involuntarily at the statue of Diana—Garden rental fees, on subscription and the selling-out of the pricier stalls to intellectual sympathizers with money. These sympathizers had not been as forthcoming as had been hoped, and John said the backers reckoned that they would probably not break even. Worse, it was looking like he was being left holding, so to speak, the books: bills had been left unpaid, and while some vendors and lenders would be happy to write their losses off in a good cause, some would not. There wasn't much he could do, but it looked like he would have to deal with the part that wasn't any fun. I said that that was because he was a good, kind, decent man who could not help but do such things for the welfare of others. He sat down on a bench that was out of the lamplight they'd been standing in, and Rosemary instinctively sat down next to him, held his arm and snuggled close. She liked him, and that was all there was to it. I think she knew I loved him, but she liked him, and when she liked people, she showed it. For his part, John liked nearly everybody he met, but felt he would, without thinking, risk his life, just like that, for Rosemary. How could I discredit such a feeling? Why would I? And, again, without thinking or any sort of articulation, he was confident that the feeling was reciprocal. It was simply the kind of man he was. Was he a daredevil? Not in any way that you would notice. Was he handsome? Yes, but not incredibly so. Was he charismatic? No. (But I loved him.) His eyes were kind and intelligent and he was not afraid to suffer, not afraid to die. And here is where I began to see things as it were peripherally. Nothing bore in on me. I could see everything floating past me but focus on nothing. Even perfectly clear shapes very near did not startle or impinge on me. They moved at ordinary speed, but seemed to drift and were quietly making ordinary noises. I could see things very far away and it was soothing to have it all so far away. It was something like being high, but I wasn't, and I was glad I wasn't. All three of us had fallen silent, listening to the shouts across the street. Once most of the crowd was inside and the Pageant had begun—you could hear the first choral shouts even in the park—we made our way with a small handtruck from the shipping dock to the tower lift. From the handtruck to the lift we moved four big boards holding red-painted electric light bulbs, a roll of electrical cord, and a little leather satchel of tools. We appeared to be handling scenery, and to be involved in ordinary stagecraft; the people milling about didn't give us a second look as we closed the iron-grill doors of the lift's little car and set off, rattling and banging our way upward. We passed up through many floors in the darkness of the elevator shaft, but came suddenly to the Parthenon-like summit of the tower's first twenty floors, and glimpsed, through the massive columns, the little streams of light flowing into the vast darkness beyond Central Park. Slowing and swaying and creaking, we went up another fifty feet into a once again closed dark space, that looked something like a miniature neo-classical bank or government building, the lift coming to a loud banging stop at its roof, which was the floor of the first of three, successively smaller balconied arcades, the last of which was the lantern, on top of which Diana rested and turned. We would have to climb narrow circular stairs now, with our awkwardly big and increasingly heavy light-boards, each of the four six feet by three.

Halfway with the first board, Rosemary, going first, said oh no sharply, and slipped. Though all she did was to sit heavily, the board came down with a crack on the top of her skull, and I was jolted backward. I let go of the board with both hands to grab the handrails, and somehow managed to hold the board on the rack of my arms and shoulders while it pressed into his throat. It was as if I were standing before the carder with an immense weight choking me. Rosemary struggled to her feet and quickly pulled the board up so that I could breathe. Satisfied that we were all right, we made our way slowly and carefully up to the lantern. We propped the board against the balustrade, and waited for John, who was carrying the second by himself. Then we went down for the third board. Halfway up, the same thing happened again: the step was somehow irregular, or slick, and Rosemary, careful as she could be, slipped. She made the same sharp sound, and I, hearing something this time in the intake of breath just before the cry, was able to ready myself, hunching my shoulders to protect my throat. Up in the lantern, we panted, and waited for John and the last board. Rosemary then went down and came back up with the electrical cord, and John set about cutting, separating, and splicing it. Then without a word she went through one of the window arches onto the ledge, a good wide ledge of about two feet, running the perimeter of the lantern. She looked up and told us she could see the splendid swell of Diana's breasts above the folds of her toga. She was all alone at the top of the city, as calm as an angel, seeing everything. John, being a man, said she should come back in: he should be the one on the ledge. I slowly pushed my end of the first board out farther and farther through the opening into the darkness. At precisely the point where I thought I would lose control of it, Rosemary dropped it lightly and quickly to the ledge, and crawled back in. A single short piece of rope secured the board to a column. Again and again and again she went out onto the ledge while I slowly slowly slowly pushed the boards out at her, thinking with every breath that something terrible was going to happen and I would be responsible for her death. Again and again and again she dropped the boards into place and popped back into the lantern with us. We were, I suppose, in awe of her. Breathless all of us, silent, feeling we were living so fully we were nearly at the edge of it, that real things were seeming less and less real, and unreal things more and more real. Then we went back down the winding stairway, unspooling cord as we descended, until we were back in the confines of the bank-like structure. Here was the utility room. The little old man who presided over it was not to be found. John cut and spliced more cord, studied a fuse box, said this ought to do it and flipped a switch. Up we went one last time up to the lantern, to see if in fact the bulbs were lit, and Rosemary hopped out onto the ledge. We waited for her to say something, but she said nothing. I thought I heard a faint whistling, and I turned to John and said, or murmured to myself, or merely thought: whistling while we work. By the time we worked up the courage, or rather the saliva, to speak, to call out her name, we knew she had fallen, knew that she was gone. We said nothing to each other, thinking somehow that if we remained calm all would be well. John went out onto the ledge. I could hear his shoes scraping around me as he made the circuit. Then he came back in. He shook his head and I began to tremble. We went down to the lift, jammed its door open, and walked down thirty floors and out one of the loading dock doors. A cab took us to Penn Station, and three days later, we were in San Francisco, reading various accounts in five or six newspapers of the terrifying lights above Madison Square Garden: NO BOSS spelled out the board facing south. NO DOGMA shone to the east, NO GOD to the north, and finally, in the west, NO FEAR. The identity of the young woman who had evidently engineered the feat was eventually revealed. Her name was Rosemary Thorndike, a well known anarchist.

SAN LUIS EL BRUJO

OR, PERHAPS ANOTHER INDICATOR OF THE NONLOCALITY OF CONSCIOUSNESS

ONE: THE DEEP BLUE SEA

Two ladies, older but in good health and fashionably, attractively dressed, sipped at glasses of local red wine and admired the landscape of ocean and distant hilly peninsulas. The wine was fast but interesting once it had settled down, if you liked turpentine. That was how the more talkative of the two put it. When they turned, the land that had been behind them, green and brown hills, seemed to fall from from blue sky and rush toward them. The green and brown appeared to cluster together Soft gray ridgelines of a range in the distance became sharper and darker as they advanced, until the one immediately before and above them them, which was dressed as if in decoration for the party with a stand of pine. It had been proposed that the group climb to that stand of trees so that the art-collecting cowboy could show them all something he thought was unique and important. Once (the talkative lady read from a pamphlet printed in green and white with the logos of many organizations) there had been thousands upon thousands of acres of those pines.

Montereys, insignis, radiata.

She pointed up the hill as if selecting some small gem or trinket. Her friend followed her finger, almost like a dog might, fixedly at the finger, then making the leap. But it was hard to say if she was pretending to be stupid for a laugh or was drawn somehow, personally, naturally, to the finger despite the long-standing effectiveness of the point—a definite, wholly intentional attention opposing what she was being instructed or asked to do, to look at, to think about, to judge and consume. It looked very much like she was doing it for a laugh, and was shaking her empty wine glass as if it were a bell. The two life-long friends stared at the pines.

The ocean crashed behind them and they turned again. They watched a pearly crystalline bank of fog form on what had been a sparkling black horizon and move without seeming to move toward them. Everything, it seemed, was moving very slowly and subtly toward them.

San Luis el Brujo, when the Mexicans had begun to put cattle and missions in Alto California and populate vast lonely beautiful places with their lonely catholic mestizo selves, had been an unbroken pine forest of Monterey pine, covering the hills from mountains to ocean—or rather, not unbroken, but a dense dark archipelago of tree-islands, from Morro Bay in the south to Ragged Point in the north.

Now there was that stand, which was coming down the hill toward them. The less talkative but comic lady, Janet, who was wearing a big curving white hat that fluttered in the breeze, had been staring at the pines long enough to become troubled. She thought they were spooky. She had just seen a frightening production of Macbeth on TV and mentioned the forest of Dunsinane to her friend. She often used sophisticated cultural references to stand up, conversationally, to her dominating friend, Marilyn, who never failed to fall silent for a significant period of time, as if in fact defeated, frustrated, irritated, envious. She was a sporting lady: her hat was simply a golfer's green transparent visor strapped around her rich lustrous silver hair, which was pulled into a bouncy ponytail over the top of the strap. From a short distance she looked like a much younger woman. Her friend was clearly old, but attractive, from any perspective or distance. It was as if she had lived a good life and it mattered.

Both women continued to stare up the slope at the pines. The sage, green with what had seemed, to the ladies, upon their arrival from Boston, like too much rain, appeared to be waving down at them as well. A stream of purple-green and yellow-red succulent flowed out of the sage and chappy down the hill, over their feet, their ankles, shins, even, in places, and over the edge of the little cliff into a churning tide pool. The ladies turned as if a tide were turning them, floating them, moving them. To the edge of the cliff. They watched as the fog bank became a vaporous, slowly drifting wall. They had to look straight up to see blue sky, or to the east over the ridges. The thick juicy ropes of succulent fig were so heavy with stored water they would probably soon let go altogether their tenuous hold on the rocks. That would account, would it not, for the odd feeling of tide tugging at them.

They appealed to the sister of the millionaire cowboy, Catherine Johnson was her name, who was herself eye-poppingly wealthy, wealthy that is, in the way only a central Californian could be: desolately so, defiantly so. Bleak. Rapacious but sad. One of her enterprises, for example, was the manufacture of the terrible wine they were attempting to cough and choke down their throats. The caterers, too, were her people. They obviously feared her, and stood behind the big aluminum urns to protect themselves from her gaze. The three ladies had met when they had been helping to elect a President of the United States. The two Bostonians, Janet and

Marilyn, had been invited to come, as a kind of treat, to a fundraiser in Hollywood. Catherine had convinced them that the land north of Los Angeles, north of Santa Barbara, was certainly one place to retire, perhaps the place if one wanted to stay put, as she mostly did. And so the ladies had come, now, to understand and to judge and to choose.

Catherine spoke of the trees and the hills. The Hearsts in San Simeon had hidden some of the castle's outbuildings and roads with Montereys. Mostly it was oak now. She could not have cared less about the trees, nor less about what her friends thought of them, what they thought of San Luis el Brujo, what they thought of her. If they came, she might find a way to consider them friends. She might find a way to use them, if they turned out to be sharper than they had so far acted. She had invited them to purchase homes because that was what she did, one of the things: bought and sold land.

"The oak is a safer tree," said Catherine. "When I was young I would hear of incidents where cones of the so-called magnificent Monterey pines crashed to the ground and killed people. I suppose that's a kind of magnificence."

She smiled without wishing to. But decided to turn the smile on her friends, each in turn receiving the full strange anger of it: the thought of the idiot unable to get out of the way of a falling pine cone the size of a pumpkin.

Her lawyer could see the smile from a good distance, even in the most murky or glaring light. He stood next to Catherine's brother, Victor, the cowboy who actually ran cattle but who in truth had spent so many millions on art that there were rumors.

If the truth as it was bandied about was in fact true. The lawyer of course knew that it was not, that there was some truth to it—the will had been changed, certainly—but that something crucial was missing from the story.

Catherine introduced her brother and her lawyer to her two new friends. Victor was well over six feet tall, lean and muscular, wore a big white cowboy hat over a tanned, lined, beautifully weathered visage which included a nearly Civil War-sized moustache that had gone gray, a colorful shirt and blue jeans. His string-tie had an imitation Chumash rock-painting for a clasp. He smoked and appeared to be at the end of the tether of sobriety. He was seventy-five years old and a homosexual. That was what he said when he shook the hands of the ladies.

Eugene Romero was introduced as the family attorney and friend of both sister and brother for more than fifty years. Janet and Marilyn immediately thought him strange, stranger even than the rugged brother, who perhaps protested too much that he was strange. The lawyer on the other was too vacant, or dreamy, or possibly he was distracted by a complicated point of law or the shenanigans of some big trial. He did not protest at all, or seem to feign a thing. He was physically as unimposing as Victor was imposing. Sometimes, when he looked in the mirror while shaving, usually at the point of slapping bracer on his cheeks, he would think yes, that's right, I am not a billboard, I'm an ordinary man. He was heavy but not fat, his hair was thin but still black and looked good on his head. He had black eyes that could be romantically distant or rigorously engaging.

"I don't practice much anymore," he told Janet and Marilyn. "I brood. 'To philosophize is to learn how to die.'"

The women dismissed him—almost making twin and simultaneous gestures of pseudo-friendly reproach. The men they had known in their lives had never given up. Naturally one paid a price for dedication, for remorselessness. But one paid. One was morally wealthy and one paid without a peep.

"You've been so helpful, though," said Marilyn, adjusting her visor so that the lawyer could see her lovely disdainful eyes, "in making this available to the public."

"Is it true, Mr. Romero," asked Janet, "that cones from pinus radiata have fallen on people and killed them." But it was not a question, evidently. It was an accusation. She wanted Catherine Johnson to be proved publicly wrong. Why she wanted this, she did not know.

"The radiant penis," drawled Victor Johnson like a gunslinger, picturesquely lighting a cigarette, and was ignored. Blowing smoke, he gestured in a childish impatient way that was embarrassing and grotesque in an older man, for them to leave the eggplant-rhubarb and apple-banana maze—the first veils of fog were already draining those colors, as if thick curtains were blowing in a breeze, a table of glazed fruit glowing and darkening as a nervous painter in a nightmare waited and waited—and mount the common brown California hill so that they might not only experience the radiant penis up close and personal but see the ominous magic he knew would scare the soupy pats right out of the old cows. It had already chastened the alcohol out of him. He felt unsteadily sober. He was uncomfortable, uneasy. Yes: he was himself afraid of everything that was going to happen. But did not know, could not say, exactly what was going to happen. Or when. Or why.

The ocean had become muted. The silently swarming fog was nearly upon them.

They began to walk up the hill. The fog seemed to come with them. As if it were reaching out to touch their backs. Then it seemed as if they were leaving the fog as a kind of billowing wake behind them. The paths through the sour fig filled with molten vapor. They could no longer see the deep blue sea—merely flashes of metal here and there.

"Since it figures so prominently in my deposition, and is typical not only of the Johnson ranch but Hearst's infamous San Simeon and this whole glorious middle third of mad lost California, let me try to give you a sense of the place."

"Deposition?" asked Janet.

"Do you mean," asked Marilyn," that this preservation is not secure."

"I am deposing myself. Perhaps it will serve as some kind of amicus brief. Of course I don't know how things will turn out. I would be a magician if I could know those sorts of things. Victor is the magician and even he says he does not know. I suppose it will only be a memoir in the end. An e-book denied even the dust of neglect."

Nobody responded to this strange muted declaration. It was as if their yacht had slowed and hove to in the bay of the island of the pine forest, and the wake of the fog was washing around them. Overtaking them like a wave, but without a sound. It was the fog talking.

"At the turn of the century—I mean the nineteenth to the twentieth, when my father and mother were children—this was all what they called "the Forest of Cambria." Monterey pines and live oaks. There is strong feeling amongst the paleobiologists of my acquaintance that these trees were here long before los playanos. Most of the pines—"

"Los what?"

Gene was not sure who had spoken, and did not care.

"Playanos. Beach people. The first inhabitants of California."

"Beach people," laughed Marilyn. The fog swallowed the laugh immediately. "Sun tan lotion? Frisbees?" She knew now that she sounded stupid, and became angry. "When was this?"

"Ten, twelve, thirteen thousand years ago," said Gene. "We know nothing about them. The earliest people we know something about would be, for instance, the Chumash and the Salinan. You may have heard these names. If you look closely at Victor's string-tie, you will see a reproduction of what, for us around here, is a famous Chumash rock-painting."

Victor, further up the hill, staggered down to them, almost running, almost falling, long, strong but old legs and knees close to giving way, to say "See? See? Chumash rock painting! It's a cheap souvenir! Anyone can have one! They're free! In the gift shop in the cave where the picture is! Would either of you like this one? I give it to you as a welcome to San Luis el Brujo! A gift of ordinary everyday magic." He slipped his tie from around his neck and pushed the clasp toward the women. Why he was still pretending to be a child was beyond everyone.

The painting was of a figure of a man and a child, or a god and a man—at any rate, a larger and a smaller figure, not much more than stick-men, the larger holding what looked like either a ceremonial wheel or large tambourine-like instrument. The figures were copper-colored and looked as if they had been etched, or scratched and daubed with rough strokes and little paint on a rock surface that was, again, eggplant-purple in the center around the figures fading into a dusty blue in which wavy white lines could be seen. "Seriously, if you'd like more than one," croaked Victor, "I've got a couple of boxes up at the ranch. I own the original. The thing in the cave is replica. You can understand why they'd want a replica." He turned away and made his way arthritically back up the few steps he had run down.

Gene continued: "...as I have already said, are gone. For some reason, they were hated and feared by the children and the children's children of the settlers of California—not only were they messy, they were dangerous: a falling cone could kill a man, though such an occurrence has never been documented, to my knowledge. Let us have magnificent oaks, they cried, and they got them. There is no question about how beautiful our oak trees are. More importantly, however, everything, prized robles to despised pinos, was cleared for cattle. Only seventy acres of our prehistoric pines survived. What we are looking at is about a half-acre of the seventy. It's one reason why the Zamboni ranch was so highly prized by all of us. In the late 1800s, the Zamboni family bought the ranch expressly for cattle grazing and it became known as the Zamboni Town Ranch. On the other side of this first ridgeline is California Highway One and our town, San Luis el Brujo, named not after some bishop in France like our neighbor just to the south but a Renaissance magus."

"Magus?" asked Marilyn. She had taken off her visor and shaken her hair loose. She still seemed angry, demanding of the truth in all things at all time.

"Magician but in the sense of wise man," said Gene. "The Three Wise Men. White magic as opposed to black. Good as opposed to evil. Scientific as opposed to supernatural."

"The town, let me get this straight," said Marilyn, "is not named after a catholic saint, but a magician. Is that right?"

"Yes, that's right. An associate of Pico della Mirandola."

Janet had just taken a survey course of the renaissance and wondered why San Luis had not figured in it. Gene, amazed, said that he did figure. Marilyn said, "Well of course he would have had to, wouldn't he. But as it was a survey for seniors, well..."

"Nearby, lost in the next range of steep hills flowing up into the Santa Lucias, is the site of another town, Cambria, which was strictly a mercury-mine settlement and now amounts to three or four ruined buildings and a sealed up hole in the mountain. These ruined buildings and abandoned mine are on the Johnson property." He gestured to Catherine, who had joined Victor up the trail, where they stood like statues with blank eye. "In 1984 representatives of the Zambonis sold the Town Ranch to a real-estate developer who planned to build a substantial residential/commercial project on the property. It was sold in 1995 through a bankruptcy auction to another developer with similar plans: Catherine Johnson.

Through the efforts of Friends of the Ranchland, a community organization formed by myself and a few devoted friends—Catherine included to be sure, most generously—to preserve the Ranch, invited the American Land Conservancy to come to our community's aid with the provision that we coordinate the transaction and fundraising. The Foundation for Small Wilderness Area Preservation helped develop the North Coast Small Wilderness Area Preservation (NCSWAP), a new chapter comprised of people from San Luis el Brujo. This organization then partnered with the American Land Conservancy, the State Coastal Conservancy, CCSD, San Luis Obispo County (to the south), Monterey County (to the north), businesses and residents to purchase (from Catherine) The Zamboni Town Ranch for $31.1 million on June 18th, 2003. Pathways were cleared, a bridge or two built, some magnificent benches composed entirely of driftwood were emplaced at auspicious spots, a hundred yards of boardwalk laid down here and there—which brings us to today, exactly one year later, and the Grand Opening you have just participated in with us so joyously. So if you stood at the precipice, where we were so happily and heedlessly drinking and eating the marvelous food and wine Catherine provided for us, turned away from the emerald grass and purple ocean and the lightning laced fog gulping toward us, you saw the essence of the Zamboni Town Ranch dream: the ocean, a cliff, a kind of turgid glazed delta of succulents gradually closed off to a stream and then a trickle by sage and chaparral thick with the yellow and red and purple paintbrush flowers of about two hundred species of owl's clover, which rises up not so steeply,

I'm sure you will agree, to these pines on the first ridgeline. Peninsulas north-northwest, on your left, and south-southeast, on your right, are terraced with rather expensive homes piled on top of each other in a way that has always suggested the ancient ports of the Mediterranean to me. Tyre, for instance, an excellent city if you are interested in illegal antiquities trading. Which we are all up to our assholes in. Begging your pardon. Ephesus. Halicarnassus. Jaffa. Carthage. Algiers. Marseille. Barcelona. Transposed to the desolate Pacific...a second ridgeline, less distinct in outline but sharply colored as the sunlight remains on it and the fog rolls in around us...quite thickly now! and a third, magically distant, as if already in the past, or in the future, causing us to look with strange guilt or apprehensiveness at the misty but still wave-forming ocean, or the ocean forming plates of flashing lead...and finally, against the blue sky--Which is now gone! Look! There goes the last bit of blue!"

They all looked: the sky turned white then dark gray.

"And that is Vulture Peak."

It is black as coal, numinous, shining like a translucent volcano. The sky around it is luminous silver. It is an unreal and terrible rampart of desolate consciousness. Gene tells the ladies that twelve thousand years ago there were no people here, and that he had no doubt whatsoever that the ones who are here now will have vanished without a trace in twelve thousand more.

"Vulture Peak is where Victor's ranch is. He and Catherine grew up there." They looked up at brother and sister but sister was gone. Victor's eyes still appeared to be blank marble. Dogs had appeared, many of them. One or two appeared to Gene's dogs, but the four, five, six others were either Victor's or the dogs of the people in the big houses on the terraces, running free.

"Where is Catherine," demanded Marilyn.

It was so quiet you could hear the fog as it came together and drifted apart. Did someone say that Catherine was gone? That Catherine was no longer there? It must have been Victor, because it seemed to come from a very long distance. Marilyn said nothing, but turned to Janet as if she meant to.

Where Catherine had been standing a hummingbird appeared to hover, appear and disappear.

The fog was suddenly so thickly upon them that the ladies grasped hands and stifled calls of concern. They had seen the white curls on the black waves for some time. Then they were gone. Doppelgängers of fog, their own eyes where the eyes of their friends had been, gaping mouths, teeth falling out, appeared to grow up from the ground around us, or step from behind wispy columns—or merely stand revealed when those columns burned whitely, silently, without heat, and disappeared. Then the ladies thought they could still hear the waves—and then could not, but then again, yes.

Gene appeared before them, smiling. He said that while they could all most certainly hear something, it was not the crashing of water on stone. If he were forced to say exactly what it was they were hearing, he would be inclined to say that it was the memory of water crashing on stone. The sun, which had been, at the commencement of the gala celebration of the purchase of the Zamboni Ranch, too bright, even, for some of them, cruelly so, everybody wearing sunglasses in any case, was now a smoking silver disc hovering in spaceless space before them. A disc of lead or tin. The sun stripped of its power, merely a strange sign in the sky, which was itself now too merely figurative. It was not the Supreme God, the Sky God, the First God or anything like a god. Everybody was gone. All that consensual reality: they got in their cars and disappeared in seconds down the two-track. Catherine's catering service had cleaned up as if there had never been so much as a celery stick eaten. And the sun was merely a mist-shrouded tin sign in the middle of the air, hung and creaking like a sign in gusts of fog for a restaurant they could not see on a street they could not see. A man appeared, someone they didn't know, drawing a string of horses and just like that they were all horseback, and moved slowly up through the choppy gray sea of fig leaves and stalks, the hooves of their horses wetly severing a magic root here and a magic root there until it seemed they were all standing still and the field of fig far below them was indeed sliding backwards, over the cliff, into the memory of the silent invisible ocean—they could only just hear it, walking the horses up the trail or it seemed upstream through vegetation becoming a flood of liquid, of a kind of blood—up through more gray sage and into another stand of pines on the ridgeline. Long pale grasses dissolving in silver clouds, deepest green trees now marble arches around the darker doors of the interior, doors that opened and closed, opened and closed, opened and closed for each passing wraith, or filmy congestion of dust and water that came and went, came and went, came and went. The castles and palaces of the Pseudo-

Mediterranean and the caves and tents of the first farmers on the coast of Peru were still solid but no longer real. Their shapes had become transparent and opaque as night, transparent and opaque at the same time, that was the key, that was how they knew things were solid but not real, the light in their eyes dim but blinding as light in a bad dream. They dismounted in a clearing where a bench had been dedicated to a benefactor. The spirit of celebration was now seen for what it had been all along, for them, false cheer, odiously false: an omen and capitulation—on the part of Catherine, who believed she could have made exponentially more money from the property and perversely saw bankruptcy looming as a direct result of this weak bowing to the good of the community—and perhaps the last straw for Victor, for whom things were going much more badly than Gene, than anybody, realized—and, by extension, for Milos, the man who had brought the horses, who was, nevertheless, so accomplished in the effectiveness of the cheer he could act out that he could not be brought low and very often succeeded in raising the spirits of those around him who had succumbed, rather than annoying and irritating them. Gene's thoughts left the memory of the ocean crashing against the shore and imagined he half-saw in the way the brain was so good at, saw but didn't see Milos speeding away on a terrible day ten years in the future—why ten years? When it could so easily be tomorrow—in his nice blue car not because he had lost everything and in his hysteria murdered Victor, who had thrown it all away, but because he had failed to...to cheer Victor sufficiently, to lift him up out of his suicidal despair. To love him. To love him in the supremely good way that everyone knew was possible but which no one could attain....

And was therefore at long last truly terrified.

An arch appeared between two pines, leading into impenetrable blackness. At the mouth of this cave, Catherine could be seen turning away and vanishing, her horse following her. Then appearing again, just his great head, his eyes white and rolling—clearly, from a distance, in waves of fog!—convulsed by something, then charging across the hill to the rest of them, where he instantly became a normal horse, a chestnut mare.

Gene said, "She likes crazy horses. Always has. A crazy horse will kill her. Will kill us all, I think, because we are getting old and because we have been hypnotized by all this for far too long. Ride up to Ragged Point and then take her over the cliff."

"Here," said Victor, "is what I've been wanting to show you." Milos, twenty years younger than Victor, stood very near his lover and lightly caressed the once-gaudy silk shirt.

He pointed at what looked like a stick, a branch, lying across the path. The dogs had been walking over it, back and forth, unconcerned, for some time. Victor stood over for it some time, examining it, getting down on all fours as if to listen to it. He motioned for the others to draw near and see this marvel: The ladies jumped back and said OHHH with their fists to their mouths. It was a three-foot-long Western Diamondback rattlesnake, stiff as a stick, straight as a ruler. Its eyes were open, and its tongue flickered once or twice.

"How horrible!" shouted Marilyn.

"What is—what is WRONG with it? Why is it LIKE that?" whimpered Janet.

"Oh take it away please!" moaned Marilyn. "PLEASE TAKE IT AWAY."

"He did not know he was dying," said Victor. "But he does now. Grandfather," he said softly, imploringly, "what have we done wrong? Where did we go wrong? Why has this happened to us?"

He picked the snake up, held it before him, stiff and straight, its tongue darting weakly.

"My baton of commandment. I merely hold it. I have no power over it. He has power over me. He says he has great pity for us. He says you will live here and your country will have a name. Living in a country that is little, not big, you will be content."

He caressed its entire length, held it out before him like a flute, older than civilization, then put its head, tongue flicking, in his mouth, held it there for a moment, then brought it out. He snapped his fingers and the snake went limp. He held it with two hands. It was a big, a very big snake. He was about to place it in deep grass when something caught his eye and he threw it up in the air as high as he could—using in fact so much effort that he fell over. There was a sharp whistling sound and they all looked up just in time to see a plummeting hawk throw out its wings and snatch the snake in its talons. Victor told them to watch the blades of grass part and swing around it, the real snake that had been alive and not clutched in the talons of a hawk, had been alive after all, hypnotized but now awake and alert and even afraid, moving away from them as it ought to have. "He is formless now, and seeks the black hole where blind he may once again find form. The hawk thinks he has a snake in his talons, but he has nothing. Nothing at all."

Marilyn and Janet, rigid as the snake had been, hypnotized too, swallowed and their heads seemed to pivot upon their larynxes.

They rode their horses at a walking pace back to town. That night they all—Marilyn and Janet, Victor and Milos, Catherine and Gene—three couples in three beds, if not in sexual intimacy—dreamed: a formlessness in a blast of lightning disappearing into a black tunnel, while they...they were sliding backwards, it was exactly the feeling one is standing on a beach and the surf is receding around your bare feet just as another wave foams and disappears in the sand— are you moving or is the world moving? Which way are you moving? Where are you going? They were moving, now they knew, they were moving backwards, the great field of sour fig had let go in its entirely and was rushing toward the cliff. They fell to their knees, became tangled in the bursting vines, blood and water dribbling between their fingers, rhythmic spurts, geysers—and then they were bound as if with ropes from an old sailing ship, as big around as...or were they snakes? Flutes made of gold, studded with diamonds, music pouring from them, rising into hysterical shrieks. And then over they went! it was fun, like a ride at a carnival! But suddenly the fun was over, and so was the fear. They went over clinging wanly to the thick juicy ropes and blinding pink cloud-masses of flower and come to rest on beds of emerald grass so bright and strange they looked blue in the clear still water of the tide pool. The silky black and white octopi caressed them with the love they had never never found and only vaguely suspected existed on Earth, true love. Starfish so strangely brilliant in the sunlight they glowed like magenta phosphorus and nuclear purple came to rest on them, like great living badges of merit bestowed upon their corpses...bestowed at this last lovely moment, just as they began their journeys to absolute decomposition.

TWO: THE GOLDEN HILLS

"Today," said Milos, holding an invisible microphone and speaking as if he were an announcer from the National Broadcasting Company with a rich upper east side accent, "is a day every bit as special, and perhaps even more important, than yesterday, when we marked the official opening of the Zamboni Town Ranch Preserve, a gift to all Americans from the citizens of San Luis el Brujo—to all the peoples of the world who love and respect the wonder and beauty of our beloved planet." Milos retained the comic accent but became sober, setting the invisible microphone aside and addressing his audience with greater warmth and intimacy.

"He's drunk," whispered Marilyn. "Everyone is." They had all been out for some time on the top of the three or four story house. One could see range after range of mountains slumping into the valley, and the loveliest gentlest blue ocean they had ever seen. The top of the so-called ranch house was flat, had chairs and tables and umbrellas like a café, and a short, very dark, broad-faced Guatemalan waiter to bring them local wine that was pointedly not horrible, and the latest appetizers that Catherine and Catherine's chefs had come across in the restaurants of Los Angeles, San Francisco, and Las Vegas. Binoculars, too, were politely handed to each guest. There were telescopes here and there on tripods four of them—and a really big one inside its own little...silo.

They were all dazed—with the exception of the apparently mercurial and gigantic Victor—and would have been quite happy were it not for the dreams that had troubled them all, each and every one of them—with the possible exception again of Victor, who did not seem troubled in the least. Which was troubling, because he was such a strange man. Terrifying, even, if he had not also feigned or been overcome by childishness.

Janet wanted to tell her friend about her dream, but could not bring herself to begin. She did not know how. It remained quite vivid but seemed beyond the reach of telling. She turned to her friend and opened her mouth, then closed it. Her friend meanly mimicked, gaping and clopping.

"You're drunk, too, aren't you," Janet mouthed back, eyebrows raised accusatorily.

"I said everyone was," said Marilyn without moving her lips. "You and I count as members of everyone. This wine, you can drink enough of it to actually enjoy the effects of the alcohol. As you know I have limited myself in the past to one glass, but I have raised the limit to one bottle." She giggled but abruptly stopped, catching it just in time as recollections of her dream passed across her face. She perceived the images as prophecies of death, of real death, her death, her imminent death. She became frightened and looked at her friend for comfort. Her friend merely re-mimicked the gaping and clop-closing of her mouth. Was it possible that these odd people had slipped a drug in their drinks? What was it called: peyote? The venom of a rattlesnake mixed in a cauldron with the paint-thinning wine of yesterday and the juice of hallucinogenic mushrooms? El Brujo indeed. Odd people, odd place, magic tricks—no golf courses, no tennis clubs. It was a laugh! We'd better get out while the getting's good, she snickered to herself.

"Today," said Milos, "we mark a different sort of anniversary altogether. On this date fifty years ago we—"

"You what?" demanded Catherine. "I'm sorry, I missed it. Did you say already?" She looked apologetically at Marilyn and Janet. "You must forgive me! My mind is elsewhere!"

Marilyn nodded. Her mind is elsewhere? She had better look to her assets! Not to mention the help. Did she have people for that? For looking after the other people who looked after the other people who—They most certainly could not be trusted—Catherine surely must know something as fundamental as that. Maybe Catherine just sat there vacantly, without a mind, snapping at flies. She was the possibly psychotic Victor's twin, after all. Maybe it was all over and she didn't care. Marilyn was tired of thinking of Catherine as the Queen of California, even as she admitted that Catherine wasn't putting on much of that kind of show, seeming rather preoccupied, rather, even distressed. At one point it looked like she was going to cry. She knew Janet had seen it too. She wondered if Janet would see it as a sign of weakness, or of humanity, or of something else all together. She thought her friend more sympathetic than herself, and secretly wished to be more that way, too, if it was possible to change one's character at such a late date.

Janet did indeed see the look, and thought reflexively of her dream. She became rather caught up in it, as if by rip-tide. Her eyes opened very widely.

Milos was as tall as Victor, and gracefully athletic in his movements, and much younger, but bald. The ladies knew there was a fashion for it, but thought that it was supposed to make one look sinister, or brutally stupid; Milos was debonair. Yes: he was jaunty and genial but moved like a dancer. An impressive but strange person who was growing stranger by the second, as if he were building to a dramatic re-enactment of a major grievance. A mime about to be struck with horror.

He tripped lightly over to Marilyn and adjusted her visor —which she had oddly retained after moving indoors to the main room of the ranch-house, a great hall of paintings and sculpture, mostly modern and strange, but striking. Milos pulled Marilyn's visor quite low on her forehead. He said she was now ready to play poker.

"Is that what we're doing," drawled Marilyn.

"YOU'RE BLUFFING!" Janet shouted, bubbling with laughter and unconcerned that she was in fact tipsy. "It's a sunny day on a ranch on top of a golden mountain with the deep blue sea spread out before us…! That's what day it is!"

"No," said Milos, quietly, sadly. "Not at all. It is not that sort of day at all."

It was a boorish come-down and everyone fell silent to honor it.

Then Milos relented, in good humor, and with style. "Forgive me. It is that kind of wonderful day and it is also another kind of day. Not so wonderful perhaps, but important."

"All right," conceded Janet, while Marilyn removed her visor.

"He's got something," said Catherine with what she had always thought was cool sexy diffidence, remarkable in a woman her age, but all the more enchanting for it, "but he's not playing a card game with it."

"What day is it," Marilyn pressed.

"On this day fifty years ago, the United states of America staged a coup in Guatemala! It was the CIA's first try at something like that, and it went super well!"

"It didn't go at all well," said Catherine.

"Just super, super well," repeated Milos.

"Luckily," said Catherine, "Guatemala had its head up its 'trade unionist' ass—note the quote marks please—and we managed with a couple of Cessnas and some radio broadcasts from Miami."

"Super, super, SUPER well," Milos affirmed.

Victor spoke in a loud, authoritative voice: "I was speaking to name deleted only last week, the State Department fellow, and do you know what he said to me? I don't know why this surprises me. He said oh dear oh dear oh dear, what we'd give to have an Arbenz now! We're going to have to invent one but all the candidates are dead!"

He had spoken too loudly.

"Arbenz," said Janet, lost but knowing her sense of herself depended totally on being able to find herself, intellectually, with regard to current events or recent history, so quickly that no one, not even a very well informed person, an expert, would notice. It suddenly occurred to her that Milos was Guatemalan—and that— "Arbenz, yes," she said to cover herself...that Gene Romero was Guatemalan too. She did not know why this might matter. Possibly something to do with illegal immigration. Wealthy Californians brought Mexicans and...and Guatemalans and...and...she failed to establish a map of Central America in her strong capacious mind...other types of immigrant...in by the boxcar and...

"Let me show you this painting. Come with me so we can look at it closely."

Everyone rose and followed Milos to another room.

The room was smaller than any other room they'd seen, and dark. Unlit but for the painting, which glowed.

It was an oil painting by Diego Rivera, one of his last. It was quite large, on linen, and was to have become a mural, but never did. The painting's background was of banana trees, a volcano, and men hefting what looked like hundred-pound sacks of bananas and coffee beans. In the foreground lay a few dead children, spattered with blood, limbs askew. The central image was of a small, finned bomb, with a grinning likeness of President Dwight D. Eisenhower engraved on it. It almost looks like a bas relief, the likeness is so convincing. Over this bomb is the long arm and deferentially leaning—almost bowing torso of Colonel Carlos Castillo Armas, who is shaking the hand John Foster Dulles, the Secretary of State. His brother, Allen Welsh Dulles, the Director of the CIA and board-member, as well, of the United Fruit Company is not in the picture. Ambassador John Peurifoy stands just behind these two major players, handing out money. Archbishop Somebody Somebody Somebody—neither Milos nor Victor could recall the man's name—blesses the ceremony and its transactions, which seem to include the dead children.

Milos allowed the group to examine the painting.

Then he said he'd found it, face to the wall, of course, in a basement full of junk in a grubby government building in Poland.

"So what?" asked Catherine.

"It speaks for itself," said Milos coolly.

"No, I'm sorry, I don't mean to be rude, especially in front of our guests! but really, so what?"

"Poland," said Janet. "How did it come—Warsaw? Krakow? Gdansk?"

"Lodz, actually," said Milos.

"Lodz! Well but how—"

"No idea how it got there. How it got out of there, that I can help you with."

Marilyn laughed derisively. "I don't think we need to know about that. That is the story of this whole...this whole place!"

"I have family there," said Milos. "Had family there."

"Oh," said Janet involuntarily. A Jew?

"Oh," said Marilyn involuntarily but not quite simultaneously. A Jew?

"It stinks in here," said Catherine. "I don't mean your family. I'm very very sorry for what happened to them, for all the Jews, you know that. But this place stinks of a shrine. Enshrined and musty dusty memories of a man who once did something brave for the good of his country and is now ashamed of it." She turned to Marilyn and Janet. "I am sorry, ladies. This is an argument of long-standing between my brother and myself. It's not as serious as it sounds." She laughed.

Marilyn pursed her lips and nodded, as if she were in a hospital room, blandly accepting mutability, mortality, infinity. Janet looked at Milos and wanted to say she was very sorry for the Jews, too, but didn't. At least she knew what had happened to them; the business in Guatemala had escaped her, if she ever knew of it. Cuba, yes, and the Bay of Pigs and Fidel Castro and the thirteen days in October—and of course the term 'banana republic' was in common usage and well understood.

Gene would have liked to speak for his client and friend—for his clients and friends, but first for Catherine. Because he loved her.

It wasn't shame or embarrassment she felt for her brother, for the man who had once "done something brave for his country" then retreated into selfishness and luxury—"I have everything I want up here," he would say, "everything. I am the man who has everything."

It was that San Luis el Brujo was a place of continuous change, and the change was incontrovertible. They had lived here and not lived here but been here anyway, somehow, and been pounded on by these waves that are almost never anything but soothing and gentle and without which they could not sleep—but which released immense amounts of energy anyway, something like two or three times a minute for he didn't know, millions of years. Billions. Milliards. Un mil millones. Gene did get lost in the figures, and in the words, he admitted it immediately and without embarrassment: He was no mathematician. He was a lawyer and a philosopher, and yes, a poet, too, since he did not think, as was also not thought by whom?—"an old philosopher in Rome"?—that one could have proper philosophy without good poetry, nor vice versa. (Santayana, that was the man, the book, the candle, the nurses he was dreaming of. The Santayana of Wallace Stevens. Lucretius. Dante. Goethe.) And he had no difficulty at all in the reconciliation of the haunting of the guilty with practical social law and order on one hand, and, on the other hand, with greater or deeper explorations of "the Universe," or whatever one chose to call it. "It." The Multiverse. Which inflated (the financial term was correct even though they were talking about background microwave radiation) just before or after— he couldn't remember—the Big Bang, doubling the cosmoses in size in a tiny fraction of a second. Or put another way, as he did for Catherine's benefit: a bank account that pays 100% interest every ten to the minus-thirty-seventh of a second— that surely was a universe she could invest in, implying as he never failed to imply that whatever she was actually about to invest in that season or day would be a total loss. Even when it was most often quite the opposite. Never missed a chance to babble at her: The Big Bang is how we believe the universe began because that's the theory that gets all the funding. When the known universe was tens of billions of light-years across in all possible and impossible directions, all possible and impossible trajectories, did that not just make the question of how to behave right here and now, in ordinarily reckoned time, in ordinarily reckoned space (which were still terrifying conundrums if you asked Gene), on Earth even more keen, doesn't it? It did for him, he wouldn't be able to sleep without the waves and the idea that his behavior mattered—and he thought it did for Catherine and Victor, too, in their very different ways. But no: Catherine reflexively denied it: "What is a light year again?" "You can't play dumb with me, Catherine." "Oh yes I can." And in the end he guessed she could. She refused to fall in a heap and worship the fifth power of a million. Catherine, Catherine, Catherine! She was a very serious woman. Laughter was for fools. Laughter lead to disaster and death. They all got lost in the numbers, but where Gene took this vastness and the measurements of the immeasurable for evidence of God or at least a call for sustained reverence for the unanswered question, she dismissed it as inhuman. It wasn't applicable, it wasn't interesting. One could not get one's head around it for a very good reason! The eternal return of the soul and words of advice from the dead, however, were eminently capable of understanding. All people at all times, she said, more or less, have believed these are natural workings as unremarkable as the transformation of an oak tree from an acorn.

But Gene Romero was just an old man, a very old man he now realized, who tried not to drink too much only because it interfered with reading too much. The book, the candle, the nurses, well, no nurses yet, but bottles, or boxes, mostly of Catherine's cheapest wines, third press mountain red in a briefcase, as his Australian clients and friends liked to put it, mixed with Tang...all of history, all of the universes, right here in a Greek ruin of a mind, looking up and up and up into the indistinct distance of ridgelines and clouds, to this grotesquely vivid mountain-top where the ranch was, all but swallowed up by sage brush. This very ranch where he stood, drink in hand, knowing there was nothing, absolutely nothing he could say, except Catherine, Catherine, Catherine...C3, he called her. C-cubed. Mrs. Wallace Johnson, née Johnson as well, Catherine Catherine Catherine Evelyn Johnson Johnson, his client and life-long friend, never had the slightest interest, in this sad affair or in any other affair, in anything but the money— Where else might these interests have been supposed to lie? She was a person of business, in a very special time and place, which was long gone even if she didn't know it, more odious times had ensued when they weren't looking, when they were hypnotized by the land they lived on. California in the Twentieth Century? They had ended the age themselves, just as their fathers and grandfathers, sober and at a crucial remove from the excesses of the Gilded Age millionaires, their fathers and grandfathers, began it: dressing up the coarsest, most simple-minded kind of lust for gold to look like civic virtue and common decency. Holiness even. The greatest of their great-grandfathers felt no compunction to be other than they were—naked villains with holy sanction—but Gene and Catherine and Victor...well, Gene didn't know what they'd been thinking. That there had to be a disguise for naked villainy that could withstand the judgments of history...? He did not know. He did not know who they thought they were, nor what they thought they were doing, nor what they hoped to get out of it, beyond the money. At the very least, Gene thought, they should have seen what was coming: California in the Twenty-first Century. A calendar would have showed them all they needed to know. That Catherine and—to a much more profound degree, of course—her brother, Victor, should have been haunted by the beliefs and values and practices of other times and places, when and where other people seemed to have ideas about who they were and what they were doing and what they hoped to get out of it, just made the plainest kind of sense.

Victor asked his guests to ascend once more to the rooftop observatory.

They did so with an air of sudden renewed vigor, great suspense and anticipation, and even nervous concern: their dreams still loomed in their minds and this after all was a man who only the day before had opened his mouth and placed between his teeth the head of rattlesnake that was neither dead nor alive, performing a trick that was not a trick, called a hawk screaming down from Heaven at two hundred miles per hour to snatch the snake out of mid-air—

Marilyn and Janet were actually afraid, but did not quite know it. As they walked up the narrow winding stairway, the light became brighter and brighter, the blue of the sky deeper and stranger, the ocean misty and dusty beneath it, the hills still green and gold but smoking—because they were afraid.

The shadow of a cloud passing overhead took them by surprise. It was so lovely, and yet they both knew, now, that they were eager to stay on the North Shore, if only to be near the children and grandchildren and—

Clouds were massing and streaming and boiling, or melting, like silver, far out at sea.

Victor was as genial a cowboy millionaire now as could be imagined. He lit a cigarette and took a glass of whiskey and water from the Guatemalan boy. As he drank it, it too was endowed with splendor.

Which only deepened the anxiety that Marilyn and Janet felt: that Paradise should be so ominous. Were they being hypnotized? Was Victor some sort of Svengali? Or that Russian…religious figure whose name they could not think of? Maybe Milos was a connection to some Eastern European unholiness and horror.

"I have everything I want," Victor was saying. "Literally everything. I love ranch life and I love art and I am standing naked in an overflowing Roman fountain of it, overflowing, finding its level then rising and falling like the tide. I own three Picasso guitar constructions and the manuscript of Stevens's Man With the Blue Guitar. Got all of Stevens that the goddamned Huntington didn't get! I have a gold collar from Ålleberg, pre-Viking, 5th century, faces of all the Norse gods worked into it. I have a very tiny stained glass window by Chagall. You saw the Maillol when you drove up. I have a hundred paintings worth a million dollars by artists you've never heard of—and I dare say never will, through no fault of your own, of course. I have a rough draft of one of the last papers Francis Crick wrote, down in La Jolla just a few years ago, on consciousness and neuroscience. Do you know what he said, by the way? Opening remark? We assume that when people talk about 'consciousness,' there is something to be explained. While most neuroscientists acknowledge that consciousness exists, and that at present it is something of a mystery, most of them do not attempt to study it, mainly for one of two reasons: one, they consider it to be a philosophical problem, and so best left to philosophers, and two, they concede that it is a scientific problem, but think it is premature to study it now. Would you like to touch a five-hundred-year-old kachina doll? You can, you may, I hope you will. You will take its strength with you. The greatest work of art I have, however, is something I'm not going to show you—or rather, I will show you only if you really want to, if you're sure." He paused and directed an encouraging smile at Marilyn and Janet. Who were unable to reply, though they were encouraged and wanted to do so, making that desire and its bafflement plain, in spite of their fear. "When we were in Guatemala," said Victor, "Gene and I, when we were adventurers in the employ of the Central Intelligence Agency, we—but hold on, getting ahead of myself. Guatemala story in the office, after the telescopes. What I started to say, what I want to say right now, what I want to ask you all, is this: this is Planet Earth, after all, the Pleasure Planet, right? Which was created for our sensual delight, right? I believe it to be. My fuller beliefs are more complicated, of course, but in the end, are we not here to float in the wonder of the universe?"

No one found a suitable reply.

Catherine seemed on the verge of it, but was denying herself 'the pleasure' of it because it was not a pleasure after all. It sickened her, what she thought was happening. Helplessly, not wanting to, she looked at Gene, who was looking at her.

Milos had disappeared.

"I have stolen a good deal of my pleasure," said Victor. "Stealing was something of a pleasure as well, and I searched my conscience, have searched, for years—all of my life I have been searching that—"

He exhaled with what looked like genuine pleasure a lungful of smoke.

"—that old conscience of mine. I decided, tentatively, early on, that I was not stealing in a sinful or criminal way, and that decision allowed me to continue and to enjoy myself to what I knew was an extraordinary depth of what is possible in the human psyche. But now I am, in turn, being stolen from." He laughed good-naturedly. "I do not know why I am surprised."

"Oh Victor," said Catherine. "You are surprised because you choose to be."

"Cathy honey," said Victor, "you are probably right."

Marilyn cleared her throat. "Of course we want to see it— if you're really sure you want us to see it."

Marilyn's courage had its effect on Janet: "Unless of course you're going to put another rattlesnake in your mouth." She tried to look comically severe.

Victor was silent for a very long time, smoking. Marilyn was sorry she had spoken and Janet was now angry. Perhaps they ought to excuse themselves to Catherine and leave. She was an intelligent, sympathetic woman and she could not understand Victor. It was possible he was simply insane.

"I was in a funny mood yesterday," said Victor. "Must have seemed awfully weird—repulsive—to you, and I do apologize. The head in the mouth is an old Mayan sorceress trick. You see it all over the world where snakes are revered. Some swami may even bite the snake's head off, you know, for the power. My personal feeling is that only a charlatan would do that, but what do I know? I too am nothing but a charlatan. But for me, you see, that was exactly what it was: a trick, something to show our unfortunate friends that they would not normally see in a trip to the Central Coast of California. What troubled me was the condition the snake was in in the first place. I have never seen a snake so straight and so stiff, dead or alive."

The ladies looked at Gene, who shook his head.

"It was a sign," said Catherine, rather abruptly, surprisingly, mysteriously. "A message." She closed her eyes and shook her head.

Victor continued: "The dogs and the horses acted as if he were not there at all. And yet you saw his eyes were open, and his tongue flickered several times. He there and not there. I've never seen anything like it. When I was a boy I would kill snakes, hunt and kill them, and if there were hawks about, I more than once tossed a snake in the air that was caught by a hawk. I had a shovel, that was my main tool, and I would flip them up in the air and smack them as if the shovel were a bat and the snake an unraveling baseball. When I learned, first hand, how well a hawk could see and how quickly he could dive, well, it was just a matter of time before I mastered a technique that let me scoop and fling a snake pretty damned high in the air. But of course they are our grandfathers, I learned much too late, and I regret all that nonsense very much. But look here, you're right to ask if I really want to show you my Mayan treasure. It is up to me, and I do want to show you. It explains a great deal. After we've taken a second look at my ranch—the telescopes are aimed at places of central importance—let's go down to my office. It will explain a great deal."

Neither angry nor afraid now, simply bewildered and feeling uncomfortably out of place, the ladies and Gene and Catherine moved to the first telescope that Victor presented with a flourish that made Marilyn roll her eyes. Janet noted that Catherine was unsteady. The Guatemalan boy refreshed everybody's drink, and these drinks were drunk rather quickly. The Guatemalan boy looked to Victor, who gestured enthusiastically. Janet saw Catherine dab at her eyes, and when Catherine saw she'd been seen, she laughed.

Was the observation deck rotating slowly? Gold and blue and gold and blue—and when Janet, who was first to look, lowered her head toward the eyepiece, she saw nothing but a rather painterly and complicated mass of color—earth tones, she thought—which became a magnified image of a bit of ranch scenery. When Marilyn looked, she had to raise and lower head several times. She came up blinking. Catherine said that she had seen it before, in a very pleasant voice. Gene murmured. Victor asked them what they'd seen, and when nobody answered, said that they were seeing something that was not there. Marilyn sighed so emphatically she wobbled. Janet touched her lightly.

"Did you see the tires, at least?" asked Victor. "What you mainly saw and did not see was a meadow. You also saw something like a cliff face, not of rock but of dirt. You did not see the best part of this ranch. Because it has fallen into the river and been deposited in the deep blue sea. Thirty thousand used automobile and truck tires—and a bunch of other shit I won't hurt myself to recite for you—were hauled in and carefully put in place in the belief that this bulwark would halt the erosion. The last thing our daddy said to us before he died was keep the ranch in the family. I thought the tires would go a long way toward honoring that wish. I have no children of course but Catherine has a clutch of them from her first two marriages."

"The tires were my idea," Catherine said. "It's very gentlemanly of you, Victor, to take the blame, but it was my idea, and I managed the operation."

"Now of course the state wants me to get the fucking tires out of the ocean," said Victor. "But I'm broke, and Catherine —honey, let's be candid—just doesn't give a shit about the meadow or the tires anymore."

Catherine dabbed at her eyes again, and again laughed. She said it was true and laughed again. Gene murmured. He signaled for another drink. Everyone joined him, the Guatemalan boy working swiftly and gracefully, and when they had finished their drinks, more or less in silence, Gene murmuring inaudibly, Janet nodding at him as if he were audible, they moved to a second telescope. Everybody bobbed up and down over the eyepiece this time. Victor looked around as if just waking from a nap and asked where Milos was.

"Well," said Catherine, "he certainly wasn't with the cattle."

"Did you all see the cattle?" asked Victor. "Standing there where they used to cross the river, staring at something? Every single one of them, standing and staring, refusing to cross?"

No one confirmed or denied this vision of the state of things at the far end of the telescope.

"Long story short, the cattle won't cross because there's meth lab hidden in the trees that were just out of the picture. Everyone knows what a meth lab is, right? That's how things are in this country now. As you drive back and forth through our little town, you may have been unimpressed. Nobody here would blame you. San Luis el Brujo is a ghost town. It's a ruin. There's not much more to it than there is to that mercury mine in Cambria. Methamphetamines go through a town like wild-fire. I say that and it sounds quaint, something a rancher would say: went through here like wild-fire. And then cap it off with some 19th century exaggeration like a wild-fire chased by a tornado round a hurricane. But all it is is money. Money and sadness. Money and despair. How much money? How much despair? Well, not too awfully long ago there was a raid and a seizure by the War on Drugs people, not too awfully far away from here, and it was a world record bust: fifteen tons, thirteen million doses, maybe four billion dollars on the street as the young people like to say. They must be talking about Salinas or San Francisco or Los Angeles because there's only one street in our town. It once was a street up and down which millions of dollars walked and talked—but not billions, not meth-money. God I want to vomit. It just makes me sick."

Marilyn and Janet both saw that he was pale and sweating.

"It breaks my heart. And there the evil thing is, there is the nightmare, there is the monster, right in the heart of my ranch."

Victor hobbled over to the Guatemalan boy. "Jimmy knows what I'm talking about. But he's on my side. Aren't you, Jimmy."

"Sure, Vic. I'm on your side."

It was an astounding thing for the small suave silent boy to say. Victor felt he had to explain.

"Of course the Mexicans are running the show and I don't just mean in Mexico. And when I say Mexicans I mean the people who employ the same three generations of backstabbing Guatemalans I employ."

THREE: THE DARKNESS OF HEAVEN AND THE LIGHTS OF HELL

Catherine drank herself senseless, so Gene Romero drove the ladies down to their B & B. They did not speak much: it was a short drive and they were all unexpectedly exhausted. Not to say drunk, but certainly having had a lot to drink. Gene wanted the ladies to understand Catherine anyway. They were friends of hers and they would want to understand, he thought; even if evidently they did not. The last thing

Catherine had said before passing out was that she remembered going to Centennial Park in Nashville, Tennessee, and seeing the mock-Parthenon. She had thought it was the original, and was scared, she said, to death, of the statue of Athena inside. She believed that Athena was talking to her, and that this voice, considered over time, was exactly the voice of her own thoughts. And over time, it ceased to be frightening. She found a theory to reconcile it with the paranormal experiences of others. Catherine saw love everywhere but the here and now. She saw it in what she insisted on referring to as "the spirit world." She was mad for meaning, for spiritual comfort, for deliverance from the land of meaningless magic, for salvation and a blissful eternity but was adamant in her refusal to think such things were possible in this life, in this world. The only measures of value she accepted were the mile and the minute and the money. Gene hastened to point out—both to Catherine at the time and to the ladies in his car—that her soteriology was not Christian, did not include a soteriomorph. It turned out that she held Jesus the Commie in deepest contempt. She had only the sworn declarations of those who had passed beyond but could thump yes and no on table—in effect: Catherine could become hysterically angry at Gene if he mentioned table-thumping in her presence. She was instrument-rated and could fly multiple-prop aircraft. She had enough hours to qualify for a commercial license if she'd wanted to. Which was part of what had gotten her and Victor and Gene to the border of Honduras and Guatemala in the summer of 1954. And she had as many lovers as she had flight hours. She was cool and rapacious—not a pious New Age ninny. She wasn't above trying to experience a sexual thrill transmitted from the far side of death, but she wanted that because she was oversexed or over-committed to the here and now—or perhaps simply disappointed in the moment with a current lover—not because she was an idiot. Her horses—she had briefly trained cutting horses in her first marriage—would not have tolerated her, much less respected her the way they did, had she been in fact pompous or ignorant in any way. She and Victor both had stayed on at the ranch long past their childhoods and worked it, along with their father—and a first generation of Guatemalans, who produced no offspring that lived—as a ranch, complete with cattle and a standard set of varying adjunct animals with goats and chickens as the foundation species. There were of course many dogs and cats as well. It was a wonderland in paradise. Nearby, a small but significant population of turkey vultures, and a little farther off, a handful of peregrine falcons—perhaps the last peregrines of central California: spirito peregrini, said Catherine. There were big loud colorful indoor birds as well, parrots and so on. The birds who lived on generation after generation, long after the passing of Mrs. Hubert Johnson, who introduced them to the ranch sometime during the Roaring Twenties, gave birth to her twins the day Herbert Hoover—a personal friend—beat nearly to death Al Smith (the governor of New York and Tammany Hall catholic who was in favor of repealing the Volstead Act!—he might just as well have run in blackface!) for the presidency, and died just after Hoover was run out of DC on a rail by you-know-who—but it was the turkey vultures, for Victor, and the peregrines, for Catherine, in which the spirit of the ranch was made manifest. The vultures had spoken for themselves in the preceding century: the ranch was situated on Vulture Peak. And when Victor learned, one day in school—it was during the War and they were enrolled at Phillips Exeter in New Hampshire—learned, via Alan Watts via D.T. Suzuki, that Vulture Peak was sacred to the Buddhists, he was, and Gene used the term advisedly, ecstatic. He left his body, came back to it, and came to believe he could do so at will, like any of the millions of shamans who had preceded him. He could not wait to get out of New England and back home. He could not wait to eat peyote and grow marijuana. But which of all possible homes was his? Fire, air, earth, water?

When the war was over and they came back, the first thing Gene saw on Vulture Peak was a wild-fire.

They were driving north, from San Luis Obispo, pondering their home, their land, pondering the location or nonlocality of their home and watching the color leach out of everything below and above them as the life-giving fog rolled in, and one of them, Gene thought it was himself (of course it was me, he said to ladies), happened to look up, to turn around, the way he remembered it, turn from talking to Catherine who had met them in Obispo and who was sitting in the back—and look through the dirty windshield up over the hills and the last few acres of Monterey pines...and saw that there was a fire burning on Vulture Peak. That's at least what it looked like, that first moment. They had all seen many fires in the hills and were all stunned at what they saw that day. Gene shouted in confusion to stop the car and in sudden sickening fear he jumped out and pointed to the limits of vision: a pillar of nearly black but brilliant smoke billowing up from the peak as if it were a volcano, immense and clearly spinning, a vortex the spiraling lines of which could be made out even at that great distance. But then, almost before they could be sure they were seeing it, it became a kind of smoky serpent, black then gray then blue, and drifted away, wasted away, rose higher as it became brighter and brighter blue and transparent and was slashed at by new currents of wind as by a samurai's sword—And then it was as if it had never been there, or had always been there.   Gene told the ladies that he thought it was there still.

After a moment, Marilyn said she was cold. It got quite cold at night, didn't it. Yes. Gene ignored the remark and continued his story. They stood there dumbfounded, Catherine, Victor, Gene, the ocean just on the other side of the highway, waves pounding silently, silently because unheard or unremarked, at their backs, fog bank rolling nearer and nearer but not seeming to move at all—until they could rub their eyes, laugh, and shake it off: a great Egyptian column of invisible fire! From the temple at Karnak directly over the ranch house on Vulture Peak! Hermes Trismegistus meets Siddhartha Gautama! Renaissance magi practicing Chaldean astrology with Buddhist detachment while Yahweh smoldered! Victor liked this idea very much. Yahweh! He said that it would become visible again, that the Chumash and the Mexicans had all in their different ways spoken of its ominous appearance and disappearance, and if los playanos could speak out of mist and dust of ten thousand years, they would say it was true, and when it did return, he would be there, close enough to make out the hieroglyphs, struggling to retain their forms as they roiled in the four elements. These fancies came readily to mind for all of us, Gene felt he must say, because while the real world was being destroyed in the war, they had been steeping themselves in metaphysics and Victor was at the height of his acquisitorial power. Gene meant "of antiques." He meant "of art." He meant of old and beautiful things that Victor and then Milos, who was just a baby at that point, in 1948, had to have. The need was strong in both of them, to have the things they wanted to have, and it was a dangerously unstable need from the beginning because Victor was the one with most of the money. It overwhelmed them, carried them off well beyond what was appropriate and inappropriate, what might be written off as carefree or even reckless over-indulgence, beyond what was legal, to what was mad—and since most of the collection was devoted to objects associated with magic or religion or whatever you'd like to call it—the nature of their pursuit or obsession or whatever you'd like to call it was perforce altered—giving lust an aura of holiness as I may have said earlier—as well as their perceptions of the nature of the objects themselves. More than once they spoke of Faustian deals—which may be written off as the hyperbole of collectors, but which, Gene felt he must assert here and now, can have a real effect on one's soul. Here and now. That is perhaps what he had been trying to suggest, or wanting to say to the ladies, the visitors, about truth and beauty and desolation in San Luis el Brujo: on the one hand, you cannot spend more than a few hours in our little town, our little countryside, and reject the reality of the soul and its universality—while on the other hand...you cannot help but feel how perilous your sense of personal well-being has become, no matter how much consciousness you may see that you share with the rock the rattlesnake the gamma ray. You can pretend, of course, that you don't share or that you don't see or that you don't care, but no one here is interested in pretense. And that in fact was the platform of Catherine's disgust with Victor and Milos: that they were playing fast and loose with things they knew nothing about. For instance: Catherine would not have hesitated a second to plow up a Chumash or Salinan—or even playano if one should ever be found—any ancient gravesite whatsoever if she had a chance to build some vacation homes upon them, but this was principled and disciplined behavior on her part: this was the material world and one dealt with, in the short while one had with material, with material! Money was merely a byproduct of one's conscientious working of material. As one's soul ascended, it became less and less interested in the material, more conversant with what lay beyond material—which was why one sought spirits out even when idiots couldn't get past the thump thump thump on the table of frauds. The bones of los playanos meant nothing, less than nothing. Their spirits were a different matter, if we would excuse the term. And if they would not excuse the term, taking her belief that matter was intrinsically evil as seriously as the Cathars in Languedoc did, well, they could go fuck themselves. She said so many times. (And Gene said so to the aliens in his car.) Matter was intrinsically evil and evil was all we had, in this life, to deal with. Anti-matter comes later. Go fuck yourself, I'm busy. Gene had bet her that she would say so on her deathbed. "Oh go fuck yourself, I'm terribly, terribly busy just now." She was so beautiful, and so unconcerned with it, that they were all thrilled, even Victor, her brother, when she told them all to go fuck themselves. Some people couldn't get enough of it. Gene meant, por ejemplo, himself: they had been lovers, it was true, but fleeting. Nevertheless he was certainly thrilled by her presence in his life, even as he held her, tenderly but critically, disapprovingly but yearningly, at arm's length, waiting for something to change—or rather, for something to cease changing, just for a moment. Catherine likewise was resigned to waiting. This was the abandoned world of trial and struggle and despair: the next life and the next life and the next life would be better and better and better.

Marilyn and Janet were so exhausted they were weak, almost unable to get out of the car, and drunk, so drunk they had become something like hypnotized by Gene's murmured nonsense. They did not get out of the car. Janet in fact, felt so serene, she said she wanted to know what it was that they had not been able to see in Victor's office. Gene was very tired, though. And yet he could not cease.

"Here I sit, retired lawyer, pseudo-philosopher, bad poet: brokenhearted...so sad sometimes I don't think I can go on, and yet, going on. Not with hope, mind you. My favorite Mexican poet is a nun—all my favorite poets are Mexicans because this is Mexico, say what you will about the fatally vexed border, this is the land of Saint Louis the Magician. Sor Juana is the only nun on my list. She lived, briefly, en el

Virreinato de Nueva España en el Siglo de Oro—and started one of her sonnets this way: "She removes the mask from Hope, and in this act of bravura sorrow, condemns it." The same poem ends in this bracing way: "You are nothing but a stumbling block on my way to death." I occupy myself with our little, brittle, and immediate laws, the more forgiving but remote wisdom of the cosmos, and the only calculation that works: beauty equals truth equals beauty. But not beauty as we've been trained to see it, not truth as we have been trained to tell it. Paint even the silliest and most amateurish images of Truth and Beauty on a pie plate and spin it ever so slowly, they become one. Even if you stop the plate from spinning they will remain mutually saturated in your mind. And where else would such a thing matter? Where else is there? No. I, living in the most beautiful place in the world, say brokenhearted and sad baldly and unapologetically, with no sense of, much less care for, literary effectiveness and knowing full well that the Estate of Samuel Beckett owns the whole notion of not being able to go on but going on. Bravura sorrow indeed: so many people gone—and is it possible I am the only one who loved them? Victor was quite sure that "love" was not available to human beings. It was real, and we could begin to imagine it, but we could not experience it: there was too much interference from all the electrochemical explosions going on in the brain, the sensual data and the consensual triangulations required to do something as simple as locate a chair and sit down on it, much less enter some kind of fraudulent business with others of like mind. The soul sensed or imagined it, yearned for it, but knew it would have to wait. When I say

Catherine was interested only in money, it makes her sound simple and mean, greedy and shallow—what I meant to say was that she is convinced, as convinced as is Victor in his way, that...that...she, that all of us, feel quite stranded in our lives. It's certainly possible to explain away that sense of exile, of being castaway, simply by standing, as we were just yesterday, on the edge of the little cliff in San Luis el Brujo. The 'beautiful desolate' behind us, the 'beautiful infinite' before. Welcome to San Luis el Brujo, dear ladies! It's all true! Desolate is not the word and yet it is the word. We were deprived in no way of either comfort or joy. Most of us were and still are filthy rich. But lonely? We must be. Just as there must be joy, or perhaps it is comfort, in desolation. Or perhaps I mean that beauty and truth must inhere in desolation and lovelessness, brooding in the twilight, rising and falling serenely for millions of years over the green-gold hills of winter, the gray-brown hills of summer, the blue and silver waves, the purple, black, green, gold, white swirl of precisely linked atoms of hydrogen and oxygen, just as they do... elsewhere. I suppose I thought things—and by 'things' I suppose I mean 'ourselves'—were going wrong at a very early age. You cannot grow up in a magical place and feel that everything is as it ought to be: magic is not like that. It's closer to say that nothing is as it ought to be, but that you are only vaguely troubled by what seems most often a classical sort of dissonance—as Mozart or Haydn would have understood the term. Or rather: dissociation, not in the psychiatric sense (hold that thought, please) but in the physical sense, of 'the usually reversible breaking up compounds into simpler substances.' We all felt we were just this side of being able to see or hear or feel that constant and simultaneous breaking up and that building up, and we all identified it as peculiar to our home, to San Luis el Brujo, to no other part of California or the country or even the globe—but I think Victor and Catherine have been altogether too careless regarding the magic, the glimpses we were given of what is invisible in nature. Now, of course, my view is directly opposed to that: they were anything but careless. They were loveless. Or perhaps I am loveless, who cannot see love anywhere. We were in Macuelizo. Castillo Armas had maybe five hundred soldiers spread out along the Honduran border. We had wished to be in San Cristobal, but El Salvador refused to let us invade from their country. So Catherine, Victor, and I were flying three Cessnas, two of which were owned and operated by the Johnson Ranch, back and forth from Mac and Florida (a town in Honduras, not 'the sunshine state,' which is where you ladies ought to live, not here) and Ocotepeque and Copán: messages, rifles, Castillo Armas, agents, etc., you name it, we were simply hauling freight. Then we got the order to go, and we, the largest force, two hundred soldiers, went across to the river towns of Morales and Tenedores—from where we supposed to breeze back along the river to Puerto Barrios, our main target on the Gulf. Well: it went very badly. We were engaged and ran quickly back to Honduras. A Guatemalan man who was flying with Victor was a Pre-Columbian art scholar who taught at the Universidad Francisco Marroquín in Gautemala City but whose main employer was our employer, the CIA, via United Fruit, and he suggested to Victor that they get the hell out of there and go to a largely unexplored Mayan ruin in Petén called San Bartolo, north of Tikal, on the Mexican border. He thought there was a pyramid there as good as buried in rain forest, with a tunnel beneath it that led to a mud-covered wall, behind which was a fresco. And indeed there was: we dug out and broke into pieces a small section of it, the Maize God looking over his shoulder while, I can't remember, haven't seen it in decades, some needy king sucks his dick with Olmec influences. Very faded, of course, mostly red and whites. First century BC. In Victor's office since 1954 AD. He gets on his knees and prays to it first and last thing each day. Milos dresses up as the Maize God and Victor blows him as part of the prayer."

The ladies got out of the car and went slowly and quietly into their B & B. Gene escorted them as far as the door but no farewells were offered. Gene walked up the very steep hill to the old cemetery in town, from which he could see the fiercely bright but tiny candle glow of a fire on Vulture Peak. The ladies would read about the rest of it for the next several years in the newspapers: either the Mexican Mafia or Milos or Victor shot Victor in the head and set his house on fire. According to a variety of investigators, Milos had a motive—he had been cut entirely out of the will—but was either the best liar anybody had ever seen, passing lie-detector test after test with ease, or innocent. These investigators also pretty much agreed that the so-called Mexican Mafia had nothing to do with it, because the evidence had been pointing at Victor for some time as the owner and operator of one of the biggest meth labs in California, where they grow on trees. The house and everything in it had been utterly consumed. The gun had exploded and melted. Victor was a pile of dust and ash. Catherine wanted the land sold immediately and to never see it again, not even when the price fell and fell and fell. She was said to have said publicly on more than once occasion that Victor had come to her and told her that it was all no good and that she should stay as far away as possible.

SADDLING THE SORRY ASS OF SELF
(OR, GETTING THE HELL OUT OF NEW BEDFORD, THEN WANTING TO GET BACK ONLY TO FIND IT'S TOO LATE)

Tuesday, January 17th

Saddling the sorry donkey of self and getting the hell out of Salem. Back to New Bedford with you, you.... What could I have been thinking, thinking is certainly the wrong word, acting on, reacting hysterically to the crazy inflammatory goads of inferior people (yes yes yes I'm sorry I wrote that), hunches, secret beliefs in which I did not actually believe, not even in a dream, for a second—well, for starters, bub, you're coupling depression that would have much stronger, better men weeping in hospitals, with what amounts to get-rich-quick schemes—you, who when it came, year after year, to placing the bet, have been steady as a surgeon—pick a different simile, Jack—careful as a riverboat-pilot, you, who have had, until tonight, a life. Why have you done this thing? What will you do now? How shall you live? Oh dear, oh dear, what have I what, bet the ranch on the Mass-Dartmouth Melvilles...? who just barely escaped being shut out by the Salem State Hawthornes...? Bet everything...? My life as a bright but mysterious figure in the cool, slick, sparsely populated family rinks of NCAA Division III hockey is OVER. I even placed a side bet with a well-known halfwit who wouldn't stop talking about the over-under and I said, hey how about this: if the Melvilles do lose, it will be a shut-out. You choose odds most favorable to your estimable self and let's put a crazy amount of money on the line. Just for the fun of it. I do not think the guy is an inferior person. And if I was hysterical, it was a very subtle hysteria indeed.

Wednesday, January 18th

Well all right, what do you know, what can I say, nick of time, discovered a priceless Andrei Rector drawing in my closet, a portrait of Anton Chekhov which I just sold to an anonymous collector who works out of a pawn shop just down the street—I know, I know, Rector's great-grandson is eating his paintbrushes in some Hollywood shithole—for quite a lot of money, enough to get me back on the road of high-stakes Division III hockey, anyway. So I'm getting the hell out of New Bedford for the umpteenth time, even though this is my home, I admit it, I feel somewhat comfortable here and know in my heart that the municipality is not at fault for my losses, heading for Providence where the visiting Western New England University Easterners are taking on the Wailing Johnsons of Johnson & Wales University. (You'd wail too if you took a puck to the prick.) And you all know, right? that I bet on these games just to pay the bills while I write my masterpiece about the ups-and-downs of a Div. III stringer for USCHO.com who stumbles into buggery on a scale that makes Penn State, etc., etc. If all goes well, I'll follow the Easterners back to Springfield, and hopefully nip over to Great Barrington and the offices of *Orion Magazine* to mess with Chip Blake's mind: take on the lineaments and gestures of the hard-boiled reporter in the midst of dangerous half-truths, pay me first, THEN I'll write ya a nice little stocking-stuffer of a Hawthornian wonder-tale that not only relates people and nature, as per the magazine's mission statement, it relates the people of 50,000 years ago to the era of the "smart, sexy, oh-so-indie" people of today. Oh I feel good again. Just to make my point clear to the Narrator of Chaos, the Lords of the Infinite Stories, and the Field of the One Story That Is All Stories And No Story, I will finish this hamburger and these french fries—or maybe not, just toss it, my heart is no longer in this food, it is in fact vile—cleanse my fingers with a moist towlette, and put on a piece for solo viol, by Captain Tobias Hume, called "Good Againe" written circa the death of Shakey, #14 of "the first part of ayres," preceded, wouldn't you know, by #12, "Death," and #13, "Life." I don't feel smart, I don't feel sexy, and I have no idea what indie means in such a context, much less oh-so-indie. 50,000 years from now, when they discover our caves, will they muse on how smart and sexy and indie we were? I am lost in smartness and sexyness and indieness. I am lost not in time, neither in space, my lord, am I abandoned; rather in consciousness. Trees are conscious, rocks are conscious, dust and ash are conscious and it never dies and it is here that I am lost, my lord. And as I listen to this strange tenuous minor sorrow that is "Good Againe," I have to wonder what Captain Hume meant, the order especially: as a soldier surely he was used to the serene aftermath of atrocity, the deliquescent beauty of corpses—and must have moved daily, psychologically and physiologically, from death to life, and once surrounded by life, was inclined to feel good againe...? This ordering troubles me: it doesn't seem right—and yet of course it is, everything dies, life goes on, and sooner or later, you are good againe. Life, perhaps, good againe...death. But when we are we ever truly good againe? Only in retrospect, only in memory. When are we truly alive? In an illusory moment. Dead? Never. The dead only seem so in that illusion plaguing the living.

Thursday, January 19th

Not the way I wanted it to go: my heart was with the Western New England Easterners, but the Wailing Johnsons scored three goals in the last ten minutes...6-4. Chastened by the disaster in Salem and happy to be alive, I wagered nothing whatsoever. Associates cocked eyebrows at me but that is a behavior I admit I have a passion for evoking. It is at least a hobby to which I am devoted. I was just happy. It was good againe to be in the RISC with 117 people, one or two of them friends, a handful of acquaintances or business associates— some of them friends, too, to be sure, of a kind—but most of the small loud crowd, to me indifferent. I am going to make the funds from the sale of the Rector last through this season AND THE NEXT. Followed the team back to Springfield, and a little further, to Westfield, where I stay in a little rooming house across the street from the cemetery. From here it's a short pleasant walk to Amelia Park, where I hope the Owls will surprise Mass-Dartmouth, mainly because I've got the bitter taste of ruin in my mouth still, and can't help but associate it, RECKLESSLY AND UNFAIRLY, with New Bedford. Because I am noting the recklessness and emotionally-driven injustice well ahead of time, I have no fear of sudden gambling. I've got problems, but they're not like that. I'll just watch the game. Even though my appetite isn't what it should be, given my return to high spirits, I'll eat some nice hot food and I'll stroll through the cemetery.

Friday, January 20th

The Owls played well last night, for 60 of us at the Amelia, but the Mass-Dart Melvilles came on steadily. My feelings about New Bedford, however, that isn't such a bad place to live, all things considered—these feelings have slackened remarkably. I have to admit it—don't I? It's a terrible place to live. I hate living there. It's just like the food I've been eating. I want to be anywhere but there, eating anything but it. My working understanding remains: my losses were not the fault of the municipality. My losses were the fault of recklessness and hubris. But I can't shake it. I don't think I want to go back to New Bedford. Ever. The flip is disconcerting, of course, but so is the knot of anxiety I feel in the pit of my stomach at the thought of going back to that miserable apartment. But no! I catch myself firmly by the wrist: nothing wrong with the apartment! Occupant to blame! In any case, for the time being...that chapter is over. Heading north. One goes east to sit with a master, one goes south for retribution and redemption, one goes west to dwell in uncertainty...and one goes north to go home. I always feel like I'm going home when I drive north, whether it's into the maw of a blizzard of sunlit white so bright it hurts my eyes or deepening darkness, the headlights dimming, the snow piling up on the windshield as the wipers struggle and slow and stop. Today, home is Castleton VT, where the Cads (one of the top teams perennially in Division

III polls) are hopping over to Southern Maine to play the up-and-down Bounders. But not before I have lunch in Burlington with my old friends, Tom McMurdo and Heather Kennedy. They are Kentuckians, the son and daughter of the last two men to run bootleg whiskey around Berea (where there's a campground I shudder, not altogether unpleasantly, to remember). Tom's the Director of U-Vermont libraries, and Heather is retired, having been if not instrumental in getting the DoD to take the scramble out of the Global Positioning System, at least ideally situated to make tons of money when they did, which she spends on sports cars. Races as well. Friend of the late great Paul Newman.

Between periods. After the game I will stay in Gorham, because the Skidmore Bookies are coming to town tomorrow, and as I think I've said before, my niece (on my ex-wife's side) Lauren went to Skidmore, and Leslie (my ex-wife) has a suite reserved for her at nearby Yaddo Rest Home for New York Intellectuals. Main reason I'm staying, though, is that southern Maine reminds me of southern Minnesota, and the intersection of the New Portland Rd., Mechanic St., and Maine St. reminds me of Larpenteur and Lexington in Roseville, where the Dairy Queen stands: the last place I saw my friend John Richardson alive. John and I go back to a country and western band in Wilkes-Barre in the late 70s and I know he's still alive, but…it's too easy, too weirdly easy for me to imagine that it was John who died in Vietnam, not his brother, on his second tour of duty, leaving his guitars to John, who gave one of them to me, which I sold to the Rector

Collector years ago. There's a Motel 6 tucked behind the Rite-Aid/Burger King mall a block of the USM campus, one of my favorite structures in the world, a long-abandoned gas station...and a little cemetery. Tom and Heather were overjoyed to see me. I mean OVER-joyed. Like I'd come back from some pointless meat-grinding and was of uncertain mental condition. They were solicitous in a way that was unnerving, off-putting. I told them about the Rector portrait of Chekhov that I'd forgotten I'd owned and they just looked at me, rather more mystified than anything else. We went to a nice restaurant, I ordered a salad and didn't eat it. Drank the whole bottle of wine before they could get to it, but didn't enjoy it, not one gulp. Heather leaned over at one point—Heather who has always told me the truth, and said, you're getting a haircut and a shave. I'm buying. I thought she was joking and managed to jolly her away from her increasingly angry determination to clean me up. But when we said goodbye, Heather poked Tom, who I could see had been wanting to say something, but I hugged them fiercely, pre-emptively, and jumped in my car and drove away, chirping the tires for the Heather. I do feel unkempt, but when I look in the mirror, all seems well enough to be let alone.

An older man of my sporting acquaintance saw me at the Burger King in Gorham, and, because you cannot hide at a Division III game, found me here. He seemed sincerely happy to see me, glad that I survived what he called the slaughter at Salem State, which is already legendary and surely must account for the raised eyebrows of people to whom I have not yet begun to speak or even acknowledge. He has always been eager to give me his money, but seemed subdued, perhaps out of respect for the fucking I took, but just out of habit, I think, he asked me if I wanted any action and I laughed and said no, no thanks, waving my hands theatrically like I always do, in a way that makes people step back or flinch but which is not my intention, I just want to watch the games from here on in. He nodded. After a moment he said, yeah me too, he understands what I'm saying, something's gone out of it. I realized that his younger brother was not standing next to him, grinning, encouraging the transfer of the brothers' money to me as he invariably has been doing for the last how many years. When my friend lumbered off (big guy, though the years are starting to hang slackly on him, and a genuinely nice guy), another man, whom I knew only by sight, paused as he was walking past me and said, "Hung himself. Nobody knows why." My spine went ice-cold and I squinted against some unlooked-for emotion or pain that surrounded my skull and throbbed. I felt a ittle dizzy. So yeah, I'm sitting here tapping out this story instead of watching the game....heading straight to Hanover when the game's over: Hanover is where my brother lives. He is a man among men. He will not have hung himself, and in not doing so, have made clear a path of righteousness. For me.

Wednesday, January 25th

In Worcester, waiting for the Stonehill Freemasons to take on the Assumption Consumptives at the Buffone, the capacity of which is something like a school bus. Hanover: hello I must be going. All well, but land mines everywhere, not the least of which is the fact that I played for Dartmouth, was in fact a captain the year the current coach was a freshman know-it-all (1978). My brother is a doctor, as were my parents, as are his wife and children. *La mère et le père du ma belle sœur* were doctors in Algeria. *Pieds noir*. Algerians! I see photographs of the father and it's hard not to think of the doctor/narrator in La Peste. When my nephew Luc was doing biophysics at Princeton, his thesis project was a design for a pipette that extracted neurons from nerve cells. So maybe you begin to see: I am very close to my brother, but never, never see him. Everywhere I go in Hanover, I see people who are amazed at what a stunning, spectacular loser I am. I am literally hard to believe. Everywhere jaws are banging on the sidewalk. I make people sad, visibly sad. Well, no, that can't be true, they don't see me, much less give a shit. I want to explain my valiant efforts in the vacuum of deep consciousness, but that would only make things worse. Same deal in Boston, where my brother-in-law is one of the 100 richest men in the city. (In his family they are all lawyers.) In Worcester, nobody knows who I am. And I like the town because it reminds me of Wilkes-Barre for some reason, where I played country music every night til four, when it was still basically a city that had been destroyed in a flood...after Dartmouth and one too many concussions on top of a pre-existing condition I don't even want to go into, and in fact never have gone into. Suffice it to say I am slow of speech and often appear confused—which is why so many people are so guiltily eager to bet with me, why I like to drive around New England in the winter and go to hockey games where maybe a hundred other people show up. And why such a life leaves weeping in wonder half the time, why I must look worse than I feel, even though I feel pretty bad, why I make people sad when I am merely in awe of them....I am making only one bet Wednesday night: with a man who was instrumental in saving the beautiful old Mechanics Hall downtown: he says fewer than fifty people will show, I say more.

Just learned that the man who built and paid for Amelia Park, in Westfield, where I was last week, died last year. Had I known, I would have gone to his funeral. Good fellow. Albert Ferst...he was 92 or 93.... Weird connection, another thing I just learned this minute: I'm listening to Levin and Kashkashian play Hindemith's Viola Sonata: it was recorded in Mechanics Hall. Here. In Worcester. Two of my favorite performers, one of my favorite pieces...no idea they'd recorded it here....small world, infinite consciousness.

It doesn't matter where you went to school or who you know at the Buffone. Owned by the Commonwealth and the DCR, one of twenty-three such rinks around the state, operated by an international group called Universal Facilities Management, who make sure the Zambonis run on time and see to it that the community bulletin board, the leaflet racks, and the little locked glass case which displays photographs of some prominent local skaters, a few ribbons and certificates of excellence from many years ago, and the main light switches, remains locked, the glass clean and clear. It's well ventilated, almost never foggy or stinky, the ice never mushy, and it's situated in Lake Park, which is a nice little park, right across Lake Avenue from Lake Quinsigamond. It's a nice building to go into and out of. This may seem like a small thing, but it is not: the spectacles with which one is presented at the constantly changing thresholds of the finite.

Seventy-one shots on goal for the Stonehill Freemasons, thirty-one for the Assumption Consumptives, and yet...and yet...it's Assumption on top, 3-2! I think you will recall that my single bet this evening was that more than fifty fans would show up at the Buffone rink (capacity thirty-five). And I was right. 235 fans showed up. I am a big winner. Still, I identified myself a couple episodes back as a spectacular loser, which means that once again the narrative has come full circle, the bus has pulled into the terminal, next stop the garage. I gotta get out. I was planning a trip out west, to Fredonia, Oswego, Geneseo, Brockport, to the wilds of SUNYAC...but I think I may keep going, all the way to Los Angeles. See if Andrei Rector's great-grandson still lives there. See if he still lives, period. Give him what I got for the Chekhov drawing. I just want things to feel right again. There was that moment of happiness, and then...nothing. Everything in the World of Right that I have patiently built up feels wrong. I should really point out for those of you too busy for arithmetic, that the above score means Bobby Bowden stopped sixty-nine shots tonight. If I hadn't been in such a funk, I would have known how hot he was, and consulted a tarot reader and diviner. I am a careful, efficient, successful gambler, but I use magic. I am after all a Renaissance Man. Just like Pico della Mirandola: a magus, a miracle! cried Hermes Trismegistus to his great pal Asclepius, how like unto an angel! Not smart! Not sexy! Not oh-so-indie! Familiar of the gods above and lord of the beasts below—or rather, the other way around, as I see it, set midway between the timeless unchanging and maelstrom of time, astral mind, body of dust and ash—a miracle! But not, I repeat, not smart, not sexy, not oh-so-indie. Christ what a planet. Give me the Buffone any day. I don't care if it's operated by the Chinese. I don't care if it's operated by Martians. It has often been said that you cannot deal with Martians, but I think you can. The anti-Martian bias goes back to hipsters, dealers, and the like, to the belief that squares were Martians and you couldn't trust them not because they were bad people but because they were not hip, they were stupid, they were not smart, not sexy, not oh-so-indie. My money is now on Martians.

Midnight, Boston Post Road in Springfield, sign for a church: STOP, DROP, AND ROLL DOESN'T WORK IN HELL. I am indeed on the wrong planet or something. Earth, right? About 50,000 years into genuine human consciousness, or 100,000 if you count the time we didn't make such a fuss about it, save to, maybe, decorate our naked flesh...? 100,000 years of confrontation with the absolute certainty that we do not know where we came from and do not know where we are going?

Words are a mixed bag at best, and using them for money is a mug's game. Consider the source: hominid hooting and barking in the trees, a whispered and screamed but fundamentally poetic response to what the thunder said. What did the thunder say? That you are alive, that you are aware of your self and your surroundings, that you are aware as well of your awareness, and finally, that you are aware of the awareness of others. Everybody around you is aware in the same ways, and of the same things, that you are aware. Most importantly, they are aware of you. You're all alive, and you're all going to die. You don't know where you came from, and you don't know where you're going, or when, or why. In the meantime? Words. Images, too, but I have a hard time conceiving of image without thought (however inarticulate and unremarked by the too busy brain responsible—solely—for both) or thought without image. Caravaggio may well have found himself lost once or twice in the umber wastes, lost in the pigment of thought without image, image without thought. But as far as I'm concerned, the two seem made for each other, and are effectively inextricable (though I can certainly imagine doing so, making "the act of extrication" theoretically possible). Much has been made, neurophysiologically and philosophically, of our word/image saturated culture. A good deal of this much may be accurately attributed to persons I am directly related to. I however do not grasp much of this much. Some believe we are in danger of losing our ability to perceive, apprehend, grasp a real thing, that a mediated thing, an image of a thing, is all that we will soon be able to understand or care about. But is that not now how it has been since the beginning? Certainly is with me, the Mendacious Mendicant of Consciousness. I have never been able to know a thing until my brain has made a picture of it, and attached commentary. The poet knows that it is good and right to want the real thing and not an idea about the thing...but knows at the same time that real things are fundamentally and instantly changed upon the blue guitar. "In the beginning was the Word": one of the most alluring but impenetrably nonsensical lines I have ever heard. The only way I can interpret it is to say that the life in the universe, the life of the universe, has always depended on a negotiation between a thing and an idea of a thing. Levi-Strauss was right: the savage mind and the technocrat mind both turn on the negotiation of the reconciliation of opposites —or at least the recognition and careful study of the relation of opposites. And Derrida was right too: the words themselves are merely temporary signs, and fall to pieces if they are not constantly examined in context. Let your brain droop just a little and it's all nonsense. I have let my brain droop quite remarkably. Brain, however, does not care for this drooping, and gives me a good talking-to, which I perceive mainly as a pain inside my skull. Brain delights in the constant transformation of context. "Taxonomy's end is not to get everything in its proper box with lid shut tight; it is the scientific and artistic and religious means of negotiating variety and the vortex of de-meaning and re-meaning." (Quoted, with permission of Brain.) Because the meanest, silliest, most ordinary and practical utterings are poetic—a response to beauty and mystery, whether we think so now or not—the use of words gives pleasure. Here I am, pleased as all-get-out, parking lot of an abandoned gas station, wee hours, western Mass, pleased as I can be. But it is an unstable pleasure, something like sex, volatile, dependent not only on the wish to have and cause orgasms, but on technique, on the mastery of technique, and the paying of constant serious attention to the terms and contexts of the negotiation —which is ongoing and always tentative with regard to conclusion and judgment. And there, friends and neighbors, in case you missed it, is the rub. "Attention must be paid to this man!" (Who, Willy Loman? Why?) Judgment must be tentative, and negotiation always in good faith. The fundamental and ongoing assumption in this book (this is a book I'm writing whether you and I know it or not) is that we live in a time of bad faith, absolute judgments, and feigned attention. The first decade of the 21st century was a time of unparalleled fraudulence, in government, in commerce—you name it and within it, the Big Lie was not only practiced, it was appealed to as if it were a kind of knee-jerk common sense. Once our Fearless Leaders saw how easy and effective it was to lie about anything and everything all the time, it caught on with the citizenry. Now it is pandemic. The deliquescent one percent, the putrefactionally wealthy, they may buy durable truths at will. The rest of us get it at the big box store, jam it in the always-to-small vehicle, rush to employ and enjoy it—only to find that it is broken and, like in the Neil Young song, a piece of crap. That sounds rather cynical, I know. But Mysterious Ambrose Bierce's original title for his infamous dictionary was *The Cynic's Wordbook*. That proved quickly unpalatably honest and accurate, forcing the publisher to opt for the sexier *Devil's Dictionary*. You can hear the pitch: it's not cynicism, it's satire! No one knows what cynicism actually means anyway! And people love the Devil, even if they acknowledge him as the Enemy of Mankind! The Devil is cute and funny if you don't take him seriously! But isn't "satire," according to the proverbial Broadway producer, "what closes on Saturday"? And since the Devil made his move because he wanted, rather than to serve in Heaven, to rule in Hell, wouldn't satire be more effective in Heaven, along the lines of the wisecracking servant, the King's all-licensed Fool? Who's going to listen to satire in Hell—especially when it's the tyrant who's the cheap-ass satirist? We must love hell. Like Malcolm Lowry: can't wait to get back. Leave the satire to the Martians.

Thursday, January 26th

I remember a time when it used to fall below zero on January 1st and stay below zero until February 15th. "There's something happening here. What it is aint exactly clear." Reading in Marge's Lakeside Inn in Irondequoit NY: "A God who is wholly in time is a God who destroys as fast as he creates. Nature is as inconceivably appalling as it is lovely and bountiful." And this, from my sometime employers, USCHO.com: "Morrisville, along with Neumann, has joined the unwanted club previously occupied by Geneseo, Buffalo State, and Potsdam: It has been cited by the NCAA for improper aid to student-athletes. To quickly review the situation — the NCAA has closely scrutinized the ratio of aid that goes to international and/or Canadian students versus student-athletes. If the ratio is found to be too much in favor of the student-athletes, the NCAA deems the aid to be de facto athletic scholarships, which are strictly forbidden in Division III. Specifically, Morrisville had the International Incentive Grants and Canadian Student Initiative Grants to boost international enrollment. However, In 2009-10, nearly 29 percent of the grant aid was given to student-athletes, even though they represented only about 12 percent of the student body. A year later, about 37 percent of the aid was awarded to student-athletes, who made up 13 percent of the general student body. Ergo, the NCAA had an issue with this program. The penalties are given to the teams that had players who received this type of aid, and for Morrisville, that was the men's hockey team. The Mustangs are banned from any postseason action this year, and are on probation through January 18, 2014. The penalties were handed out by the NCAA Division III Committee on Infractions. "Obviously, we're disappointed, disappointed for our kids," Morrisville coach Brian Grady said. "It's been a frustrating year, right up to the latest unfortunate set of circumstances. The kids have really been tested with adversity since September to now." Some of the issues which schools have had with all this is the change in how the NCAA interpreted these rules, the lack of information the NCAA provides for good ratio numbers, the vague warnings the NCAA provides schools, and how many years the NCAA looks back on. Nonetheless, the NCAA has decided on this path to even the playing field amongst Division III schools, and all colleges will have to abide by these rulings. Like I mentioned in the past, there is a very good chance other schools will run afoul even if they have heeded the warnings and cleaned up the present, considering that the NCAA can look back into the mists of the past, a number of years at least. In the meantime, Morrisville must move on like the teams in the past had to. In fact, a number of players were on Morrisville the year Geneseo was banned, allowing the Mustangs to get into the SUNYAC playoffs for the first time. But more so, Morrisville remembers the way Geneseo handled the situation, virtually running the table the rest of their season. "Can't say enough for the way Geneseo responded and finished the year," Grady said. "That's what we look at as an example. I think our kids handled it well this past weekend, putting together a very strong effort. That was satisfying. "Every day is a challenge. We still harp on the same things — hard work, discipline, integrity, playing for each other. For the underclassmen, they want to send the seniors out on a winning note, as well as set a base for the program."

I used to write such news reports. It seems like good, honest work to me. I don't know why I quit. Happened across a scale in some bathroom somewhere and stepped on it: I think I was once a little on the heavy side, I'm a big guy, I always went into the corners and came out with puck—but now I think I'm a little on the thin side. I looked at myself in the mirror while the shock was still on my gaunt hairy face: you're as thin as a Martian, I said, quietly but aloud.

SUNYAC (that's the NY state university athletic conference) is greasy and fast. I much prefer driving around New England (ECAC East and West and Northeast, NESCAC, MASCAC

—the Mass state colleges) but I make the drive across the Empire State because (a) I like to see a bit of a great lake now and then—Superior is my childhood home; (b) the first opera I heard—*Rake's Progress*—and liked was on the radio one beautifully sad bleak gray day in Sodus Point; and (c) there's an incredible amount of action to be had. SUNYAC likes to import thugs and snipers from Canada. It's a completely different game. I don't like it nearly as much, but if one is a gambler...

Friday, January 27th

Great game between Cortland and Brockport: firewagon-hockey. 6-5 Cortland in OT but it should have been 6-5 Brockport, end of regulation. "They're calling it a hand-pass!" nearly everyone shouted at the same time (500 of us!) It wasn't a hand-pass, and Brockport should have won. It was a bad, bad call—but everything was happening so fast, there were so few whistles, shifts were running long because you just could not get off the ice. If Michael Northrop hadn't called me out of the blue and made a joking reference to the over-under at the Penmen/Freemasons game tomorrow (zero, a dry fellow is Nawthie, fond of puns) in Foxboro, I would have stayed out of the way and not made the zillion dollars I did make, because if there's one thing I can smell it's defensive teams going to pieces and about to roll the firewagons out. It was the only kind of hockey I could play. Full-speed into the corners and le melee grande and BOOM out he comes, old Doc Lumberjack they used to call me, hale and hearty, a healer, but now I am the Admonitory Martian. I look terrible! But I wanted to keep to myself not just because it's clear I have to stop living this way, but because a non-hockey-related event was playing odd, unpredictable games with minds of the locals: a big brash overbearing loud bullying couple who have had their nose and fingers in everything that happens in Brockport for I dunno, ten years, were convicted of voter fraud in the village council elections last fall. I heard there was quite a scene at the courthouse, and they are both going to do some time. The news cheered and emboldened me, while it had the opposite effect on my companions: confused and feeling pushed about awkwardly, they made stupid bets. But now here I am in the Gingerbread B & B, unable to sleep. Mrs. Michael Tingelhoff, owner and proprietor, has a great library of old books and films on VHS here, old sheet music ("Fifteen Miles On the Erie Canal"), a couple of pianos and guitars. They were left to her by a friend who died—doesn't read or listen to music herself. I just watched *La Dolce Vita*. Could I have lived that sort of life here, now? I mean a bad but sweet one? I think I could have. I don't know. After Fellini I got really sad, the Big Sads were upon me without warning, listening to Roy Buchanan and "The Messiah Will Come Again," that it occurred to me my blood sugar was low or something like that, because I don't think I've eaten much in the last week, not remembering it if I do, anyway, a week without food seems not only possible but a positive good, but maybe not months and months of haphazard eating...I do look terrible, but I feel great!—and I perked right back up with *Don Giovanni* for

Mozart's birthday. It is what is after all termed a "dramma giocoso." It is not a metabolic stabilizer, it's music. Nevertheless: it is true that I have not eaten much: flipped through these pages, noting only the untouched salad in Burlington, and the burger and fries I trashed...wherever that was. It was in my head just a second ago and now it's gone. I have no desire to riffle back and get this fact straight. I have never been one for record-keeping. It can't be "good" that I'm not eating, but I can't say that I don't feel "good." In fact I dare say I feel better. To hell with food if it's just going to make you feel not good. I have lost some weight, and that is always exciting to an old athlete. Possibly I will return to fighting weight if I keep up the fast, stop drinking, get some exercise. (I have all but stopped drinking, the last being the tasteless, effectively alcohol-free Finger Lakes red I guzzled in Burlington. Right out of the bottle, just to see what Heather would do.) Tomorrow I'm going to walk along the tow path until I'm tired, really tired. I will listen to Thomas Hampson sing the Songs of America, volumes one and two, and I will feel good, because I am an American who likes to sing songs.

Saturday, January 28th

The Lift Bridge Bookstore in Brockport is a nice bookstore, a good bookstore. There's a beautiful mural, outside above the windows, running the length of the building—fifteen feet high by maybe fifty wide, bright blues and yellows and greens of the rolling open land along the famous canal, a barge drifting toward the lift bridge, happy people in rocking chairs on the barge, or working, or playing a fiddle, a carriage and horses trotting along, big round trees bursting with fruits and flowers, simple lines, stylized figures, a little bit on the cartoonish side but only in a good way. Mrs. Tingelhoff has a big framed photograph of it, taken from the roof of the building across the street. There is a small crowd on the sidewalk outside the store, listening to a stocky man at a podium read from a book. The man is me, the book is Insider's Guide to Division III Hockey. Mrs. Tingelhoff, who looks and acts like my grandmother in jeans and tennis shoes but who is less than five years older than me beckoned me as she stood before this photograph. "When you came to my desk yesterday," she said, "you scared me." I chuckled. "Scared you?" "I didn't," she said firmly, "recognize you. Look at the way you looked only a few years ago." "2005?" I asked. "I don't know what year it was. But just look at you. You've let yourself go or something's terribly wrong," she blurted, tears forming, "and I'm so sorry. Is there anything I can do?" I took a moment, hoping she would interpret it as an indication of sincerity and thoughtfulness. "Look how heavy I was," I said, pointing at the photograph. "I've lost a little weight and—" she snorted and dabbed at her eyes, one two blink blink, "—and I've grown a beard. No wonder you didn't recognize me. But honestly, I'm fine." She looked at me for quite a long time, I thought. She was actually searching my face. "You frightened me when I looked up, because I did know you, it's true, but what I saw wasn't you." She threw herself at me and we hugged warmly, again for quite a long time. Then she broke it off. "You've got to get a grip," she said. "Whatever's going on, you have got to get a grip. Promise me now! That you will get a grip!" I smiled, held my hands up beside my head, made gripping motions. I don't know what made me say this, but I did say: "I had the best hands in hockey." "Please," she says, "stop calling me Mrs. Tingelhoff." I mean, I was joking, I wasn't making a genuine plea for her to remember me as I remembered myself, I think it's actually a line from a movie. Her home, the Gingerbread B&B is, as its name suggests, a very pretty place. But it's not all frosting. Every room gleams with dark wood, brilliant white curtains that crackle with the faintest movement of a body through the air, the clearest, thickest glass... "Didn't I, Mrs. Tingelhoff?" In what I took to be consternation, she turned a lamp on and off: it was like lightning striking. "You said you were working on a novel!" she cried. "Everybody seemed so enthusiastic! There was a chance you were going to be on—" "There is no dignity in novel-writing," I said quietly. "Not anymore there isn't." "There's no what?" she demands. I go into the library, as if I've had quite enough, but am too much of a gentleman to say anything harsh, or even faintly reproachful. Which is true. That is the sort of fellow I am. In the library, which Mrs. Tingelhoff had done in greens and browns in a way that suggests an aquarium, I sat down in a big soft chair and paged through Wallace Stevens's *Harmonium*. I said to myself, now this...this is truly worth a lot of money. You all know I was kidding about the Rector drawing: it's a beautiful drawing, Andy is eating his paintbrushes, the pawnbroker made the usual remarks about the frame being worth five bucks and I smashed the glass right there in his shop, took out my lighter and set that lovely gift from my suffering friend ablaze. I don't know why. But I do know that I let it burn, and the broker let me let it burn, we both watched it, and then I went outside: sweet home, New Bedford, lord I'm comin' home to you, here I come, Beddy Bedford. The *Harmonium* was a first edition (I don't think there was a second), and it was signed by Stevens, inscribed to Mrs. Tingelhoff's grandfather. I stood up, having surprising difficulty, and walked out of the library with it. Then I walked out of the Gingerbread B&B with it, and with it, walked into the Lift Bridge Bookstore. I told the young woman at the register that I was looking to sell some books. She called the manager. The manager didn't even blink: "You're the man who wrote the book about hockey, aren't you?" and she gestured toward the windows, to one of which, in a corner, the lower right from our perspective, was taped the photograph of me reading from *Insider's Guide to Division III Hockey*, and a cardboard-backed poster of the book itself. "This book," she said, as if we were talking about my book, "is worth thousands of dollars. Maybe ten thousand dollars. And I believe it belongs to Mrs. Tingelhoff or did she—?" "We were arguing about how much it would fetch," I said sternly, "and I brought it in to you for a second opinion. CALL HER UP!" I said. "SHE KNOWS I'M HERE!"

Sunday, January 29th

Much Ado About Everything: an Oration on the Dignity of the Novelist: that is the book I will now write. I will say there is more dignity in writing online picks of the week in NESCAC than in the writing of a novel. I will say I can no longer write. I am unable to write anymore. I will write, but I cannot. Once I could write; now, it is not possible. Words fall from my hands to the floor. "You may write," someone said, "or you may not." I do not possess the requisite skill to write. I must write, and yet it has become clear that I may not. I am not allowed to write. Something is keeping me from writing. My will to write has been undermined. The structures of language have collapsed. These signs, these symbols, these hieroglyphs, these scratch-marks—they no longer have the power to animate my mind. The torpor of days without writing is killing me. Why may I not write? Why can I not write? If I know and do not act, then I am either tired or a coward or simply lazy. If I do not know and do not act, then I am merely a witness to some disaster I have no part in. If I do not know and do act, who will tell me what I have written? I won't know. I will not be able to see it. Your right to write has been revoked. It is no longer permissible for you to write. Writing privileges have been revoked. You are being punished for not writing when you could. You thought that writing was something that happened in you because you were special. It is not. You are not. The Universe does not make these kinds of distinctions. You cannot write because you have damaged yourself, broken something, let something die. It is not magic. The ground of reality, the field of being, the cloud of unknowing: I can no longer write. I have no faith. I no longer believe in writing. It seems childish, trivial, vain. "One often hears of writers who rise and swell with their subject, though it may seem but an ordinary one. How, then, with me, writing of Leviathan?

Unconsciously, my chirography expands into placard capitals. Give me a condor's quill! Give me Vesuvius' crater for an inkstand! Friends, hold my arms!" My brain, that three pounds of electrified, superbly-trained jello, has been thumping against my skull, in what I think is a subtly mocking reaction of the way I bang my head—analogically—against the wall. At first I thought a helicopter was landing on the roof of my house; then I thought a large insect had become trapped in my ear; then I thought it was an artery about to blow like a fire-hose out my ear. Finally it settled into a regular thumping, coming, I was sure, from one or both of the temporal lobes. What do the temporal lobes do? I wondered. Keep time? This was a kind of 3/4 time, an old country waltz. Which reminded me of a joke about 5/4 time that I could not remember. John Richardson: how did it go again? "The memoirs of the mentally ill are full of confused action, failed promise, and grinding pain; they do not tend to make good narratives. The writing of the other patients horrified me, as I struggled to suppress my own compulsion to write about myself." I read that in *The Midnight Disease*, by Dr. Alice W. Flaherty, a Harvard doctor who is or was a neurologist at Mass General. My note is dated 2004. I also say that I am surprised I do not know the good doctor. I wonder how she's doing, now I mean. In her book, it sounded like she was in worse shape than I am apparently in, but, you know, rose up from her torment, got a grip, wrote her book, and is living I hope happily ever after. Je ne peux pas écrire. Ich kann nicht schreiben. No puedo escribir. Ég get ekki skrifað. Jag kan inte skriva. Jeg kan ikke skrive. Non posso scrivere. Scandinavian and northwestern

Mediterranean. These are all the languages in which I can work out simple sentences like: I cannot write. It's all I ever wanted to do. Hockey was just a game, and I was up to here with doctors and lawyers.

Monday, January 30th

The NCAA sanctions have left Morrisville in a state of collapse and despair. The Buffalo State Bisons scored nine straight unanswered goals and I said okay, that's it. These teams must not be allowed to dramatize the daily crises of the Sad & Admonitory Martian. I intimated as much a couple of weeks ago, I think, and now I'm sure. I hoped to see my friend Lara Hubel, and sell her (give to her) a fake William Gaddis notebook, but she's on the North Campus and halfway through the second period I knew I had to get the hell out of Buffalo. It was snowing, and I knew that if I blinked, eight feet of snow would come down at once and strand me there. The notebook is explicitly a fake, but it's my imitation of Gaddis and it's not too goddamn bad. Lara is a Gaddis scholar, and I thought she'd find it amusing. Anyway, just like that, the swiftness of desire is pure magic in my experience—here I am in Sudbury, in the province of Ontario, despite the ridiculous difficulties of entering Canada these days (the unkempt appearance and dazed attitude never mattered in the good old days...), and will stay in Canada, moving west, as long as I can. Then south to Los Angeles. I know a guy there who once ran a hedge fund AND wrote for *Law and Order*. I think he was actually some kind of "story manager," marshalling the scenaristos. Seems strange to me, but that's the way it goes, I guess. I am going to get him to pay for a lobotomy. One flew east, one flew west.... Yes. I will apologize to Andy's face for burning his drawing, and get Tom Smuts to buy me a lobotomy. His wife invented a television show and they have billions of dollars. More than all the doctors and lawyers in the world combined. And yet...and yet...perhaps I shall not require one: I'm not eating. I'm paying attention to it and am absolutely sure. It disgusts me now. The momentary spasm of desire is quickly apprehended as disgusting as everything was before the spasm and will be after the spasm. There is a food trailer on the southwest edge of town, just before the big cut they made through three billion year old rocks for the Trans-Canada, that specializes in poutine. I once drove to Sudbury just to get a plate of that particular poutine from that particular trailer. I slowed as I drove past: just made me feel sad. I don't understand how I could have been so...so what. Carefree? Hungry? Possessed of a keen wish to live life to its fullest?

Friday, February 3rd

I have been staying most of this week at the Victoria Arms B&B in Regina, Saskatchewan, because Manitoba was simply too crowded and too hectic! Alberta is just going to be worse: Edmonton AND Calgary?? The Tar Sands Megalopolis of Athabasca, Peace River, and Cold Lake?? 54,000 square miles of molasses almost ready for the family car?? but mainly because I am paying weird, necessary homage to the White

Sisters, Regina and Victoria, who control the fates of hockey games more than they let on. For instance: now that I am here in Regina, my go-to darkhorses, the Salve Regina Whites of Newport RI, who have struggled to win a game a year for the last twenty years triumphed resoundingly against the Suffolk Insufferables, one of my least favorite teams for reasons I won't go into but which involve schadenfreude on the most piddling level, at my favorite rink, Portsmouth Abbey, before an ideally sized crowd of 125. The owner of this B&B on what used to be a rock farm on the outskirts of town is a classmate of mine from Dartmouth, James Klassen, but when I checked in, I was told he was out of town and would be for some indeterminate time. A strange woman then confronted me. "I know who you are," she said. "I know all about you." This was somewhat disconcerting, especially given the impenetrable blackness of her eyes, but explained without too much difficulty. I was about to ask her who she thought she was, Mrs. Michael R. Tingelhoff? when she stopped me with an abrupt hand gesture. "My name is Regina White." I started to say that I had a friend named Regina White, but she stopped me again, palm of her hand almost touching my nose and lips and chin, quivering in the air. "I am not your friend," she said. "You have debts to pay."

I e-mailed Regina, I wrote on her facebook page, I even called her, though I loathe telephones: not a peep. Maybe she's out of town. She lives in DC but often goes back to Fort Dodge to get off the grid, to hole up, to ask herself, she says, where she went wrong. It hurts to hold my pen, it hurts to tap the phone, to click the miserable fucking little keys, it hurts to walk and to talk. Maybe I'm worse off than I thought: Regina's evil double makes absolutely no sense if I step back from it even one little step. It is excruciatingly painful, however, to step back. Perforce I allow everything to happen as it will. To step back from anything, to step back from life? What more bizarre challenge could I set myself? "One is usually afraid of things that are overpowering. But is there anything in man stronger than himself? We should not forget that every neurosis entails a corresponding amount of demoralization. If a man is a neurotic, he has lost confidence in himself. A neurosis is a humiliating defeat; worse, one is defeated by something 'unreal.' Doctors have assured the patient long ago that there is nothing the matter with him, that he does not suffer from a real disease like cancer. His symptoms are quite imaginary. The more he believes he is a malade imaginaire, the more a feeling of inferiority permeates his personality. 'If my symptoms are imaginary,' he will say, 'where have I picked up this confounded imagination in the first place? And why should I put up with such a perfect nuisance?'" (Jung, in a book just handed to me by JK, who says he has been here all along, checked me in, hugged me, conversed at length with me, etc.)

Of course I'm sorry that I'm not in Boston for the Beanpot...this is the first time I've missed the tournament since 1981. On the other hand, a lot of people who used to eagerly await the Beanpot no longer do. The tournament doesn't have the...the...the what, I don't know, it doesn't have it. I'm not alone in thinking so. BU and Chestnut Hill Community

College will play what is to them just another HEA game, Northeastern will throw its sticks to the ice, c'mon boys to hell with this, and Harvard will resume their careers as diplomats and what have you. Doctors, lawyers. And of course things are psychically dicey here in Regina. Jim K, who more or less gave it all up to return to his Mennonite roots in "Palliser's Triangle" (so called by early Canadian geographers, who figured the place as good for nothing agricultural and a little spooky to boot) informs me that, yes, they do have some kind of paranormal/pseudoscientific phenomenon manifesting itself every now and then, most often in the form of someone either looking like or identifying itself as a profoundly trustworthy person in the observer's life, one of the least likely persons, in other words, in the observer's life, to level judgment or make accusations—doing just exactly that. So he and I are going to follow the live-blog and let the Manichaean forces overhead finish whatever it is they are doing....

Regina, the real Regina, not the city in Saskatchewan where I am currently resting or the hockey team in Newport, called me yesterday to confirm what Jim and I had come to believe reading the liveblog of the Beanpot: in the evening game, Northeastern came out, skated around in lazy circles and said, basically, don't want to play this stinkin hockey game. And didn't. She also asked me to stop invoking her, at least as a deity, in the neurotic little morality play (rather, monologue from dear diary) others call facebook updates. She said her sister Vicky was very troubled over her unwilling participation in anything Manichaean. I apologized profusely, saying I had lost track of what I was saying on facebook and what in my diary. I had meant to play fast with one and loose with the other. Meanwhile, Jim (who is a doctor and a Mennonite pastor—don't think I mentioned that—as well as the owner of vast portions of Palliser's Triangle here in SK) decided to move me out of his B&B (where I was "frankly worrying the other guests") to an abandoned farm northeast of Saskatoon, near Carrot River, which he uses as a retreat when his spirit is racked. Five little buildings in a single row, each about the same size, no bigger than the average livingroom, though the barn has a mow and the house a second floor. He also said John Richardson had called him (they know each other from long ago as well, when they were dating twin department store heiresses) and would be joining me. This is a little hard to believe, but welcome news in any case. John owns about twenty or thirty barbershops/beauty salons in the Twin Cities, but spends most of his time reading Plato with two other Plato freaks who are also in his country band, which goes back to Wilkes-Barre PA, when I sang with them. He is going to open up one of the compartments of his mind and teach me something about despair. While I wasn't looking, Dr. Jim managed to get some vitamins and protein into me. He said relax, we're just going to get you high. I don't know if I was or was not. High, I mean. The sudden vitamins and the landscape alone could account for how I felt for...however long I felt it. The sky was and remains far too blue to be real. Did/Does my disbelief mean I was/am high? That the doors of my perception have been cleansed? Or smudged. The line that separates air from earth is weirdly vivid: there's no snow on the ground, but the vegetation that should be brown is singingly golden. There is nothing else here but the blue and the gold. The shacks are so weathered, gray, and falling down that they seem insubstantial, here, then not here. The windows are filthy and cobwebbed but the line and color outside is so fierce it makes the windows glow like varnished oil-paintings. Why is there no snow on the ground?

WHY IS THERE NO SNOW ON THE GROUND?

It's all some kind of wretched trick. Play along, play along! What can it hurt? What harm can it do? I have to admit, the body feels better when to it proper attention is paid.

Friday, February 10th

This is the gist of what John said to me when he finally got to Carrot River. I thought at the time that he was paraphrasing Plato because he has that philosopher nearly memorized, but I didn't ask. I don't interrupt when he speaks like this: "It is hard to think of a thing more out of time than nobility. Looked at plainly it seems false and dead and ugly. To look at it at all makes us realize sharply that in our present, in the presence of our reality, the past looks false and, therefore, dead and is, therefore, ugly; and we turn away from it as from something repulsive and particularly from the characteristic that it has a way of assuming: 'something that was noble in its day,' 'grandeur that was,' the rhetorical 'once.' But as a wave is force and not the water of which it is composed, which is never the same, so nobility is a force and not the manifestations of which it is composed, which are never the same. Possibly this description of it as a force will do more than anything else I can have said about it to reconcile it to you. It is not an artifice that the mind has added to human nature. The mind has added nothing to human nature. It is a violence from within that protects us from a violence without. It is the imagination pressing back against the pressure of reality. It seems, in this last analysis, to have something to do with our self-preservation; and that, no doubt, is why the expression of it, the sound of its words, helps us to live our lives." When he was done, he closed the book and still it did not dawn on me that he was reading, not remembering. "What a terrific memory you have," I sez. "What, are you some kind of actor?" "I have been reading from a book," sez John. "Oh have you," sez I. "I have indeed," sez John. "Name for me the author of this book from which you has been a-reading." "Let's see if this rings any bells for you, you fucking dope, you ignoramus, you—" "Name of author, please," sez I. "Wallace Stevens," he sez, "your old pal." "Oh gee," sez I, "first it's Carl Jung and now it's Wallace —" He fished around in a bag. My bag. Pulled out *Harmonium*. "Bells?" I was sure I had returned to it to Mrs. Tingelhoff, and averred as much to John. He sighed. I remain sure I returned it to Mrs. Tingelhoff. It seems more likely to me that John had a copy of his own.

February 17th

I do not understand why John was so angry with me. Whatever the reason, I was forced to flee Carrot River, and I have to thank Jim for restoring enough health to me so that I could in fact drive a car, could in fact flee. Left to my own devices, I would not have been able to flee Carrot River and the full weight and horror of John's wrath would have fallen upon my desiccated head and withering limbs. Instead, I am in Hollywood!

February 29th

Leap year this year. Hollywood has been cold and gloomy: Saskatchewan seems like a dream. At least I was taken care of there. I'm kidding! I found Andy's apartment without any trouble at all, like I'd been doing it every day for years. Pulled right in. Door was open. Somebody said Andy was sleeping and made elaborate shushing motions at me. Then left. Slammed the door. Asshole. Weirdo. Typical Hollywood Asshole slash Weirdo. I went into the bedroom and sure enough, there was Andy, either sleeping or dead. I was too tired myself to really rigorously call his bluff. SMACK! and a needle do not necessarily mean the guy is dead or even high. He has been using heroin archly, deftly, for at least two decades. I find it really hard to believe he would let it kill him. I turned from his bedside with an air of having done all I could do, and happened to glance at the slightly warped full-length mirror that is hung on the closet door. Gloomy neon light, shiveringly cold, shouts in the street below. Is it Hollywood or Disneywood that is the Greatest Place on Earth? Screams. I said aloud, "I find it really hard to believe you would let it kill you!"

March 1st

Andy is not dead. He held himself over me with great difficulty and said that he found it really hard to believe that I would let it kill me. I tried to tell him about his drawing and what I'd done, but he wouldn't let me get a word in edgewise: really hard to believe that you would let it kill you really hard to believe that you would let it kill you really hard to believe that you would let it kill you hard to believe that you would let it kill you hard to believe

March 2nd

Hard to believe indeed. I am going to die writing. "Wilt thou then hesitate and think it a hardship to die? Thou for whom life is well nigh dead whilst yet thou livest and seest the light, who spendest the greater part of thy time in sleep and snorest wide awake and ceasest not to see visions and has a mind troubled with groundless terror and canst not discover often what it is that ails thee and goest stray tumbling about in the wayward wanderings of thy mind?" What have I written? Can't read it, but must have written it. Is my literary estate in order? I

NIGHT, MYSTERY, SECRESIE, & SLEEP

I

Night, or the European

A strange little tune, breezy but suggestive of the inner lives of clowns, one associated perhaps with ice-skating, with red-cheeked young men and women holding each other's hips and hands while their bladed feet cross snicking and rasping according to the metronome of what is possible, over the thin ice of what is not, dance hall rhythms inconsequent in themselves but burdened in some incomprehensible way and accompanied by such dark and unlooked-for harmonies as one can hear only in silence and the presence of death. And yet there they are, the bright bouncing notes, the music of happiness, of the bracing pleasure that comes of exercise in cold weather, of delight so general and ubiquitous it can be mistaken for air. No one knows why this music is playing. No one standing on the wharves on this windy cold brilliant night can say with certainty where in the darkness of the sleeping town the music comes from, nor can they imagine who is responsible. It is as if they are being encouraged—now, at this moment of ecstatic, sorrowing departure from the old world to the new, when everything that must happen has happened, when it is too late—to believe their lives will turn out all right in the end. When will the end come? The music seems to say that no one knows because it is best not to know such a thing. The music seems to say it will be there until that very second, that paradoxically split and split and infinitely split second when everything ceases to be, the music, the wind, the smell of the person next to you, the lap and crash of water on wood and stone, the moon in its crowd-pleasing trompe l'oeil seeming to shoot from cloud to cloud like a cannon ball but moving in true black empty space in a perfect circle around the spinning world. Yes, the music of creation promises to be there until annihilation, but no longer. No one in the queue believes in the heaven that is the reward of faith—it seems rather the remorseless consequence of faith, the heaven of blinding deafening justice, the heaven of arbitrated recompense for suffering and pain-wracked belief in the power of faith. All in the queue are Christian. All in fact are peculiarly devout and passionately sober Christians who have sworn never to dance or play cards—drinking of alcohol and cursing are for the barnyard only. And yet all have worshipped Jesus Christ in fantastic smoky churches that stank of manure and decaying pine needles, the architecture of which were not based on the cross or the convergence of all things rising but on antler of reindeer and horn of ox, on an immense ash tree in the center of the universe from which the god of gods hung himself by the neck for nine days in the hope of knowledge beyond cause and effect. The happy piping that comes and goes on the wind, swallowed up in string quartet darkness and sudden tympanic crash of surf only to be borne up like spray, speaks to them, all of them, secretly, insinuatingly, of the mischief and license in which only the owners of land may indulge—in which the good and the beautiful may perish at the hands of the gross, the popular, the ignorant, only because goodness and beauty rise naturally from such decay. All, and there are hundreds if not thousands in this murmuring and rustling chain of human beings, profess a belief but hear something else in the music. The gangways sway and sag with the weight of their passage from the torchlight of the wharves into the dark of the ship—as if despite the compelling optimism of the magical music and the promising snap and flutter of ethereal sail, the idea of so many all at once were not just another, more mysterious way of seeking the misery at the last turning of every road, at the summit of all endeavor.

The disappearance of people continues for some time. If in fact they are entering the rooms of the ship, it must be a ship vastly more large than is suggested by the shape of the thing above the waterline.

Soon there is no one on the wharf. And yet the ship rides too high. If there ever were people aboard her, there are no longer. One last person remains on the threshold, back brilliantly lit against the darkness of the hold. The gender and age of the last passenger cannot easily be remarked: an effeminate young man or masculine young woman, someone very old upon whom time has marked itself only in the most abstract ways, a dissolution of the eye, a crackling parchment around bones too prominent, a smell of ether and waste...or a child to whom language is new and incantatory grown monstrously heavy of frame, bones still soft and sinuous as muscle but long, flesh smooth and fragrant but simian and despairing in its repose, its silence and watchfulness and calm.

At last what had seemed in the beginning a simple acknowledgement of mutability, this pause and faint turn of head and hooded glance, a single note on the transitory nature of love and affection, of the end of something—a moment, an epoch, a thought, a life—the simple pause, ceasing of movement or resumption of volitionlessness, the failure to take the next step or successful return to rest even upon the threshold, the maw, ancient mouth, and faint contraction of the muscles of one side of the neck, the expansion of the muscles of the other, now seems a subtle but irresistible demand for audience.

The Player of the Music approaches, down the narrow winding streets of the mountain town, visible for moments in flares of gaslight and fog, repeated in the black mirrors of windows, obscured by brick and wood and cobble, horse and wagon and barrel, smoke and stink and snow.

The passenger's apprehension of the presence of the Player becomes more and more clear until it becomes possible that there is no ship, no wharf, no town, no wind, no moonlight. There is only the cloying manifestation of the passenger's faint resistance to the Player or perhaps the sticky residue of its presence, the consequence of resistance, oatmeal, cabbage, vomit. . . long squirming, steaming, faintly squealing and sighing coils and loops. . . viscera, anathema.

The passenger understands—is a believer, after all—that it is too late—a believer in order and wisdom beyond sensation and experience... but comes to think... somehow...that departure is perhaps not inevitable.

Turns a quarter into the wind and music.

Turns another quarter. This ear is deaf—in an ordinary and miraculous way—to music and feels only the buffeting of the wind.

Acknowledges the possibility of descent cleat by cleat down the gangplank.

Begins this most extraordinary refusal and descent in the face of not only music but the Player of Music and the belief that ascent is not only good but inexorable, remorseless, relentless.

The abomination and the heartbreak—mind and heart assailed—of this turning, the terror of a journey that must be undertaken—these mount like bile and acid and undigested barely torn flesh in the gorge of the passenger with each elimination of perspective—as if the descent were into a quagmire of corruption and vomitus... not a flight from inevitability and the lingering smell of coercion that all the passengers murmured against—filled all the while with that happy happy music.

Moving in and out of gaslight, disappearing for heartbreaking seconds then reappearing in a blaze of lamp and nimbus of moisture only to vanish yet again, appear again, vanish again, appear again, vanish again, the passenger descends the gangway and runs, falling to hands and knees at wharf's end, seeing the black water but hearing nothing, seeing that his numb hands are bleeding but feeling no pain, no slickness of fluid, sucking salt air in through flaring nostrils but concluding it has no smell, concluding that the old country has been lost over the black line of the horizon after all, lost in that furnace of stars and soil.

II

Mystery, or the Indian

Children children unspeaking unmoving small faces great need relentless need relentless cold eternal cold the snow never ceasing the wind always screaming everything dead white earth black now white trees green now white sky blue now white sea gray now white perfect white as far as the eye can see my eye further still still dead white everything has disappeared

no food nothing to eat everything buried dead white no life no movement the fires cooling the children hate us for the failure the children hate us for giving them life the children hate us a tree explodes from the cold deep in the white forest this island once a refuge once a light once alive now dead no manitous all dead all fled we are abandoned

I am looked to in this absence I am begged I am feared I have power greater power in this absence the imperfect world assails me I was not warned I was not taught assailed by madness thrust I was thrust into it called they say I was called heedless a loner a lover of the dreamworld helpless and crazy in this one called to power and drowning in it now magnificent and lethal no warning no teaching I should not have been called should not have answered when called die like the rest of them helpless and crazy they hate and fear me offer me pipes simple ceremonies long elaborate lies communion and manifestations of powers in the imperfect world pipes and esteem good will then hate and fear in the imperfect world now perfectly white

small ones relentless gaze and innocent hatred knowledge too soon of the imperfect world dying first dying fast here is my answer here it is as it was presented to me here is a judgment here is a vision here is a power I grant a movement in the whiteness and silence and stillness the tree explodes who can deny it and I am told I hear and I see and I say here is food at last eat it

eat them eat the children eat the children eat the small faces the smallest first and the dead the smallest dead first then kill in order small to large small and already dead then larger and more alive eat eat eat they are food now eat them they belong to us eat them all hot dark rooms of meat and satiation to walk about in empty rooms all spirit flown I will be the bear whose hunger is simple

all this introspection and wandering is killing me berries nuts bark and worms my bowels are in an uproar my shit is like so many sharp stones clearly I have been driven to this place beyond madness by the avenging manitou of the small ones and the bigger ones who ate them unlike the others a mystery boiling up out of nowhere no one knew him no one could warn me it's clear he must be associated with the white people

I have wandered now for years been the bear been alone been feared driven away hated been the bear and lived in my mind for years now trying to dream my way back to hot summers on the island lots of food children everywhere welcomed everywhere in every residence reading fires with languid assurance shaking the tent sucking disease from their bodies with my short clever tubes tapping them pleasantly with my clever little mallets

I am desolate and singular I am an anomaly wherever I go whatever I say whatever I eat the thing now is clear I must become white must solve the mystery find the new force find the thing in the darkness so clear so invisible behind the tree behind the sun locate the disease the menace the death and then come what may

I will learn their language language is everything learn the words and get them right the rest is laying on of hands and tapping with mallets and sucking with tubes going through the motions I will learn this long and vivid language and start a newspaper attract attention and disease and death then come what may I will see it as it is for what it is

III

Secresie: an Arcadian Duet

European Utopian: I got off the ship and I fled into the forest. I sought the lakes and dark trees of the interior, of the north. Logging is monotonous and hard but I felt safe. I felt pursued, you see, by the horror of the world, by life and death. It's well-known that the people who lived in the northern forests of my country were protected in their isolation from disease, from the various epidemics, from the plague, but they paid a terrible price for it. In the deep cold and darkness, the light of Christianity became chalky and nebulous. The old beliefs were like gravity, like tide. Lunar light washed gray the glow of candles in the smoky wooden churches and the old gods could again speak to life and to death. The old gods understood horror and revelation, but these poor bastard farmers, they wanted to live in a modern country, they wanted to succeed. They wanted all to be barons. In the darkness the old gods are shredding their poor brains. YOU CANNOT SUCCEED! SUCCESS IS A LIE! shout the old gods, and they rip the limbs from one farmer after another. With their exploded heads and dangling arms they crawl into the city or the hold of a ship bound here. Where they will still talk of success. They will become the mad kings of their tiny fortunes, adrift in dinghies of dreams. Around them will swirl poisonous consciousness. Lightning will crackle across the dark sky like the hot white blood of their fellow men drawing near.

Wandering Shaman: My life! My life has been one of false and fatal dreams. A pernicious education. Blazing eyes and missteps. Overweening pride. The life of my people. . . ? Terrible, indeed yes. The weather is often cruel and the other tribes dull and stupid. There are always hunting problems to be solved, illnesses to be understood, cowardly or duplicitous leaders... aberrant shamans... the indifference of the cosmos... random visitations of forces, cosmic forces, that we will never understand... a constant state of deprivation and isolation. And now, now we feel abandoned. So little of the little we knew applies anymore. Perhaps it's only me. Perhaps my people feel none of this. Perhaps that is why I was debased and driven off. I used to believe—I was trained to believe—that I was a conduit of those vast and unknowable forces, that I came closest to understanding the nature of our existence and was therefore obliged to speak and to act accordingly. But something happened to me.

For many years, the years when I was being taught, I would awake each day with fresh bruises. In my dreams I was beaten up. Every night I was taken away and beaten by mysterious manitous. These blows are you education. That was what they said. We beat you and you learn. Have not the people already begun to fear you? They fear the bruises, new each morning. Where could he have gotten them from? They know you walk with us at night. The wounds are a part of the vision you were given at the start. They are a part of the sickness you must suffer. They are the reason you must withdraw from society. They are your only connection to the spirit world. Without them you will never be a shaman. I accepted the beatings but something happened to me.

My people were cold and starving to death. I suggested we eat the children. Either I am very powerful or they were very eager. I don't say this to excuse myself. . . but they traded surprised looks for a moment, then. . . gobbled them up, more or less.

IV

Sleep: an Aria in Alpha Waves

I have spoken to everyone on the planet. Many souls swirl in dissipation. God will call them all from Chaos. Reform them of ether and love. We will all live in the City of Light, the realm of pure, blinding light, the light that blinds from within, that shines through our eyes into the outer darkness, illuminating it, peopling it as the damned are forgiven. Come. Repent. Be blinded and follow me. Do good. Ascend. There are three tasks.

May I tell you a secret? I've told no one else, not even my companions. I think I have discovered how to extract gold from lead. Yes, I learned it in a dream. Saw the molecules dancing and spinning at incredible speed, splitting and recombining. I went to the laboratory, first thing, because I was full of doubt. I do know that I have seen things I would have been better advised not to see. I see messages written everywhere, from the Powers, from the Player of the Music. The question remains: are these messages false or true?

Answer me this: Why does sulphate of iron in a solution of cloroaurate of sodium precipitate metallic gold? Because iron and sulphur are included in the composition of gold. All compounds of sulphur with iron that occur in Nature contain some gold, more or less. I have begun to work on solutions of ferric sulphate. Or I would, if only I could get to San Francisco. Lead, refined in a melting pot lined with bone ash, always yields a little silver, and this silver invariably contains a minute amount of gold. I have concluded that, as calcium phosphate constitutes the most important part of bone ash, it should be the essential factor in the production of gold from lead.

But there can be no utopia. There can only be this world. I severed myself—we both did, did we not, in our different ways, like rotting arms green and stinking from our people? We have severed our gangrenous selves and become wanderers. And yet we were born to listen and to heal. So you see I am confused. Are you confused as well?

All the knowledge now returning all the language all the people the land my home winter over at last a number of good stories have been told in the smoke and the fire no harm done the children are laughing and playing I know everything as I used to know it know everything have been alive forever and will not die never die cannot die walk up into the sky and the hot sun I should rise up from my death because I can and comfort the wounded around me here because that was why I was called but this death it cannot be denied feels good to me it feels right and certain and sound it is pleasant green trees dusty and brilliant flickering blue water translucent the figures walking to and fro beneath the silver explosions of light upon its surface old friends working and laughing and drifting deeper and deeper the black earth moist and slippery and crumbling with bone and ash of the fallen the sky is strange yellow and gray a giant eye forming in the swirl of lead colored clouds purple clouds green clouds the eye perhaps of the maker, the player but I should comfort the wounded if I can I no longer think I can and yet I will I will comfort them if I can

Redlands California, December 2001

I would like to thank, with all my heart, those editors who first published these stories: Brigid Hughes at *A Public Space*; Sven Birkerts, Bill Pierce, and Billy Giraldi at *Agni*; Jim Hicks and Michael Thurston and Ata Moharreri at *Massachusetts Review*; Elise Proulx at *Litquake*; Troy Ehlers at *Minnetonka Review*; Vincent Standley, MT Anderson, and Joanna Howard at *Third Bed*; and Andrew Tonkovich at *Santa Monica Review*.

Gary Amdahl is one of many pen-names used by the Norwegian writer Jalmar Lillygreen (1783-1842), now known primarily for his translations of Stendhal.

CPSIA information can be obtained at www.ICGtesting.com
Printed in the USA
BVOW072217111212

307873BV00001B/5/P